My Sister's Child

ALSO BY CAROLINE FINNERTY

In a Moment

The Last Goodbye

Into the Night Sky

My Sister's Child

Enjoy!

Caroline Finnerty

Caroline Finnerty

POOLBEG

Published 2015
by Poolbeg Press Ltd
123 Grange Hill, Baldoyle
Dublin 13, Ireland

© Caroline Finnerty 2015

Copyright for typesetting, layout, design, ebook
© Poolbeg Press Ltd

The moral right of the author has been asserted.

A catalogue record for this book is available from the British Library.

ISBN 978-1-78199-944-8

Printed by CPI Group (UK) Ltd, Croydon, CR0 4YY

www.poolbeg.com

About the Author

Caroline Finnerty lives on the banks of the Grand Canal in County Kildare with husband Simon and their three young children, Lila, Tom and Bea as well as their dog Sam. As well as contributing to magazines and newspapers, she is the author of the novels *In a Moment*, *The Last Goodbye* and *Into the Night Sky*. *My Sister's Child* is her fourth novel. You can find out more about her on www.carolinefinnerty.ie

Acknowledgements

To all at Poolbeg, especially Paula & Gaye for their guidance on this book and getting it onto the shelves. To my agent Sallyanne Sweeney for your support and encouragement – I'm looking forward to working on many more together.

To Dr. David Walsh of the SIMS clinic who took the time to help me with my research in relation to donor-assisted conception and also Emma Morrow & Noelle Byrne for helping me with my midwifery questions and for sharing some of the courageous work that they do. I will put in my usual damage limitation clause here: any mistakes, liberties or inaccuracies are 100% my fault.

A special mention must go to Annemarie McBrearty who bid on my books as part of Authors for Nepal to help raise funds for the people affected by the dreadful earthquakes. I'm delighted that together we could play a small part in assisting with the relief effort.

To the booksellers, bloggers and librarians who put my books in the hands of readers – big, big thanks. I couldn't do this without you.

Also the people who pick up my books and get in touch with me afterwards. It never fails to blow me away that people actually take the time out of their lives to contact me, so thank you so very much.

I am lucky to have made friends with some really talented writers but I have to give a special mention to the lovely

Margaret Scott and Janny Peacock – thank you for all your chats and support.

To my ladies: Rebecca, Catherine, Michelle, Carol, Camilla, Louise, Gemma, Pam and Jenny. And not forgetting all the Musical Tots mammies too, now that some of our little ones are moving on we'll have to replace the tea with wine.

To my family who mean the world to me: Mam & Dad, Niall & Nita, Dee, Tom – a line in the acknowledgements could never say it all but I love you. And a big special mention has to go to my in-laws Mary & Neil, who are so supportive and really go above and beyond for us all.

Lastly, but by no means least, to my husband Simon and my children Lila, Tom & Bea, who have enriched my life in unimaginable ways. I couldn't do it without you; you're the best xxxx

For my beautiful sister, Dee

Chapter 1

Longing

She was dreaming of the baby again. She could still feel his weight in her arms when she woke from the dark recesses of sleep and had to look to make sure that he wasn't really lying there in the bed beside her. She was disappointed to discover that of course he wasn't. She felt so sure that she had been holding him this time. He had been breathing so evenly; the rise and fall of his small chest in time with her own breaths had felt so real to her. As real as the cool cotton sheets that were now brushing against her skin. His scent seemed to linger in the room and she could almost still feel his silky covering of hair underneath her fingertips.

The baby was a boy, it was always a boy, and she wasn't sure if it was the baby that she'd lost, the baby in her dreams. Or maybe it was David or another baby entirely. He never cried, he just slept peacefully, and she knew that it was because she was there to comfort him.

As Isla Forde lay back against the pillows, she let herself imagine how it would feel to have him growing inside her and to know that they were joined together for life. She liked to do it from time to time. She liked to imagine how it would feel to lift him gingerly from his pram or to rub his back in rhythmic circles to bring up wind. How would it feel to be the person that he would run to if he were scared? Or to be the only one who could make it all better if he was upset?

Was this what people meant when they said that they were longing for a baby? She had always wondered what that felt like, the longing. She had heard people describe it as a gnawing hole inside their tummies, pulling deep down into their groins, like a chain grounding them to earth that made them yearn for motherhood. She reckoned that it must be a pretty strong feeling because it had kept the human race populated for two-hundred thousand odd years depending on which side of the evolutionary debate you fell in with. Sometimes she thought she could feel it, she thought she could hear it calling her but other days she wasn't so sure. How did you ever really know? She had watched people take the plunge and they all experienced that strange thing that happened to her sister Jo after she'd had Réiltín, where our animal instincts take over, and she wondered if it would happen to her too? She had heard people say that as soon as your baby was placed into your arms you felt a rush like no other. Her mother said that the day she brought her older sister Jo home from hospital she had sat down in her armchair feeding her infant baby from her own body and she had never felt more in touch with nature. Like everything and everyone had just slotted into its rightful place, like the way her back fitted in between the cleavage of the cushions, her first-born baby was sitting rightfully in her arms.

Isla got up out of bed and tiptoed across the floor. She pulled back the curtain and peeked out at the clouds, which were heavy and full above the frost-tinged street below. The snow hadn't yet arrived. She let the curtain swing back into place and went into the bathroom. Climbing over the side of the bathtub, she turned on the shower. The water pummelled against her scalp, until the skin on her chest turned red. Steam rose around her until she couldn't see through the glass anymore. She rubbed shower gel over her body and let the water wash it away. She thought back to the dream again and she felt a shiver run down her body. It always left her disturbed for a long time afterwards. It lingered in her head and wrapped itself around her thoughts like smoke for the rest of the day. She felt as though it was trying to speak to her but what was it trying to tell her? *What are you trying to say to me?*

When she came out of the shower she wiped away a circle of steam that had worked its way up along the mirror. In it, she saw her cheeks were rose pink. She brushed her teeth and swept her damp hair up into a bun. Then she dragged the black pencil-eyeliner in an arc across her eyelid and curved it upwards with a flick, before doing the same on the other side. She dressed quickly and stood back to look at her reflection in the mirror before leaning in again to slick some Vaseline over her lips.

She threw on her parka and opened the flat door. The usual chemical smell met her. Her small one-bedroomed flat was over a dry-cleaner's. She hurried down the stairs to the front door and stepped outside. A cold wind sliced through her, whipping loose strands of her hair against her face. Pulling her hood up, she walked along the row of Victorian houses to where she had arranged to meet Jo. They were going for a walk along the strand before work.

A lid of ice covered each puddle on the footpath. It gave her a childish thrill to break each one and hear the crack of ice, followed by the splash of the puddle underneath.

When she reached the steps that were their meeting point, there was no sign yet of her older sister. She looked out over the sea wall where the slate-grey water mirrored the dark and threatening sky overhead, merging into murkiness somewhere on the horizon. The red-and-white chimneystacks of Ringsend looked hazy in the distance. Eventually she saw Jo coming with her small straw basket in her hand and her dog Oscar on his lead.

They greeted each other and took the stone steps down to the sand where Jo unleashed Oscar and they watched as he darted off up the beach. They walked after him until Jo stopped to bend down and collect fronds of kelp, which she put into her basket. She would take them home and let them dry in the sunlight on the kitchen windowsill until they were curled and crisp, before eating them.

"I had that dream again last night," Isla said as Jo righted herself and they continued walking.

"What dream?"

"The one about the baby!" Isla said, throwing a stick for Oscar. They watched as he dug his paws into the flattened strand and tore off after the stick, scattering sand, powdery like Demerara sugar, in his wake. "It's really strange. That's the third time now that it's happened."

"You probably were watching something about a baby on TV before you went to sleep," Jo said dismissively as she bent down to collect some more strands of brown-green kelp.

"But don't you think it must mean something? I mean it's the exact same dream every time! I'm not sure if it's David or someone else."

Oscar was back, stick in mouth, with brown sand matting his shaggy grey coat. Isla took the stick and fired it onwards. He bounded along after it.

Jo was down on her hunkers on the sand again, separating fronds of seaweed; she turned and looked up at her younger sister.

"Honestly, Isla, you don't have to make everything so dramatic! It's just a dream!" Jo, who worked as a solicitor at Lawson-McBride-Williams Solicitors and who prided herself on being the very epitome of level-headedness, sighed.

"Yeah, you're probably right," Isla said quickly, feeling stupid. "I always read too much into these things."

The sisters kept walking on until they reached the tower, which marked their turnaround point. The wind was head-on now and it pushed them back as they walked. It swirled inside Isla's hood, ballooning it out until her ears were stinging. They didn't bother talking, as they knew their words would be lost on the gale. They reached the bottom of the steps and climbed the well-worn slabs until they reached the top.

"Do you want to come back for a juice or maybe a coffee?" Jo asked.

"Nah, I better head on."

"Oh, I forgot to say it's Réiltín's birthday on Thursday –"

"Yeah, I know – you didn't think I'd forget it, did you?" Isla laughed.

"No, of course not." There was a defensive edge to Jo's tone. "I was just wondering if you wanted to come over for dinner that evening?"

"Sounds good."

"Great – well, will we say around eight?"

"Perfect."

"Okay, we'll see you then – have a good day."

They said goodbye as a jogger swerved around them on the path, breathing out clouds of white as she ran.

As Isla continued on to the café, she couldn't believe that her niece was turning fourteen – the years were just flying past. She didn't normally allow herself to think about how Réiltín had come to be; she felt it wasn't fair to Jo. Usually, whenever the thoughts entered her head she pushed them back out again but she could never help herself on her niece's birthday. It was always a day she found bittersweet. It was a day that made her think back over everything, especially now given her own desires to have a child.

She rounded the corner onto St John's Street and saw Greg, the owner of the café where she worked, putting up the sandwich board with the daily specials outside the door. He had a knitted hat pulled down over his ears and strands of his black wavy hair were poking out from underneath it. She could see his face break into an easy grin as she approached.

Greg's wasn't like the newer cafés down on the waterfront, the ones that had canopies and little Parisian-style tables out the front. The ones that served boards of antipasti, paninis and bagels, macchiatos and soya-lattes, to the time-pressed workforce in the surrounding office blocks. No, it was a proper greasy-spoon café that served rasher sandwiches, beans-on-toast, egg-and-chips and that type of thing. The walls were covered with plain square white tiles and little blue-and-white gingham curtains framed the windows. Isla had been working there for nearly three years and she had yet to experience her usual itchy feet.

"Morning, Isla," Greg said when she got closer. "It's a cold one today." The lines at the sides of his clear blue eyes crinkled as he smiled.

"It is – it's Baltic."

She pushed open the door, went inside and hung her coat up in the small passageway out the back before hooking an apron over her head and coming back out front.

It wasn't long before the first of the day's customers started to come in. The place soon filled up and they were kept going serving plates of food and cleaning tables off.

Mrs O'Shea and her friend Mrs Price, two little old ladies who had been meeting there for the last twenty years, came in then. They had a habit of reminding Greg that they'd been coming there before it was even called *Greg's*. They sat down and Isla served them their usual: a pot of tea and a fried breakfast for Mrs O'Shea and scrambled eggs on toast for Mrs Price.

After the morning rush had died down and Isla started wiping down tables, she noticed a young girl sitting at a table over by the window. She was holding her baby on her knee, bouncing him up and down while he giggled heartily. She couldn't have been any more than seventeen but Isla watched her as she cared for him ably. Even though some would argue that she was still a child herself, she knew what to do with him and it was clear to Isla that she cherished him. Was it purely instinctive, she wondered? Would she be like that too if it was her baby? She thought again of the baby in her dreams and felt a familiar tightness in her chest. The urges were getting stronger. The need to connect with something outside of herself felt more powerful than ever. She wasn't sure if it was because of the dreams but she was feeling a longing that was like nothing she had ever experienced before. It felt like an insatiable hunger growing inside her, a hunger that wouldn't rest. Her body ached for a baby.

"Penny for them?" Greg said, coming up beside her.

"Sorry, Greg, I was miles away," she sighed.

They made their way back over to the counter.

"Where were you – lying on a sandy beach in Barbados or diving in the Great Barrier Reef?"

"I was almost at the top of Everest when you interrupted me!"

"Well, it's cold enough, that's for sure! You look tired, Isla . . . are you okay?"

"I didn't sleep very well last night."

"Have you stuff on your mind?" His tone was concerned.

"No, I just keep having a really strange dream and it keeps me awake for hours afterwards."

"What's it about?" Michelle asked over her shoulder as she unloaded the dishwasher. Michelle was into dream interpretations. She liked nothing more than spending a morning analysing what they had all dreamt the night before.

"It's just this one I keep having about a baby." Even thinking of it now made her feel unsettled. She had a heavy feeling in the bottom of her stomach, like there was a stone sitting in it.

Greg raised his head from the till and looked at Isla with widened eyes.

Michelle turned around and laughed. "It doesn't mean she's going to have a baby, love – it's a sign of new beginnings."

"Really?" Greg asked, sounding disappointed.

"Yeah, it's a sign of something new happening in your life."

"We're out of napkins," Isla said.

"I saw a box out the back earlier – top shelf, right-hand side," Michelle said.

Isla, glad of the excuse to escape for a minute, went out to the storeroom. There had been no mistaking the hopeful look on Greg's face when he thought that she might be pregnant.

Isla and Greg had a thing, if you could even call it that. They had been sleeping together for over a year, usually after a night out. The thing was, though, they never used protection and she was starting to wonder if maybe there was something wrong with her. Was she, at the age of thirty-eight, like the arbiters of doom also known as the medical profession would have you believe, a barren lady? Were her eggs drying up? Was she just not dropping them any more? She had thought a few months back that she might have been pregnant; she had felt light-headed and nauseous when she woke in the mornings and she didn't get her period that month – but it was negative when she had done a test.

She opened the door to the storeroom and scanned the shelves full of catering supplies until her eyes landed on the box she was looking for. She took it down and also grabbed a bag of wooden coffee-stirrers because she had noticed earlier that they needed to be replenished.

"So are we going for a bite to eat at the weekend or what?" Michelle asked when she came back out front. "My mum has offered to take Jamie and I could really do with a night out."

"Well, I'm on for it," Greg said. "What about you, Isla? Will you come . . . I mean, if you haven't already got other plans?"

"Yeah, why not?"

"Where do you want to go? The usual?" Michelle asked.

"Sounds good to me."

"I was just thinking, Isla," Greg said, "If you're tired and want to head off after the lunchtime rush, that's okay."

Isla saw Michelle looking at them with raised eyebrows.

"Ah, thanks, Greg, you're very good. I'll be fine though."

"Wait 'til you have kids keeping you awake at night – then you'll know all about tiredness!" Michelle said snappily.

The baby came back to her again that night. He was lying beside her, working hard to make perfect O-shapes with his small mouth. Then he smiled, reached out, took her finger and held on to it tightly. He was calling to her.

Chapter 2

A Birthday

Milk
Kale
Washing powder
Meat
Reschedule Réiltín's orthodontist appointment
Milk
Kale
Washing powder
Meat
Reschedule Réiltín's orthodontist appointment

Jo Kingston's to-do list for the day kept looping in her head as she pressed the button on her juicer and watched as it angrily buzzed to life. She watched the berries and the kale as they swirled together in shades of purple and green. Suddenly she remembered that she needed to leave cash for her cleaner, Aurelia, so she tacked this onto the end of her list:

Milk
Kale
Washing powder
Meat

Reschedule Réiltín's orthodontist appointment
Money for Aurelia

She looked out through the French doors where the wind moved like a silvery wave across the garden. When the juicer stopped, she tipped in a shot of fresh wheatgrass and poured the mixture into two glasses. She drank one herself and set the other on the table beside the empty bowl and spoon which she had set for Réiltín.

"Morning," she said as she heard someone come into the kitchen behind her. She swung around to see her husband Ryan there. "Oh, it's you!"

"Morning." He was reading something on his phone. He didn't look up at her.

"Any sign of the birthday girl?" she asked.

"I think she's just finished in the shower."

"How did you sleep?"

"Fine."

"I've asked Isla over for dinner later."

"Great, what time?"

"Around eight."

"So what are your plans for the day?"

"Meetings all day. Will you be able to collect Réiltín from hockey? It's just I've a meeting at four and I've a feeling that it might run on."

"Sure." He was winding the cable of his laptop around the battery pack and putting it into his briefcase.

Réiltín entered the kitchen then with eyes still half asleep, dressed in her uniform.

"Happy birthday, darling!" Jo sang.

"Happy birthday, Little Star," Ryan said, leaning in to kiss his teenage daughter on the forehead where she had slumped into the chair adjacent to the place that her mother had set for her at the breakfast table.

"I can't believe you're fourteen," Jo said wistfully, sliding the bowl further down the table to position it in front of Réiltín, followed by the spoon and the glass of juice. "My little baby is growing up all too fast. When I think of how tiny you were when you were born and how we weren't sure if you'd even make it . . . but here you are, Little Star, amazing us every day."

"Mum!" Réiltín groaned in pretend embarrassment but Jo knew that secretly she loved hearing the story of the day she was born.

"Right, I'd better go," Ryan said. "Have a great day, birthday girl. I'll be picking you up from hockey."

"See you later, Dad."

As Ryan picked up his briefcase, Jo waited as she did every morning for the kiss on the cheek or even just the 'bye' that never came any more. Her heart sank as he turned and walked out of the kitchen. She listened to his footsteps over the tiles of their hallway, followed by the slam of the front door.

It would be nice if he still gave me a kiss goodbye – not every day, just sometimes, she thought.

"*Urrrgh*," Réiltín said as she picked up the glass of green liquid with leafy bits suspended in it, jolting her mother out of her thoughts.

"Come on, love, it's good for you – lots of antioxidants. Now, what cereal do you want?"

"Coco Pops."

"Réiltín, you know I only allow that on the weekends! Porridge, Rice Krispies or Cornflakes?"

"Rice Krispies."

Jo walked into the pantry and took down the box from the shelf, came back out and filled Réiltín's bowl with the blonde cereal grains.

"I thought we'd have burgers and chips tonight seeing as it's your birthday?"

"Woohoo, Mum, we really are celebrating!" Her tone was sarcastic as usual. "Is Isla coming over later?"

"Yes, I already asked her, don't worry! So did you get all

your homework finished last night?"

"Yes, Mum," she answered impatiently.

Jo watched her daughter as she ate her breakfast: her thick auburn hair that never seemed to sit properly no matter how much it was brushed; her porcelain skin, without a trace of a freckle or blemish; her bright green eyes with their veins of hazel. Every day she would look at her and drink in her beauty. She was their miracle baby and Jo would never forget it.

"What are you looking at, Mum?" Réiltín asked grumpily, snapping her out of her thoughts.

"Oh sorry, I didn't know I needed permission to look at my own daughter!" She smiled indulgently at her.

"Weirdo." Réiltín exhaled heavily. "I'm going to brush my teeth." She stood up and pushed her chair back from the table.

Jo sighed and started gathering up her papers and putting them into her briefcase.

"Did you bring your hockey gear?" Jo asked when Réiltín came back down the stairs a few minutes later.

"Yes, Mum."

"Did you remember to pack your lunch bag? I left it in the fridge for you."

"No, Mum. I'm going to get it now," Réiltín said impatiently, going to the fridge.

"Right, let's go then." Jo belted her woollen coat around her waist and slid her hands into her black leather gloves.

At the school gates Jo applied the handbrake and Réiltín leaned over to give her mum the usual swift kiss on the cheek, so quick that some mornings she missed her face entirely and kissed the air instead.

"See you, Mum."

"Have a good day, my love," Jo said and then Réiltín was gone.

Jo didn't pull out immediately like she usually would in a rush to beat the traffic on her way in to the office. Instead she sat there in the car and watched as her daughter walked towards the school gate, her hair rising up in a wild tangle on the wind. She looked on as Réiltín met a friend, then stopped and chatted easily. Jo admired how easily her daughter could make friends. She wished she could have been like that as a teenager. She wished she could be like that now. Réiltín got that from Ryan. Sometimes her daughter seemed so different from her that it scared her. Being social didn't come easily to Jo. 'Introverted', she believed was the term for it. She wasn't like her husband; he needed to be around people. Whenever he was driving he had to be talking to someone on speaker-phone. When they went out for dinner, he would charm the waiter and by the end of the night the couple at the table beside them too. When they used to go on holidays before they had Réiltín, they would be friends with the whole resort by the time they came home. Ryan needed to be surrounded by people whereas sometimes Jo would rather eat her own arm than try to make conversation with a stranger. Charismatic people were born with the gift, Jo believed. People warmed to them wherever they went. In shops people were friendlier to them and helped them pack their shopping, people let them jump in ahead of them in queues. They had people eating out of the very palms of their hands. Everyone loved them, *she* loved them. She felt the familiar wave of anxiety start up in her chest again but she forced herself to silence the thoughts. Then she released the handbrake and pulled out into the traffic with her to-do list looping inside her head all the way to the office:

Milk
Kale
Washing powder
Meat
Reschedule Réiltín's orthodontist appointment

She had left the money for Aurelia so at least that was crossed off her list.

Chapter 3

A Gift

It was somewhere around two years after they had first started to try for a baby that Jo realised that something was up. Her periods had always been regular so she'd never thought there would be anything wrong with her. She was in her twenties; she hadn't left it too late. She had gone along to her doctor who referred her for more tests and scans which showed that she had severely polycystic ovaries and the eggs were just not getting to where they needed to go. She had tried various treatments and fertility drugs unsuccessfully until she was advised that their only other option was to try IVF. So Jo began injecting herself with hormones to switch off her pituitary gland; the medical term was 'down-regulation'. Then there were more hormones to start it back up again so they were in control of her cycle and could extract her eggs, mix them with Ryan's contribution and wait to see how many embryos were made. The first time they made two embryos and they decided to implant one so that they had a backup if it didn't take, which it didn't. She was upset obviously but she also knew that only one in four IVF cycles were successful so they put it behind them and said they'd try again with the remaining embryo that was frozen in a straw in a tank of liquid nitrogen at the clinic. But it didn't happen for them. It was third time unlucky as well. Jo had had to go back through all the drug-taking to stimulate her ovaries and the egg-harvesting stage again. The in-vitro fertilisation resulted in three embryos. They decided to transfer two that time to try and boost their chances but that didn't work either. Then came the jackpot or so she and Ryan thought: they had their fourth round of IVF and both felt really positive about that one. That was the one where on the law of averages it was going to work for them. Statistics were in their favour. And it did work until Jo developed a bad pain and a scan showed that the baby was ectopic so she had to have emergency surgery and was lucky not to lose her ovary. But despite all that she still felt strangely positive because of the fact that they had been able to get pregnant. She felt they were finally on the right track and that soon it would be their turn. But it wasn't to be that way.

They were already several years down the line of trying to conceive a baby by the time Isla had become aware of the situation. It was a few months after their father had passed away and things were still strained between the sisters. Their dad's sudden death had created a rift between them.

Isla, who was still living at home at the time because she couldn't afford to move out, had got up as usual that morning. Then she had noticed that her dad wasn't up for work, which she'd thought strange, as he was normally an early riser. She had let herself gently into his room to check on him. The room was tidy as it always was. His clothes from the day before were hung neatly over the back of the wicker chair and light flooded in around the edges of his curtains. It was then that she saw that he had passed away in his sleep. A massive heart attack, they said.

Isla was devastated. She had been very close to her dad. Of course Jo was upset too but Isla took it particularly badly. In fact, the depth of closeness in their relationship had only become fully apparent to Jo after he had died.

Jo had always felt that her dad and Isla were as thick as thieves; they had a similar calm personality where they would weigh things up in their heads before speaking them. They were more sensitive too – it was like their hearts rested just under their skin and could bruise more easily than most.

Isla was annoyed with how Jo began to put their dad's affairs in order after he died, like life just moved on, but Jo was annoyed with Isla's monopoly on the grief. It angered her that Isla didn't seem to think that anybody else might have been grieving for their father because she was so completely absorbed in her own world of grief.

Then Isla had lost her job in a busy office. After their dad died, she just hadn't shown up and eventually after several months they'd had to let her go. Jo couldn't believe it; she was grieving too but after taking a week off she was back at her desk again trying to keep it together, whereas, to her, Isla was wallowing in it.

One day Jo had called over to tell Isla that she thought that they should sell their childhood home, 6 Lambay Grove. Isla had pulled back the door to let her in and barely responded to her greeting. Jo had noticed that her hair was looking wilder than usual and her thumbs were poking out through the holes that she had made in the bottom of the sleeves of her ancient grey cardigan. Their dad had bought it for her when she was fourteen. Like all of Isla's clothes it was well worn to the point of being threadbare but she only seemed to buy new clothes out of necessity.

When Jo told her why she had come, Isla had gone ballistic. She couldn't believe that Jo would sell their childhood home. Jo's response was to ask how she intended to pay her share of the inheritance tax due on the house, especially now that she had no job. So the house had gone on the market and after solicitors' and agents' fees and taxes were paid, Isla's share of the proceeds were transferred into her bank account. Isla didn't know what Jo had done with her half of the money – she guessed that she probably bought stocks and shares or did something equally sensible.

After the house was sold Isla had nowhere to stay so she lived in Jo's seafront house at Sandymount Heights for about three months until she found her own place. But, although they were under the same roof again, it was hard not to notice that something had shifted between the sisters.

One time Jo was late home from work and Ryan and Isla were drinking cans of beer in the sitting room when she came in. Jo had been horrified.

"What's going on?" she had said. "It's like a student squat in here!"

"We're just having a few drinks, Jo," Ryan said, straightening in his chair.

"Every evening this week I've come home to find you two drinking and laughing in here."

"Sorry, I didn't realise there was a law against laughter!" Ryan had said sardonically.

Jo rounded on Isla then. "I can see you're working really hard on job-hunting!"

"I sent out a few more CVs earlier –"

"Jo – it's seven thirty on a Wednesday evening – how could she be out job-hunting?" Ryan said. "Leave her alone."

She had stormed out of the room, up the stairs and into her room. Ryan had followed wearily and had eventually managed to calm her down.

The next day Isla had gone out and got a job doing face-painting in the play centre near to Jo's house. The money was dire but she wanted to show Jo that she was making an effort. She had been working there for two weeks when she was on her way home from work one day and saw Jo's car in the driveway. It was only half past three, which was odd because

18

Jo was never home before she finished work. She let herself in with her key, walked down the hallway and straight into the kitchen where she saw Jo sitting at the table with a pregnancy test in her hands. Her eyes were red and puffy and her cheeks shone with tears.

"What's wrong, Jo?" she asked gently.

"I can't do this any more," she had said. "This is hell."

"Are you and Ryan trying to have a baby?"

"Trying, but failing spectacularly. I really thought that this would be my time."

"How long have you been trying?" Isla had asked.

"Four years now – we've had five rounds of IVF and it hasn't worked. You always have it in the back of your mind when you can't conceive – 'Oh well, at least there's IVF – that'll sort us out'. It's like a safety net waiting for you . . . but what I hadn't expected was that it wouldn't work for us."

"Oh, Jo!" Isla had put her arms around her sister.

"I really thought I would have had a baby or at least be pregnant by now!" Jo had sobbed into Isla's hair.

Suddenly it had all clicked into place for Isla. Jo's terrible mood-swings, her tears and depressions, her secretive behaviour when she was trying to hide that she had an appointment. The mysterious tablets and nasal sprays she'd been taking.

"I'm sorry, Jo, I wish you had told me earlier – you shouldn't be going through all of this on your own. It will happen for you – chin up, you have to stay positive."

Isla had hurried up with her flat-hunt and moved out, because she knew that Jo and Ryan needed space as a couple to work through it alone and she was sure it didn't help having her living in the house with them. She could tell that their marriage was starting to suffer. She watched the distance grow between them as Jo ploughed ahead with treatment after treatment while he stood idly by, afraid to even suggest taking a break. Jo became obsessed with research papers. She would spend hours trawling through scientific journals seeking information, which might give her some new insight into why she couldn't get pregnant. Then she would bookmark their pages and present them to her consultant at her next appointment. She liked to be in control and Isla knew that was her way of coping.

Isla had watched as Jo kept her chin up and stayed positive but it still didn't happen for them. She had watched as a broken Jo picked herself up again and again as another cycle failed, until Isla couldn't bear it any longer. She didn't know how Jo, as the person going through it, was able to cope with the disappointment.

They had become closer once again after Jo had confided in her. Their squabbling after their father's death was put to one side and Isla made an effort to be there for her sister. She watched Jo injecting herself directly into her stomach and it made her want to hurl. Jo had told her that that was the easy bit – it was the awful wait to see if it had worked that was so much worse. Isla had a new level of respect for her sister. Back then she could never have imagined feeling such a desperate need to have a child that you would put yourself through all of that, almost to the point where you became a different person.

It was on their eighth failed attempt that Jo had heard the banging on the front door and tried to shut it out. It kept hitting off her head and she had to put her pillow over her ears to drown it out. She had heard Isla's voice then, calling up the stairs to her, getting louder and more frustrated as the minutes went on.

"Jo, I know you're in there so open up this minute – don't make me kick in your door!"

That had almost made her laugh – the thought of the birdlike frame of her younger sister thinking in that insane head of hers that she could kick through the heavy wooden frame of her Victorian front door.

"I swear, Jo, I'll kick it down and, if I can't, I'll call the Gardaí and get them to do it for me!"

And Jo knew that she would too. She had dragged herself up off the bed and gone down the stairs. She caught sight of her face in the standing mirror beside the door – a hideous reflection stared back at her, red-raw and swollen from tears. She took a deep breath and opened the door to Isla.

Isla said nothing and instead just threw her arms around her sister, hugging her tightly until Jo started to cry.

"Let's go sit down," Isla said eventually.

Jo followed her sister into the living room and sat down on the sofa.

"I don't know about you but I could murder a glass of wine right now," Isla said.

Jo didn't argue as Isla went into her kitchen and opened the fridge to take out a bottle. Jo could hear her opening drawers looking for a corkscrew. She didn't have the energy to tell her that it was in the third drawer on the left from the cooker. Finally the clattering stopped and she knew that she had located it.

Isla returned with two glasses and sat on the other end of the sofa where Jo was sitting with her legs curled up underneath her.

"Ryan called me," Isla said simply.

Jo nodded. "I can't do this any more. I can't keep going through this." She dabbed at her nose with a tissue as she felt the upset build up inside her once again.

She couldn't ever remember feeling so desolate in her entire life. Everything, every single thing that she had ever done had always been of a high standard – whether it was exam results or projects in work. But all of those things she had been in control of. Whenever she had a task to do, she could control the outcome to the standard that she wanted through hard work, but this time no matter what she did she couldn't make her body improve its own eggs. She had tried dieting, focusing on maintaining a healthy body-mass index, she ate superfoods. She abstained from alcohol for over two years. She had tried acupuncture and yoga. For someone like Jo who was always a high achiever, trying to accept that there was nothing she could do to improve the situation was very difficult.

Having been through it seven times before, she had known bad days, but now she found herself feeling a despair that was so acute that she never would have thought a feeling like it was possible. Every failed cycle had been awful but the last one was really bad. It was soul-destroying and just really, really sad. She was sad for herself and sad for Ryan. She felt she had failed him. He had been so good throughout it all. He had never complained about what he was missing out on when his friends or colleagues became fathers and Jo couldn't give him the one thing that both of them so desperately craved which seemed to come so easily to everyone else. He had kept strong when Jo was going through an inner turmoil of self-loathing and a feeling of failure so awful that it was akin to wanting to claw off all her own skin and climb into someone else's body. But that time it was different because it had marked the end game for them. That was the imaginary line that they had drawn under it all, the one she had never really believed they would reach and now there they were.

When Ryan had come home from work that evening, she had told him to go. She had thrown him out of the house. She knew that it was cruel and selfish but she couldn't face seeing his disappointment on top of her own. So she had made him walk through their front door and outside into the rain, which was coming down in diagonal sleet. The hurt written on his face, as he turned back to look at her, had cut deeply. Even as she was looking at him, she knew that that image of her distressed husband would probably stay with her forever. She knew that they were both thinking the same thing: *what had they become?* But she couldn't let him come back. She loved him too much for that. She could not give that good man everything he deserved in life so she had to tell him to go because she knew that he would never leave her. He had obviously contacted Isla and told her what was going on which was why she had shown up and threatened to break down the door.

"Come on, Jo, you're strong. You've said before that you couldn't go on but you've managed to keep on going." Isla squeezed her arm. "Maybe you should take a break for a while?"

"You don't understand, Isla. That was my last chance. My consultant didn't want me to have another round after the last time. He believes that the reason the IVF hasn't been working is probably caused by inferior egg quality and he doesn't think that it's a good idea for me either physically or emotionally to keep on putting myself through it when the chances of success at this stage are not in my favour. And Ryan agreed with him. He said we have to draw a line under it at some stage. He only agreed to go ahead with it the last time on condition that it was our final shot."

When they had told her in the clinic that her eggs were substandard, she had taken it badly. She saw herself as a failure, that her own body had failed her. It was definitely a depression of sorts although she didn't realise that that was what it was at the time. She had to mourn the fact that their journey was over, that a genetic child wasn't going to happen for them. Ryan had been adamant that they were done with IVF. As well as the emotional toll it was taking on them and on their marriage, it was financially ruinous even with their large salaries. Somewhere deep inside her, in a dark, hopeless place, she knew that Ryan was right. She knew that their marriage probably wouldn't withstand much more. She felt like a gambler choosing a colour on the roulette table – just one more time, *this will be my time* – except she always seemed to choose the wrong colour.

"Well, maybe he's right. I hate seeing you like this – I hate what the whole 'trying for a baby thing' is doing to you."

"Do you think I like it? I don't have a choice in it! This is the hand that I was dealt. Jesus, I feel so cheated at the hoops that I have to go through to have a child of my own and it comes so bloody easy to everyone else!"

"So is that really it? Don't you have any other options?"

"Basically, no. If I choose not to have any more IVF then I will never have a genetic child of my own and my only other options are adoption or egg donation."

"Well, if you want eggs you only have to ask me!"

"Jesus Christ, Isla, how can you be so flippant? Have you any idea of what I'm going through here?" Jo was insulted by her suggestion and she was also angered by how casual Isla could be about something that she knew was so incredibly difficult for her. Although Isla was always there with tissues or to pour the wine when she was going through her treatment, sometimes she would say something so utterly insensitive that it was clear to Jo that she didn't have an iota of understanding about what she was living with on a day-to-day basis.

Jo was still reeling at finding out that she wasn't pregnant and she couldn't even begin to think beyond that and, yes, she wanted to have a baby, but her *own* baby.

"Oh I'm sorry, Jo, I wasn't thinking. You know I didn't mean to upset you – I just want to help. Sorry – that was probably really thoughtless of me."

But in the weeks afterwards, as the long, dark days went past, even though Jo had brushed her off initially Isla's words had stayed in her head. She had planted a small seed in there and, after the benefit of some time and perspective, it didn't seem as ludicrous a suggestion as it had seemed at the time when she had first mentioned it. Having to use a donor was not what she wanted at all, not by a long shot, but at that stage it seemed to be the only way she could get to have her own child. She wanted to be pregnant herself; she wanted people to admire her bump and to offer her their seat on the DART; she wanted to be able to hang scan pictures on her fridge and point out the obscure shapes to her friends. She wanted to feel labour pains and the tenderness that came from breastfeeding. She wanted all of that. So although adoption and egg donation were not roads that she really wanted to go down, they were the only two options open to her and her heart was leaning towards using a donor. The more that she thought about it, if she had to go the donor route, wouldn't it better to have Isla's eggs as opposed to some anonymous donor with no genetic link to her whatsoever? She and Isla were sisters; they shared the same parents and the same genes. If you thought about it, what was the difference in the genes that went into making Isla's eggs when she was in their mother's womb as opposed to Jo's? They came from the same place; in fact, when the eggs were being dealt out Isla's eggs could just as easily have been Jo's eggs. It all came down to random biology. And did it really matter where the eggs originated when it would mean that she had a chance to have a child of her own? And she would finally be able to give Ryan a child of his own. She needed to put herself second in all of this. This was a chance for him to have his dreams come true.

Suddenly the idea grew on her and she became excited by it. She decided to do a lot of research on it first before mentioning it to Ryan. She knew that he might find it difficult to get his head around it. She made an appointment to meet privately with her consultant Dr Collins to listen to his advice. After an hour in his clinic she had soon discovered that there were lots of women worldwide just like her trying to come to terms with the fact that this was their only option and learning how to accept it. She suddenly didn't feel like what she was contemplating was that extraordinary. It was happening across the world every day but people just didn't talk about it. Her consultant had also discussed the issues surrounding using eggs from a known familial donor or else going down the anonymous donor route. That had been a tough decision for Jo. If they decided to use an anonymous donor, she felt that it would be easier to forget about the origins of your baby if the treatment was successful. Once that egg had been fertilised and implanted, she imagined that you could switch your head off and forget it ever happened because the donor wasn't in your life and no one need ever know except for her and Ryan. Whereas if she was to use Isla's eggs, was she going to be reminded of the fact that Isla had donated her eggs to them every time she looked at her child? On the big features Jo knew that she and Isla were quite different but they shared certain things like the fullness of their lips and the arching curve of their eyebrows. If you looked closely enough, you'd know that they were sisters. She wondered would the child have Isla's auburn hair with its soft curls that never seem to know which way they wanted to fall, or would he or she have Ryan's thick dark strands? But she knew that having a genetic link with her child was important to her.

When she finally felt ready to tell Ryan about what she was thinking, she was a bit deflated by his initial reaction. She thought he'd be excited, ebullient even, at another chance to have a child of his own. She knew that she would have been if Dr Collins had phoned her up and said 'Hang on a minute, Jo, before you rush off there lining up egg donors – there's this new treatment that might just work for you'. But instead Ryan had been wary. He had lots of questions – first and foremost, would the child be Isla's or theirs? She knew that he was getting confused with surrogacy so she had patiently explained her research into it as if she was instructing one of the junior solicitors in the firm. She told him that under Irish law the donor would relinquish all rights to the baby with the act of donation and that it was the birth mother who would be the legal mother on the birth certificate. She would carry the baby; it would be her blood that would flow through it, her body that would nourish it. "And," she had said, handing him a research paper that Dr Collins had given her, "did you know that the birth mother's genes will affect how the donor egg's genes are expressed?"

"What does that mean?"

"Basically, if Isla had that exact same foetus growing inside of her, it would be a different baby because it would be her body that would determine which genes get turned on and off in the baby and it would be the same for me if I was carrying the baby. Isn't nature fascinating?"

"And how difficult would the treatment be from her point of view?"

"It would be the exact same as what I go through with an IVF cycle. So first she would inject herself to make her body shut everything down and then she would have drugs to stimulate egg production. The eggs would be harvested and then that would be her bit done. Then in the lab they would fertilise them with your swimmers and just like what we've done before, the resulting embryo would be implanted into me and we would hope and pray to every god above that it takes and that we get a baby at the end of it all."

"And what if we went through all that and it didn't work out?"

"I don't want to think about that but, yeah . . . it would be awful for us and also for Isla having gone through all of it too."

"Do you think you would resent her, if it didn't work? Would she resent you?"

"We're sisters, we're closer than that. I hate the thought of her having to put her body through what I've been doing for so long, but it's a once-off – if it doesn't work then that's it – I wouldn't ask her to do it again."

"And if it worked what would we tell the child? Would it know that Isla was its mother?"

"You need to change the way you're thinking about this, Ryan. She wouldn't *be* its mother – it'd be *our* baby – yours and mine! But we wouldn't tell it anyway. No one would know except for you and me – and Isla obviously."

"Oh, I don't know, Jo . . . don't these things always come out in the end?"

"Well, neither of us would say anything and I'd trust Isla with my life."

"But wouldn't it be a bit weird? It's like me having a baby with my sister-in-law for god's sake!"

"You wouldn't be having a baby with her – it'd be my baby. She would be only giving us the egg. It only becomes a baby after it's fertilised and is growing inside my body. It's not a baby with just Isla's egg – it is you and me that make it into a baby. We would be its creators because it would never exist in the first place if it wasn't for us wanting it so badly."

"Is it even legal to do this?"

"It has been happening for a long time. At the moment in Ireland there are no laws really governing this area yet so it's a bit grey."

"Ah, Jo, come on! Doesn't it all sound a bit crazy? A bit far-fetched? Like we're messing with nature?"

"It's our only option, Ryan – it's either this or we remain childless."

"We could adopt?"

"Do you know how long you have to wait to get a child? There are so few children given up for adoption these days. You could be waiting for years and you're still not guaranteed to even get a child at the end of it and you can end up in a legal nightmare if you decide to venture abroad. I really think we have a great opportunity here, Ryan, and we have to take it."

She decided not to push the issue any further with him and instead gave him some space to get his head around it all. She bided her time before bringing it up with him once more a few weeks later. When he raised the same concerns again, she had all her arguments ready to convince him.

"I just think we need to accept the hand that we've been dealt," he had said.

"No, we don't, Ryan."

"We can still be happy, Jo – we can still have a really great life together. Just because we can't have children doesn't have to mean that we're living a poorer version of the lives we could have had. We have each other – it can still be great if you want it to be!"

"Please, Ryan, there is one more option open to us and I really want to try it. It's our last chance and, if we don't at least try it, I think I will always wonder what might have been and regret it for the rest of my life."

"But it's not just us involved – there's your sister as well."

"Ryan, please, just one more chance, that's all I want. If it doesn't work then that's it. I'll raise my hands in defeat."

"But I've heard that so many times already, Jo!"

"Well, if you want to be the one to stop me from experiencing the joy of carrying my own baby then so be it."

She had stormed out of the room and gone upstairs and bawled. Why were they being tested like this? Why did the whole thing have to be so hard and stressful? What had she ever done to deserve this? She had tried hard throughout her treatment to be strong and not to let herself fall into a 'why me?' puddle of self-indulgent pity but sometimes it was very difficult.

Ryan had come upstairs and pushed open the bedroom door a while later. He came over and put his arms around her on the bed and she had sobbed heartily into his shoulder.

"I hate seeing you like this, Jo . . . so if it's what you really want and you're sure about it, we can do it." He had sounded hesitant. "Once Isla is fully on board and understands completely what would be involved in it."

"She is, well, she will be – I know she will."

"Okay then, if that's what you want . . . if you're sure, and Isla too, we'll do it."

She threw her arms around his neck, breathing in his scent, and for the first time in a long time they made love.

Jo knew she now needed to talk to Isla and make sure that she'd meant what she'd said. She knew that Isla could throw words around carelessly without considering their meaning. She was worried that she had jumped in as usual on the spur of the moment. But it was like someone had thrown her a lifeline in an ocean of despair, so she took it, practically snatched it out of her younger sister's hands and was now clinging on desperately to it.

Isla had been surprised but happy when Jo called over to her flat to talk about it one evening after work.

"I thought you'd completely discounted that idea?" she'd said.

"I had – you were about ten steps ahead of where I was at that point but, after I had time to think about it properly and rationally, I realised it's the next best option. I've had time to accept that I'm never going to have a genetic child of my own but this is pretty close."

"Well, I'm glad. I feel really happy that I can hopefully – I mean if everything is okay with me – that I can help you in some way."

Isla hadn't seen it as any big deal: Jo wanted a baby, she needed some eggs – she had some. They had the same parents, so she figured it was the same difference.

"I really hope so, Isla. I couldn't face any more setbacks. I'm pinning everything on this – sorry, I don't mean to put you under pressure." Jo had laughed nervously.

"Hey, don't worry, this is going to work. I just know it is."

Jo laughed and hugged her close. "God, I hope you're

right. Thank you so much, Isla. I will never, ever forget what you are doing for us. Ever."

They didn't tell anyone what they were about to embark on. They went back to Dr Collins, the three of them, at the very earliest appointment that Jo could get. It had felt strange consulting as a trio instead of the duo that Jo and Ryan had been working as for so long. They did initial tests on Isla to make sure that she was healthy and didn't have any potential fertility issues herself.

When they all looked good, Isla had to go through the counselling which was a requirement of the clinic. Jo knew that legally it was part of the protocol but it still made her nervous in case they said something to Isla that would trigger a change of mind and cause her to back out of it. But Isla didn't and she signed the paperwork. Jo drafted up a confidentiality agreement, which she made Isla sign but Isla knew that that was just the solicitor coming out in Jo.

Then the clinic had encouraged Ryan and Jo to discuss what, if anything, they would tell the potential child about how she or he was conceived. Jo was adamant that she didn't want anyone to know but Ryan was unsure. He had asked how a child would feel to find out when it was older that it was conceived using a donor? He felt that its trust in its parents would be completely damaged and the fact that it had been this big secret might make it think that its parents were ashamed of its start in life.

"At least if you tell it when it's young, it grows up with its conception as part of its identity and it shouldn't be any big deal," he had argued.

However, Jo was completely opposed to ever telling the child, so he let it go.

When they had all the issues ironed out, they were good to go and it was time for the drugs. Isla took the medication she was given on the days she was told to. She had to give herself a daily injection to shut down her reproductive system, which seemed crazy to her, but it was explained that it was so the clinic could be in control of her cycle – most importantly, over when she would drop those eggs.

Isla hated needles. It was not the injection itself but the anticipation that she found awful so Jo had offered to come over at the same time every day to do it for her. It also allowed Jo to make sure that Isla was doing everything as she was supposed to do it. Jo was finding the lack of control hard and the fact that she was relying on her sister, who could be flaky at the best of times, to get it right was making her anxious. A side effect of the injection was that Isla's body thought it was going through the menopause and she was experiencing all of those symptoms. She would wake up at night with her sheets soaked through with sweat. She would have to go outside the back door in work to cool down when the heat from a hot flush became too much. And the pounding headaches too. But she knew that it was nothing compared to the torture that Jo had put herself through for years. She had watched her sister go through some very dark days so a few weeks of injections and a few hot flushes were nothing to moan about when you thought about it like that.

Then they harvested Isla's eggs and that was her part over. They mixed them with Ryan's sperm and it resulted in two embryos. One was implanted into Jo and they made the decision to freeze the other as a backup in case it didn't work the first time and, if it did work, then it potentially could be a future brother or sister to the first child.

They had another horrible wait then to see if the treatment had worked but when Jo woke up feeling nauseous even before she had done a test, she had dared to hope. Thankfully the embryo had taken and, when a second pink line had appeared where there had only been a single line for so many years, she rang Ryan at work in a teary, trembling mess.

The next phone call she made was to Isla.

"Thank you for this gift, Isla – I will never be able to thank you enough."

Jo would never forget her reply.

"I've got a good feeling about this, Jo. You're finally going to get your baby."

Jo had liked the fact that she had used the word 'your'.

Chapter 4

Little Star

As the weeks went on Jo had tentatively ticked them off on her calendar. She did not want to get her hopes raised but for once it seemed that everything was going well inside her womb. She had been extremely anxious during the first twelve weeks. She would continuously run to the bathroom just to make sure that there was no bleeding. She was so worried. It wasn't until she got through the first trimester that she finally dared to believe that it might just happen. That at last there might be a baby in their future.

Soon her belly had started to push forward and she was so proud when she finally had a bump to show off. It finally felt real. People in shops admired it, colleagues in work offered to carry her heavy files to and from meetings. When she met up with friends, they said that pregnancy suited her. She loved joining in conversations with other pregnant women in the office who were complaining of backache or of the poor choice of maternity clothes available to them. She had been overhearing those conversations with a heaviness in her heart for so long that she was now embracing the chance to finally be one of those women who chatted idly in the lift or stopped by the photocopier to discuss their pregnancies. She was basking in the attention. She had wanted to be that woman a long time and, now that it had arrived, she was relishing every minute of it. Everything in her life finally was perfect: she had Ryan and they were soon to be parents.

It was almost going too well. Then their baby had decided to arrive at twenty-seven weeks, which was a frightening experience for any pregnant woman but, when you had gone through all that they had been through at that stage, it was terrifying.

Jo had been feeling off that day and had gone home from work to lie down. She had called Ryan to tell him and he had said that it was just stress – that she was doing too much in work and needed to think about throttling back now that she was entering into the third trimester. She had agreed with him and made the decision to leave the office at five o'clock every day. She had gone home and climbed into bed. She felt so heavy and every part of her felt achy like the very worst flu. She had slept for about an hour and when she woke up and got out of bed her waters had broken. She rang Ryan in an awful state and he came home and took her straight to the hospital. They admitted her and gave her drugs to try to stop her baby from coming but the baby was insistent and was born less than two hours later. The midwives announced she was a girl and Jo caught a glimpse of a tiny pink thing before she was rushed away immediately to the special care unit. She could remember Ryan squeezing her hand so tightly that it hurt.

Then she had started to haemorrhage. She was shaking and shivering and felt so very cold. *The cold, the cold.* She remembered saying to Ryan, "I'm so cold. I need a blanket. Can you get me a blanket? I'm so cold." Her teeth were chattering wildly against each other. She could remember looking down and seeing the colour red, bright poppy-red, soaking into the white sheets, and then she felt it form a warm sticky pool underneath her. She had looked at Ryan who had blanched as if the blood was running from his own body instead of hers. She remembered the alarm on the face of the midwife in the room with them. Ryan had started stumbling backwards until he found himself sitting in a chair with his head in his hands. Then the room had started to fill with people. Midwives, people wearing green scrubs, they all came running into the room.

She could remember that the colour of the blood was so rich she almost thought it was beautiful. She was transfixed by it as it seeped across the cloth. She would pick a point on the starched white sheet and watch as the blood journeyed towards it. Then she would pick another one further away and do the same thing again. They were all running around her, talking in panicked, pressured tones to each other. She could hear the snap of latex gloves being pulled on. Machines beeping. The redness had now reached her toes and the shivering was getting worse.

She wanted to sleep badly like she had never needed to sleep before. Her body needed rest but she was being frustrated by a midwife who kept talking to her and asking silly things like where she lived and what colour car she drove. She knew now that they were trying to keep her awake. She could hear Ryan, somewhere on the periphery, asking what was happening over and over again but nobody was answering him. She wanted to ask where the baby was and whether or not she was okay but she couldn't make her mouth form the words. Instead, all she could hear was the rattle of her own teeth, enamel on enamel. They were pulling at her heavy arms, inserting needles and cannulas without any consideration as to whether they might have been hurting her. They pumped blood into her from plump plastic bags filtering down through tubes that led into her body but it came out again just as fast. The redness had now made its way down over the sides of the bed. They reached inside her trying to remove fragments of the placenta and they didn't care if it was hurting her. She looked down over the side of the bed and saw the blood pooling onto the grey vinyl floor.

Ryan had told her that next they were running with her trolley down to theatre and thrusting a clipboard with a form in front of him asking for his consent to the surgery with the possibility of a hysterectomy if they were unable to stem the blood flow. He had signed it without hesitation. She knew that he didn't have much choice: it was either consent to the hysterectomy or have a dead wife with her womb and ovaries intact.

Then they lowered a mask down over her face and that was the last thing she remembered.

Ryan had often told the story of an awful wait where minutes turned into hours and he didn't know if his newborn, much-longed-for baby was dead or alive, or if his wife – the person who brought this much-longed-for baby into the world – was dead or alive.

Jo lost her womb and ovaries on the operating table – not that it mattered to her of course. They had proven themselves more than dysfunctional over the years.

When she had come around, she could remember reaching up and trying to pull the mask off her face. She could remember seeing Isla's concerned face; she could see the worry in her eyes as they looked down into hers. She looked tired, thought Jo. She didn't remember it but she had asked if her baby was alive before falling back asleep again. The next time she came round, she saw Ryan. His face was grey and tired and he looked older somehow. Again, she asked where her baby was and the nurse came in and sedated her. When she was lucid, Ryan told her that their daughter was alive and Jo would never forget how hearing that news felt. Even without knowing her condition, to hear the words "our daughter" was so sweet to the ears. She didn't care about the pain or the weakness or the disorientation of being in a white room with wires and tubes: Ryan had said the words "our daughter". She didn't think that any medicine the doctors could have given her would have made her as determined to get well again as those words had done. When she was a bit stronger he had told her that the baby had almost died twice on them. Ryan hadn't known who to go to – whether he should sit outside the operating theatre as surgeons battled to save his dying wife or in the neonatal intensive-care unit where the newborn infant that she had given birth to was fighting for its own life. He had watched in horror through the glass partition wall as they worked on the baby, large hands working on a tiny body. They had managed to resuscitate her on her way out of this world and brought her back to them. Twice.

By the time Jo was well enough to see her for the first time, she was five days old. Jo could still remember seeing a tiny red baby. She hadn't expected that but her skin looked raw, like a case of bad sunburn. She imagined it would hurt her if they touched her. The nurses told them she was very sick and, although she was stable at that point, she was not yet out of the woods. But there was no way Jo could let her go – they had fought so hard to get her, *their daughter*. They had been down such a long road at that stage, that only to get her for a few days and then to have to say goodbye to her would have been too cruel a fate. So she prayed and prayed for her to get better. And miraculously she did. They told Jo that she wouldn't be able to breastfeed her, that her body would be too weak to produce milk after what she had been through but she asked for a pump and she persevered with it. She kept on pumping until the droplets of milk grew into a trickle and then a steady stream.

Then they realised that they had been calling her "the baby" for two entire weeks. They were still a bit detached and were too afraid to name her. It was like they both thought that they would be tempting fate by doing something like that. But one day the nurse looking after her had chided them gently, saying that the baby should have a name, so they had decided to call her Réiltín, which meant 'Little Star'. Whenever Jo looked up at a star in the night sky, she was always amazed by the fact that the light that she was seeing had been emitted millions of years ago and that she was looking at history rather than the present. It reminded her of how small we all are on earth. It used to give her comfort when she was going through her fertility treatment because there was a bigger picture out there which we could only hope to catch a glimpse of. As humans we thought we knew so much but there was a whole galaxy out there, which we knew nothing about. It gave her hope that miracles could happen and when she had held her baby daughter in her arms for the first time she knew that that was exactly what had happened: she had her own star.

Jo grew stronger and was discharged from hospital and she and Ryan went home together, feeling weird and guilty too, like a huge part of them was missing. They went in to the hospital to see Réiltín every day and gradually they began to see improvements: she began to gain weight, breathe by herself and develop a swallow reflex, which they were told was important for feeding. Finally, almost ten weeks after she was born, they were told that she was doing well and once she gained some more weight they would be able to take her home.

Jo knew that she would be indebted to Isla for the rest of her life. Never could she have even begun trying to find the words to thank her sister for her selfless gift. The gift of a child. For allowing Jo the privilege of being able to give Ryan a child of his own. And in all of her wildest dreams, Jo never could have imagined that it would be as amazing as it was. Any worry that she'd had about loving Réiltín less because she wasn't her genetic child was unfounded. From the first time that she was allowed to hold her, she had known that Réiltín was *her* baby.

The day she finally brought Réiltín home from hospital, she was blown away. She was frightened, amazed, scared, in love, disbelieving that she was finally there in their home. She worried that her body would not be able to give this weak little baby all that she needed to grow. She worried whether, after their long wait, they were really up to the challenge or if they were going to fall at the first hurdle. She had a few panicky nights where she literally would not sleep because she was watching Réiltín with a sense of wonderment and awe but also an undertone of panic. But everyone told her that it was just nerves – apparently it happened, especially when people had been through the wringer to have a baby like she had. She supposed that it was a trauma of some sort.

Chapter 5

Anchors

"Hey, Isla!" Réiltín jumped up off the sofa and ran out to the hallway to throw her arms around her aunt as she came in through the door that evening.

"Happy birthday, Réilt! Cool hair!" Isla said. "Show me?" She ran her fingers through Réiltín's thick auburn hair, which was now streaked electric blue.

"Don't encourage her, Isla – it looks terrible," Jo said as she came into the kitchen.

"When did you do it?"

"When I came home after school."

"Of course, it would have to be permanent!" Jo said.

"Mum, I am fourteen years old!"

"Only as of today, Réiltín!"

"I just want to play around a bit. It's not forever – it will grow out."

"Well, your school will not be happy – you know it's in the rulebook about dying your hair. Don't blame me if you get a note home!"

"Relax, everyone does it, Mum!" Réiltín protested.

"So what are we having for dinner?" Isla asked.

"I'll give you a clue . . . Réiltín's favourite . . ."

"That's easy – burgers and chips!"

Jo smiled. "I hope you're not too hungry – it will be another half an hour or so – I got delayed finishing off the icing on the cake."

"Here," Réiltín said, thrusting a mobile phone into her aunt's hand. "Look at my new phone."

"Very nice! It beats my old brick anyway," Isla said.

"That wouldn't be hard! I still don't know how you survive without any apps."

"Well, I just breathe in and breathe out. I find that usually works," Isla said, laughing.

Réiltín laughed too, linked her arm through Isla's and led her into the living room. Jo watched as they fell down to sit side by side on the sofa.

"I love this one," Isla said, looking at the screen.

It was an old episode of *Friends*. Jo couldn't stand that show with its childish humour and phony canned laughter. She felt a pang inside her. A pang of what, she wasn't too sure . . . it wasn't quite jealousy . . . but it wasn't a good feeling either . . . She loved how close her daughter was with her sister but, if she was really honest, she wished Réiltín could be like that with her, just sometimes. But all she seemed to get from Réiltín these days was a roll of the eyes whenever she said something or monosyllabic answers whenever she asked her a question. She knew it was all part and parcel of being a parent to a teenager – she had asked her friends recently if they were going through the same thing with their children and she smiled now as she recalled how they had all tried to trump each other as they recounted stories about how awful their teenagers were to them. Stories of raging arguments and of devious lies were swapped with conspiratorial relish. The worst by far, though, was one mother who discovered her son had been stealing money from her purse. Jo had come away from that conversation feeling relieved. It seemed she actually got off very lightly with Réiltín compared to the way some teenagers behaved towards their parents.

"Would you mind fetching a bottle of red from the cellar, love?" Jo asked Ryan who had come into the kitchen. Their Victorian house had a basement wine cellar, which was one of the selling points the estate agent had pushed hard on when they had bought the house.

He didn't bother to reply as he vanished out of the room. He came back up a few minutes later with a bottle, which he uncorked and let sit on the table to breathe.

"Dinner's ready!" Jo called as she set plates of burgers and chips and a large bowl of salad down on the table.

The four of them took their seats and began helping themselves.

"So any plans for the weekend?" Jo asked Isla.

"Well, I'm going for a bite to eat with the work crew on Friday night and I have Vera's baby shower."

"Vera Rowland is pregnant?" Jo asked.

"Yep, she's due next month."

"What age is she? She must be nearly forty?"

"She'll be forty in September."

"She was lucky," Jo said.

"Why, Mum?" Réiltín asked.

"Well, because as a woman gets older it can be hard for her to conceive a baby. After forty, a woman's fertility falls off a cliff."

"You're nearly forty, Isla – well, nearly thirty-nine," Réiltín said, turning to her aunt.

"Damn it!" Isla said, slamming the palm of her hand theatrically to her forehead. "I knew I had forgotten to do something!"

"Well, you'd better hurry – you've only got a year left!"

"If the baby would be like you then no thanks," Isla said, laughing.

"Harsh, Isla!" Réiltín replied with pretend affront.

"Well, I'm not sure if they teach you in biology that you need a woman *and* a man to have a baby?"

"Hmmh, I can see you might have a problem there all right. We really need to get you a boyfriend!"

"Well, cheers, Réiltín, you're really playing a blinder today!" Isla replied.

"But I don't get it. I know you're good-looking and men think so too – isn't she, Dad?"

"Absolutely!" Ryan said, looking mortified. He took a large gulp of wine.

"You see! You'd need to be blind not to notice it, Isla."

"Now that's enough, Réiltín – eat up your dinner, please," Jo interjected.

"Yeah, well, life is complicated," Isla sighed. "It's not like in the films. It's not that easy to meet someone, you know."

"You should try online dating," Réiltín continued. "You know my friend Georgie? Well, her mum tried it after she broke up with her dad and it worked! Now they're getting married and Georgie is really happy about it because he has a son the same age as her and he's hot! They're all going on honeymoon together to Antigua so she's packed lots of bikinis."

"I can't believe I'm getting dating advice from my fourteen-year-old niece!"

Réiltín turned to Ryan then. "Dad, do you have any single friends for her?"

"Eh . . . I'll pass, thanks, Réilt."

"Yeah, you're probably right" Réiltín said with a world-weary sigh. "They're all stuffy bankers anyway."

"Réiltín!" Ryan said, laughing. "Will you leave poor Isla alone? She doesn't need advice from you. I'm sure Isla has lots of men interested in dating her . . ." He looked as though he wanted the ground to swallow him up.

Jo felt a tinge of jealousy grow inside her. The familiar pang that seemed to be reserved just for Isla. "Okay, can we all please stop discussing Isla's love life?" she said, more snappily than she had intended.

For her whole life, everyone fancied Isla. Even when they were growing up as children in Lambay Grove, their neighbours had all had a soft spot for her – girlfriends and boyfriends, they all wanted to be with her because that was where the fun was. Jo had often wondered what was it about her younger sister that made men flock to her. She wasn't conventionally beautiful. She never dressed up or made an effort with her appearance. God knows Jo had tried hard enough over the years to get her to take more care with how she looked. Jo used to try subtlety to get her to update her wardrobe by buying her new pieces for Christmas or her birthday, a new sweater or maybe a dress but she had never once seen Isla wearing the things that she had so carefully chosen for her. Her hair wasn't styled – instead its long strands hung loose and wild around her face. She wore the same clothes all the time, faded jeans and baggy sweaters over them, clothes that were too big and hid the thin frame underneath. But even Jo could see that there was a certain fragility about her, a vulnerability that men felt the need to tend to. They wanted to mind her, care for her. It had been happening their whole life.

"What about Greg in the coffee shop? He totally fancies you," Réiltín was saying now.

"No, he doesn't!" Isla felt the heat making its way up her cheeks.

"He so does! You should see how he looks at you!"

"Well, anyway, I'd hate someone to accuse me of trying to sleep my way to the top."

Réiltín leant in towards Isla and punched her arm playfully.

"Okay, that is quite enough, everyone." Jo was stern.

They all looked down at their plates and continued eating their food.

Chapter 6

Frustration

On Friday night Isla walked down the street to the small Italian, where she had arranged to meet Greg and the others from the café. She pushed open the door and saw that the restaurant was full of groups just like theirs, some roaring in laughter, others drowning in forced camaraderie. She squinted across the room to see if she could see anyone. Eventually she spotted Greg standing up out of his seat, waving over to her. He looked smart, dressed in jeans, shirt and jacket, and she knew that he had made an effort. His sandy hair was styled up carefully. He never usually wore gel in his hair.

"Hi, Isla," he said when she reached the table.

She said hi to Michelle and Fran, a college student who worked part-time, usually at weekends.

Michelle handed her a laminated menu. "It's a set one, darling, so you don't have to make your mind up," she said, laughing.

Greg filled her glass with yellow wine and the four of them raised a toast and clinked glasses. The background music was a loop of saxophone covers of eighties easy-listening classics.

They ate and, as the wine loosened them up, they joined in

when Lionel Ritchie's 'All Night Long' came on.

"Who's coming for one more?" Greg asked after he had settled the bill.

"Go on then," said Michelle, "I don't get out that often so when I have a baby-sitter I'm making the most of it! What about you, Isla?"

"Yeah, why not?"

"Fran?" Greg asked.

"I said I'd meet a few of my mates," he said sheepishly.

"Ah, we're not cool enough for you," Greg said, laughing. "I get it."

They left the Italian and stepped out into the cool night air.

"The forecast said it's to snow tonight," Michelle said.

"It's too cold to snow," Greg said.

"That's the most illogical thing I've ever heard!" she responded. "Doesn't it snow in Greenland and Antarctica and all those other places and they have much colder winters than anything we're ever likely to experience?"

"I suppose so," said Greg.

"It's very late – we don't normally see snow in March," Isla said.

"Blame global warming!" Michelle said as assuredly as a person who had spent a lifetime studying meteorology. "It's got all our seasons muddled up."

They strolled down the street until they reached McFadden's. As soon as they pushed open the door of the pub the sound of drunken laughter hit them. It wasn't one of the cooler places that had sprung up all around the area recently. The walls were still covered in purple velvet-effect wallpaper and the Formica tables were from the eighties but they always had a good night there.

"What'll you have? The usual, is it?" Greg asked them as they sat down at a table.

"Yeah, a beer would be great, thanks, Greg," Isla said.

"A Bacardi and Coke for you, Michelle?"

"That's the one."

He signalled the lounge boy over and ordered the round. They looked up at the stage where a yellow-blonde woman with a weathered face was singing Blondie's 'Heart of Glass'. Her chorus of followers swayed their arms back and forth.

"*G'wan, Joan!*" someone roared. "You're the Debbie Harry of Rialto!" This was followed by a cackle of raucous laughter.

Later, Greg moved closer to Isla when Michelle went to the toilet. She picked a beer-mat off the table and folded it in two as she chatted with him. They watched Michelle coming out of the bathroom and stop to chat to someone at the bar. After a while Isla said she was going outside for a cigarette. She had given up the year before but still smoked whenever she was drinking.

"I'll come with you," Greg said quickly. "No point in me sitting here like Billy-no-mates while Michelle's off up at the bar."

She grabbed her coat from the back of the chair and they went out the back. Greg flipped open his packet and pushed one up for Isla. She took the cigarette and put it between her lips and he held his lighter out for her until the end of her cigarette glowed orange. She raised her chin towards the sky and exhaled a long plume of tarry smoke onto the cold night air. Greg lit up one for himself then. The snow had finally started to fall.

"Looks like Michelle was right," Greg said, nodding at the flakes that dithered on their lazy descent to the ground. He paused for a moment to take a drag on his cigarette. "You look very nice tonight, Isla."

"Do I? Thanks, Greg, so do you. Is that a new jacket?"

"It is – do you like it?" He started to pinken.

"I do, it suits you."

"I got it in the shopping centre at lunchtime earlier. They were having a sale."

She nodded. "Well, it's a good buy."

They fell silent for a few moments until Greg spoke. "There's been something on my mind that I wanted to ask you about."

"Go on."

"You know the other day when you said you were dreaming of a baby . . . I thought you might have been . . ." he paused, "you know . . ."

"Pregnant?" she finished for him.

He nodded.

"Well, don't worry, I'm not."

She looked away from his gaze and flicked her ash onto the ground where a light dusting of snow had lodged, like someone had gently sieved icing sugar over it.

"But that's what I wanted to say to you – I wouldn't mind if you were." He turned her around to face him and took her free hand in his. "Honestly, I've been thinking about it and it would be great. I'm probably jumping ahead of myself here . . . but it got me thinking about it and if you were . . . we'd work it out. We could move in together – I mean, only if you wanted to, of course . . . For what it's worth I think we'd be good parents . . ."

"You're right, we would be good."

"So you're definitely not then?"

"No," she said sadly.

"Oh . . . I see. Do you think you would like to have children, Isla?"

"Yeah, I would." She had never admitted that to anyone else before. "I really would."

He nodded in agreement. "I always saw myself as a dad. I thought I'd have a whole football team by now but it hasn't happened yet so who knows if it ever will?"

"It's different for men – you don't have that clock ticking, putting a deadline on things."

"Yeah, but who wants to be the geriatric dad in the playground?"

"I suppose that's true."

She really wished she could make things work between them; she liked him so much that she wished a relationship between them were possible. He was kind and considerate, he wanted to have children – he was perfect for her. But there was something inside her stopping her from letting it grow into something more.

It reminded her of a conversation she'd had with her dad before he died. She remembered he was sitting on the bottom step of the stairs, pulling off his steel-toed boots after a long day in the factory. She knew by the heaviness of his steps as he'd entered the house, the invisible weight that seemed to be loading down his movements, that something was up with him.

"Bad day?" she had asked, sitting down on the step beside him.

"Ah, it was all right, *mo ghrá*, but the supervisor called me in for a chat . . ." He had exhaled slowly.

"Why?"

"Ah, sure I'm not as fast as I used to be – my times are slipping. The young ones that come in, you should see how fast they go – I can't keep up with them – I'm slowing everyone down and then they all have to stay late to get the orders out because of me." He was referring to the assembly line where he worked inserting components into other components, which was monitored to the second to keep the production line going.

"You've worked there for over thirty years, Dad – that has to mean something to them?"

"It doesn't matter – it's all quotas and production targets these days. It was a different place when I first started there. I'm not able for it any more."

She leaned in and rested her head on his shoulder. "I'm sorry, Dad."

"Sure it's not your fault, Isla love. So anyway, enough of listening to your old dad feeling sorry for himself – have you

50

no young man taking you out somewhere fancy tonight?"

She laughed. Her dad said the same thing to her almost every night of the week. "I keep telling you, Dad – it's slim pickings out there."

"There must surely be a nice man out there somewhere for you. What about that Martin fella you were seeing for a while?"

"Ah, he's too nice."

"Now how can that be a bad thing? The man who gets you will be a very lucky lad. If you ask me, you women are all mad. Do you know your mum said the same thing to me about being too nice once?"

When he'd first met her mother she was working as the boss's secretary in the office up on the balcony that looked down over the factory floor. He would see her walking in and out to her office and she would take his breath away. She had long shiny brown hair in waves down her back when all the women in the place had their hair cut up short. She always dressed in skirts and high heels and she wore lipstick when none of the other girls in the factory did.

Isla had heard the story many times and had always found it hard to reconcile the former glamorous version of her mother with the woman she remembered in her head. The woman who wore slippers with dresses, and wellington boots with shorts. She knew that was why the whole business with his timings in the factory had upset him so much – because it was more than just a job to him – that place was his life. It was where he had met her mother and it held a lot of good memories for him.

"I didn't think a man like me had a cat in hell's chance with a woman like that but we got talking and eventually I plucked up the courage to ask her out and that's what she said to me – 'You're too nice for someone like me, Dennis,' – and sure didn't we get married and have three beautiful children together?" His voice had been tinged with sadness.

51

Isla often wondered how her dad had been so happy with his lot. He'd had a wife who barely acknowledged his existence and a job he was much too clever for, and yet he never seemed to expect or want more. And that was exactly the reason why she couldn't allow herself to get into a relationship with Greg. She couldn't do that to him. Live a lie with him. Give him half a life. He deserved someone better than her, someone who could love him back just as much he loved her.

After last orders Greg offered to walk her home. Michelle lived on the way so they dropped her off first before continuing on their own. The sound of their steps along the pavement echoed in the night air. The snow seemed to make everything sharper, crisper.

They went back to his place on the South Circular Road and Isla followed him down the narrow hallway, squeezing past his flatmate's bike, which had left streaks of black along the white painted wall. She followed him into the kitchen and sat down at the table. It smelled like sausages. There were always food smells in Greg's place. He put the kettle on to make a pot of tea. Isla lit up another cigarette while it boiled noisily.

Through the window she could see the streetlights reflected off the bright whiteness outside. She watched the flakes as they rushed now against the glass, falling steadily and persistently. What is it that transfixes us about the beauty of snow, she wondered. It was almost like everything had gone quiet, the whole world had gone still as if cloaked in a blanket of silence and, for a time, everything looked at peace. It was perfection for a while until it started to melt, leaving dirty brown slush everywhere.

When they had finished the tea, they went up to bed, creeping up the stairs so as not to wake his flatmate. Isla lay back on his springy double bed, with its plain navy cotton duvet cover and two matching pillowcases while he was in the bathroom brushing his teeth. She looked around the small room at his built-in wardrobes where he had hung clothes on the corners of the doors so they didn't close properly. When he came back in he put on a Bowie CD and switched off the lights before undressing. Then he leaned over her on the bed and started tugging off her boots and then her jeans. She sat up and pulled her T-shirt off over her head and tossed it onto the floor. He started kissing her passionately, eating at her lips, her neck. He traced his fingers gently over her collarbone. She could feel his hardness pressing against her thighs. He worked down lower, his lips grazing delicately over her skin before coming back up and kissing her deeply again. She was ready for him. She pulled him close.

"I love you, Isla," he said as they lay there afterwards, their skin clammy with sweat.

"No, you don't."

"I do. I love being with you. I love this. I love you." He propped himself up on one elbow and turned to look at her.

She could just about make out the contours of his face in the light coming in behind the curtain from the street outside the window. A long curl fell in front of his forehead. She reached out and brushed it back off his face.

"Why won't you give it a chance?" he said.

"I'm sorry, Greg, I don't know why – I just can't . . ."

He lay back down on the bed with a heavy sigh. She could feel his body tense with frustration. They lay there in silence for a few minutes until Greg rolled over. Isla lay wide awake, staring at a triangle of street light that was escaping at the top of the curtains. Why did she do this? She had a closeness with Greg that she didn't have with anybody else – it felt like he was the only person in her whole life besides her dad who had truly accepted her as she was.

Isla didn't sleep well that night. At one point she woke up with a start and sat upright in the bed beside Greg, her heart hammering, her breathing quick. The sheets were damp with sweat underneath her. She had dreamt of the baby again. He had smiled this time. His rosebud lips moved up at the sides and he smiled at her. It was like he was calling to her.

Chapter 7

Vera's Baby Shower

Greg had been unusually off with Isla as she had sat on the edge of his bed getting dressed the next morning. After she had tied the laces on her boots, she had leaned over his mound in the bed to give him a kiss but he didn't turn around to say goodbye to her. He had never been like that with her before. She had let herself out and continued on home to get ready for Vera's baby shower.

Now, as she came through the revolving door of the hotel, a huge display of fresh flowers standing on a polished mahogany table greeted her. All around her were guests on plush sofas taking afternoon tea. She squinted around the foyer to see if she could catch sight of Vera.

A traditionally dressed doorman came over to her. "Can I help you there, madam?"

"I'm looking for the baby shower for Vera Rowland?"

"Oh, yes, that's taking place in our conservatory. Turn right here and go straight down to the end of the corridor and follow the signs. They're all seated there already."

"Thank you," she said nervously.

Isla walked over the wool carpet, thick underfoot, and

followed the directions she had been given. She had come to a fork and hesitated, unsure whether to go right or left, when she felt someone come up behind her.

"Isla?"

She turned to look at the speaker. Her blonde bushy curls were ashier in colour now, and she looked smaller in height too. The American twang that was once so strong to the ear had softened.

"Mrs Rowland? Oh my goodness," Isla said. "How are you?"

"I'm good, thanks, Isla – how've you been?" She hugged her warmly. "Gosh, I haven't seen you in such a long time. What have you been up to?"

"Not a lot really."

"You're so good to come. I was thrilled when Vera said you could make it." She kissed her cheek. "We're just in here."

Isla followed behind Julia and the blow-dried heads of twenty women turned around from the long table to look at her. She immediately felt self-conscious as she took off her green parka jacket to reveal a grey T-shirt layered underneath a cardigan, jeans and a pair of Converse, and wished she had made more of an effort with her appearance.

Vera was seated at the head of the table. She used the arms of the chair to push herself up and came over to greet Isla with one hand across her bump and the other on the base of her spine. She waddled slightly as she walked.

"Isla! I'm so happy you could come!" she enthused and threw her arms around her friend.

"I wouldn't have missed it." But the truth was that Isla had been dreading coming from the moment she had read Vera's email.

Vera was a paediatrician working in the children's hospital and all of her friends were either doctors like her or lawyers or company directors and, well, Isla had odd-jobbed since she had left school, usually earning the minimum wage or thereabouts. Isla's life hadn't really moved on since school. It was like someone had pressed pause on the sixteen-year-old Isla but Vera's tape had kept on playing.

Once Vera and Isla had been inseparable but, the more time marched on, the more it seemed to wedge them further apart, highlighting the different paths their lives had gone down. Although they had been best friends in secondary school, today they were very different people.

"You look amazing, Vera. Really, really great."

Her bump looked like a perfect basketball had been attached onto her abdomen. She was dressed in an elegant red wrap dress and high heels. The sun that was slanting through the glass panes of the conservatory lit up her face. Isla noticed how Vera's fingernails were manicured and she found herself putting her own hands behind her back. She couldn't help but think back to their school days and how much Vera's appearance had transformed. Gone was the grungy girl who only wore black, heavy eye make-up and hair dyed a different hue of red every week. The woman standing before her now was sophisticated and poised.

"I see you still haven't given up the heels then," Isla said, pointing at the four-inch-high court shoes on Vera's feet.

"God, no! I've done everything else by the book – no alcohol, no unpasteurised cheeses – I've stopped wearing underwire bras but I draw the line at giving up my heels!"

They both laughed. Vera linked Isla's arm with a squeeze and turned her around to face the table. "Everybody, this is my friend Isla! We were in school together."

Isla had met Vera on the first day of secondary school. She had noticed her in her oversized denim jacket and black nail polish, getting out of a Mercedes Benz car, which were a rarity in those days. A glamorous woman with a poodle-like blonde perm, who Isla had presumed to be the girl's mother, had come rushing around from the driver's side, grabbed hold of her by the shoulders and pulled her into a bear of a hug before proclaiming loudly in an American accent "Good luck, my angel!" so that everyone in the yard could hear. The girl in the denim jacket, who looked the furthest thing that Isla had ever seen from an angel, had pushed her away disgusted.

The second time she saw her was when their English teacher handed Vera a bottle of nail-polish remover and a wad of cotton wool with the instruction: "Take it off." She did as she was told without argument as if she knew that this was going to happen. After the class was over and they were all supposed to be making their way to double French, Vera had stopped in the corridor, rested her back up against the wall, folded one knee up underneath her for balance and then took out a small bottle of black nail varnish from her schoolbag. Isla had watched in fascination as she began to paint her nails again. She purposely hung around outside the classroom door and waited until the girl went in ahead of her and then she made sure she got the seat beside her.

"What's your name?" Vera asked as Isla sat down on the chair next to her.

"Isla."

"Nice to meet you, Isla. My name is Vera and I hate it – parents!" she said with a shrug of her shoulders as if it explained everything.

She was born in New York. Her dad was Irish and her mum, Julia, was American. They moved over to Ireland when Vera was twelve. Vera's parents were forever embarrassing her. Not intentionally but it just seemed that way to Vera. "Vera, don't tie that belt too tight on your jeans or your ovaries won't grow," Julia would warn or "Vera, what date is your period due again?" She said 'due' pronounced as 'doo'. "Lemme know so I can buy your tampons when I go to the store later." Her mother would comfortably walk around the house in her bra and knickers and not feel awkward if she saw Isla sitting at the kitchen table drinking a glass of juice. And when she got older, it wasn't unknown for her mum to slip a condom into Vera's bag when she was going out somewhere. She was an only child and they worshipped the ground she walked on.

Vera was a Morrissey fan and had become a vegetarian like him. Isla had experimented with it briefly but she didn't have the willpower.

It was Vera who taught her how to kiss. They were sitting on the floor up in her bedroom one day when Isla told her she was worried that when the time came for her first kiss she wouldn't know how to do it. She was worried about how you would breathe – how fast should your tongue move? Should it dart in and out or move around in a circular motion?

Vera had shrugged and said, "You can practise on me if you want."

"I can't do that!" Isla was horrified by the suggestion. "You're a girl!"

"Duh! That's how all the girls back home learn but if you're too prudish then . . ."

"No, I'm not – okay, let's do it then."

"What, you really want to?" Vera suddenly didn't seem as enthusiastic about the idea.

"Yeah, if you say that's how all the girls in New York learn, then what's the big deal?"

"Okay. So close your eyes,"

Isla sat back against the bed and did as she was told.

"Now tilt your face slightly upwards, yeah . . . okay . . . just down a teensy bit . . . okay . . . come closer . . . now stop."

The next thing Isla felt was Vera's warm mouth covering hers, her tongue parting her lips as it started to search out hers. The taste of Wrigley's Juicy Fruit chewing gum. But instead of it being disgusting, as Isla had thought it would be, it felt strangely good. She relaxed her shoulders and moved her hands up into Vera's lemon-scented hair.

Then she heard the groan of the door opening, followed by, "What are you two doing? Oh my God!"

Isla opened her eyes to see Jo standing there, looking at them in horror. She quickly pulled away from Vera and stood, using the bed to lever herself up.

"We're not lesbians, I swear to you, Jo! . . . Vera was . . . em . . . she was just teaching me how to kiss, you know . . . to practise . . . for when I'm kissing *boys*."

Vera was still sitting on the floor, clutching her stomach, snorting out big bellyfuls of laughter.

"I'm sorry, you guys –" she tried, before breaking off into peals of laughter again. "I'm sorry but –"

"So you think this is funny?" Jo said, putting her hands on her hips, turning to her in mammy mode.

"Don't worry, Jo, Isla's not a lesbian," Vera said, getting up off the floor. She turned away from Isla and said in a mock-whisper to Jo, "You should see the way she gets off with guys down in the bowling alley! Trust me, you have *nothing* to worry about."

And then she sauntered out of the bedroom. They heard her making her way down the landing before she traced her steps back and stuck her head back around the door. "See ya tomorrow, Isla!"

Then they heard her laughing all the way down the stairs.

Life always seemed to be exciting whenever Vera was around. She was like a stream of colour in a grey world.

But when Isla decided to leave school in fifth year, even Vera, who spent every weekend outside the fur shop near Grafton Street drowning the ladies coming out with red paint, was shocked and tried to convince her not to do it. But she just couldn't stay there any longer; the conformity had felt like a tightness constricting her whole body. She couldn't follow rules; she hated the regulations of school – being told what to do, what to wear, how much study you should be doing. It all felt counter-productive. It was like a blindfold tied over her eyes, a gag across her mouth. It felt unnatural for her to be there. She never seemed to be able to answer a question in class like her classmates could. Vera seemed to be able to abide by the regulations more than she could. When Isla had asked her about it one day she said, "You have to play the game, Isla, do what they tell you. Let them think they're in control of you and it makes your life easier. It won't always be like this for us, you know." But Isla couldn't stick it, she had to leave. She felt as though she was useless at the whole thing. She was doing all pass subjects except for art and she knew she wouldn't even get the points to get into art college because all of her other subjects would let her down. There was no point in wasting her time and fulfilling everyone's expectations of her, so she dropped out, more to Jo's horror than her dad's.

Vera would call over on her way home from school and fill her in on the goings-on. She would do impressions of the teachers until Isla was laughing so much that she had to tell her to stop or she might wet herself.

On the day that the Leaving Cert results came out Vera called over as she did every day on her way home from school but on that day she had stood in the doorway to Isla's bedroom looking sheepish. She wouldn't look her in the eye.

"So how did you get on?" Isla had asked. "Let me guess, sub three-hundred?"

"Actually, Isla, I got five-six-five."

"Five-six-five?" Isla had repeated in disbelief, wondering if she had heard her right.

Vera nodded.

Isla was shocked. Then she felt guilty for feeling that way when she should have been happy for her friend. It seemed that after Isla had left school in fifth year, Vera had put her head down and worked hard. Her parents had paid for extra tuition in sixth year too. She went off to Trinity to study medicine the following September and dropped the denim jacket and black nail varnish.

Isla knew that that was when the distance had set in between them. Vera would invite her out with all her new college friends but Isla didn't feel like she fitted in with them so she would make excuses not to go. They still saw each other, though not as often as they used to.

"Let me introduce you to everyone," Vera was saying now, jolting Isla out of her thoughts. "This is my friend Sandra from the hospital" (she pronounced 'Sandra' as *Sondra*). "This is Annabelle – we were in med school together – and of course you remember Jane."

Isla did remember Jane; she was another med-school friend of Vera's. She and Isla had both been bridesmaids for Vera at her wedding to Mike three years before.

"Hi, Isla," they chorused back to her.

"This is Louise – we met in antenatal yoga – she's due two weeks after me, isn't that exciting? And this is Mike's friend's Tom's wife . . ."

And on and on the introductions went until Isla's head was spinning.

Isla eventually sat down at the last remaining place at the table between Mike's younger sister Lisette and another doctor friend of Vera's called Stacy. She remembered Lisette from Vera's hen party – she had been good fun. When everyone else had cried off to bed at midnight, Isla and Lisette had gone on to a nightclub. Isla had flashbacks of dancing to some really bad eighties music and falling backwards against a wall – then when Lisette had tried to pull her back up, she had fallen down beside her and they both had sat on the sticky tiles, laughing hysterically. Then there was something else to do with a rickshaw, which had seemed hilarious at the time but it was all fuzzy now. Lisette had fallen asleep in the taxi on the way home and Isla had to get out to ring the doorbell to get her mother to take her into the house.

Lisette lifted a bottle of pink champagne from the centre of the table and leaned over to fill their glasses. Stacy's hand automatically shot out to cover the glass. "Not for me, thanks, I'm driving."

She turned to fill Isla's glass then. Isla went to stop her because she was worried she wouldn't be able to afford it. "I . . . eh . . . might just get a beer actually."

"Jane left six bottles of this stuff on the table and I'm the only one drinking it – the rest of them are all on mineral water." She pointed her finger accusingly around the table. "Now are you going to help me or not?"

Isla smiled. "Okay, go on then."

"That's more like it, sharing is caring," Lisette said, filling Isla's glass with the pink bubbles.

"So, what do you do, Isla?" Stacy asked.

"Oh, nothing as important as you guys . . ."

Stacy's eyes were fixed on Isla, wide with curiosity, demanding more.

"Well . . . I . . . eh . . . work in a café."

"How nice."

Isla knew she was just being polite.

"Would I know it?" Stacy asked.

"I doubt it – it's on St John's Street."

"Oh . . ."

An awkward silence hung in the air between them until Lisette filled their glasses up again.

Lisette and Stacy chitchatted throughout the meal. Isla wasn't good with new people. She tended to get nervous and, instead of conversing, her head would start looping, trying to think of something else to say. Then the other person would have said something but she would have missed it because she was too busy trying to think of something to say next.

Jane stood up from the table and tapped the side of an empty glass with a spoon to get everyone's attention. She wore a navy blazer with a cream silk blouse tucked into slim-fitting jeans and high heels. Her brown hair was blow-dried in glossy waves, her make-up obviously carefully applied but subtle.

"Here are a few little treats we had made for you, Vera.

You might as well eat these guilt-free while you can!" She laughed, flashing perfect white teeth as she presented Vera with a stand of cupcakes, each decorated with iced baby faces, nappies and bottles.

"Oh my God, thank you! These look too good to eat!" Vera said.

"Now I just want to say a few words about our dear friend Vera," Jane continued. "Don't worry, I won't keep you too long. Firstly, thank you, everyone, for coming today to celebrate Vera's baby shower. I met Vera on the first day we started med school together and since then we have stressed about exams, exchanged notes, cried through bad boyfriends and more bad boyfriends." Cue laughter. "And then we rejoiced when she met Mike." Cue more laughter. "We were bridesmaids for each other's weddings. Then Vera did me the honour of becoming godmother to my first-born son, Laurie, two years ago." She turned to face Vera then. "Vera, I just wanted to say, from the bottom of my heart, thank you for being such a good friend to me."

Isla watched as Lisette gulped back her champagne.

"I think I can safely speak on behalf of all the women in this room today," Jane went on, "to say that you truly are an amazing person, you will be an amazing mother and from the bottom of all our hearts we wish you and Mike every happiness on your journey into parenthood together. It will be the best thing you ever do. So let's all raise our glasses to our dear friend Vera!"

They all stood up. "To Vera!" they said, clinking glasses.

Then everyone clapped. Jane beamed around at her audience and sat back down beside Vera who was dabbing away tears from the corners of her eyes.

"Jesus, I think Jane would actually push the baby out for Vera if she asked her to!" Lisette hissed into Isla's ear, causing Isla to splutter the champagne out of her mouth.

Stacy looked at her in the way you would look at a child

who was misbehaving at the dinner table. Isla wiped a dribble of champagne off her chin.

"Do either of you have children?" Stacy asked when the murmur of chatter started up again.

"No, it's just me on my lonesome," Isla said with a sad smile.

"Me neither. I just never met the right person," Stacy said wistfully.

"Well, I'm only thirty-four now so I still have a bit of time to go," Lisette said assuredly, "but if I'm still single by the time I'm thirty-nine then I've decided that I'm going to go it alone."

"What do you mean? Use a donor?" Isla asked.

"Uh-huh." Lisette nodded decidedly as she sliced her knife through the middle of a cupcake decorated with a sugar-paste baby's face.

"Really, you would do that?" Stacy asked open-mouthed.

"Come on, you're a doctor! Surely you must know that is happening all the time?"

"I work in ophthalmology, so I don't actually," Stacy said with a smile.

"Well, I don't see what the problem with it is – if your car is broken down and you can't fix it, you bring it to a mechanic – if your house needs work you call a builder. Why shouldn't it be the same if you want a baby and you can't do it yourself? You get help!"

"I suppose so . . . but my goodness it's a big step, isn't it?" Isla said.

Lisette shrugged. "Well, I guess it all depends on how much you want to have a baby." Then she brought her cupcake up to her mouth and bit into the half-head of the baby.

Jane announced then that it was time for everyone to pass their gifts up to Vera to be opened. They watched as Vera carefully unwrapped presents in soft neutral tones and yellow and green pastels tied up with ribbons, bows and lace trimmings. One after the other she held up tiny outfits to be admired. Little vests and babygros, tiny soft-soled shoes, cardigans and snowsuits, baskets full of expensive-looking creams and organic lotions too. Vera thanked each of her friends in turn and each one modestly replied that the gift receipt was in the box should she need to change anything.

Then it was Jane's turn. She presented Vera with a large gold envelope.

When Vera opened it, she gasped, "Oh my God, Jane! It's too much – I can't take it!"

It was a voucher for a hotel break.

"Nonsense, it's so important to have a babymoon," Jane said sagely, nodding to the other mothers around the table, who were nodding back at her with gentle murmurs of agreement.

"There was no such thing as a babymoon when I had Vera and I'm pretty sure we all did okay," Julia said, laughing.

It was Isla's turn next and she was mortified following after Jane.

"It's only very small . . ." she said as Vera pulled on one end of the bow she had tied it in.

Vera unwrapped the paper and held up the tiny bonnet and mittens, which Isla had knitted in cream lambswool. She had known that any gift she could have afforded would have looked paltry compared to the gifts that would be lavished on Vera so she had decided to go the homemade route instead – but, beside all the other gifts, they looked so plain, even old-fashioned.

"These are just gorgeous, Isla," Vera beamed. "You are too bloody creative – it's not fair! Thank you, Isla, thank you so much."

"Very crafty!" Jane enthused but Isla couldn't help but notice a smirk on her face.

They finished up soon after and said their goodbyes.

"Do you want a lift, Isla?" Julia asked.

"No, no, I'm fine – it's only a ten-minute walk."

"I'll drop you home."

"Honestly, I need to walk off some of that food."

"No, I insist."

Isla watched as Vera and her mum hugged goodbye, then she sat into Julia's passenger seat.

"God, I need a drink after that," Julia said as she pulled out onto the street. "Jane is a little bit . . . intense."

Isla laughed. "She means well."

"Do you know what – I always thought she was jealous of you."

"Of me?"

"Well, of your friendship with Vera. I think she's part of the reason that you and Vera drifted apart over the years."

"Oh, I don't know . . . Vera and I are very different people now."

They chatted until they reached Isla's flat, then Julia turned to her and said, "I know people move on and things change but Vera still counts you as one of her best friends. You do know that, Isla, don't you?"

Isla nodded. "Sure."

"Okay, well, you look after yourself."

"You too – and I can't wait to hear that the little one has arrived."

"Thank you, Isla."

Isla got out of the car and opened her front door. The smell of chemicals hit her as it always did whenever she opened the door but it seemed even stronger today. Jo was convinced that by living there Isla was exposing herself to unknown carcinogens. She was always telling her that it was dangerous to her health.

Isla climbed the stairs and opened the second door at the top, which led into her flat. She plonked herself down on the sofa.

She couldn't help but think over what Lisette had said. She was almost thirty-nine – time wasn't on her side any more.

How much longer was she going to put up with the deep ache inside? She couldn't keep waiting and hoping that she would fall pregnant with Greg. If it hadn't happened already then there must be a reason why.

She *needed* to have a child. It was like a deep hunger inside her. She couldn't stop it. Maybe she needed to look at it differently. Was Lisette right – was it time to take matters into her own hands?

Chapter 8

The Next Step

On Monday morning Isla pushed open the door to the café. Greg was just lifting the chairs down from the table tops, getting ready to open up.

"Morning," she said.

"Hi, Isla – look, I'm sorry about the other morning," Greg said sheepishly as he followed her out the back of the kitchen where she was hanging up her coat. "I shouldn't have been like that. I was just frustrated . . . I wish you would give us a chance, that's all."

"I'm sorry too, Greg." She looked around and saw that besides Greg there was no one else in yet. "Where's Michelle?" she asked as she tied an apron around her waist.

"She texted me to say that she's running a bit late – her ex didn't show to pick Jamie up."

Neither of them mentioned the other night again, not out of any lingering awkwardness but because they both knew that they had to separate work from what went on in their personal lives.

As she got on with the day's tasks, Isla couldn't get Lisette's words out of her head. They had been swimming around

69

inside her brain since the baby shower. Could it really be that simple? Lisette had tossed them out with wild abandon like it was the perfectly obvious answer to any single woman who was yearning for a child but, when she thought about it, could *she* do that? She really wanted to hold a child in her arms but doing it that way . . . well, it was insane, wasn't it? What would people think – people like Jo and Greg? Even with people who didn't know her too well, how would she explain being pregnant when she wasn't really even in a relationship? But another part of her said if she really wanted a baby so much, which she did, then couldn't she do it alone if she wanted to? What was stopping her?

The door opened again and a council worker came in and handed her a notice, snapping her out of her thoughts.

"What does it say?" Greg said over her shoulder.

She felt the heat rise up along her face and her heart started thumping. "I haven't got my glasses on."

"You and your glasses!" he teased good-naturedly. "In all the years I've known you I've never seen you wearing them! Give it here to me."

She handed the sheet of paper over to him and watched as he read down through it.

"I don't believe it – more bloody road works! Honestly, we'll be out of business if they rip up this street again!"

"I'm sorry, Greg, he never showed!" Michelle came blustering through the door, prodding little Jamie along in front of her. "I'm going to kill him! I didn't want to let you down by ringing in, so I hope you don't mind that I brought him with me – my sister is going to swing by and pick him up soon but she lives on the other side of the city. He won't be any trouble, I promise." Her face was flushed.

"No worries at all. Grab yourself a cup of tea, calm yourself down and I'll sort this little fella out." He turned to Jamie then. "Hey, little man, how about we get you doing a big important job?"

Jamie looked up at Greg wide-eyed and nodded his head eagerly.

"We could do with a bit of help with the washing-up, couldn't we, Isla?"

She nodded. "Absolutely! If there's one job I hate, it's the washing-up!"

Greg pulled a chair over to the sink and signalled for the boy to climb up. Then he filled the sink with water and lots of washing-up liquid so the bubbles rose up around the rim. Jamie started to giggle. Greg gave him a few cups and plates to play with.

"How about you mess around with the bubbles for a while and we'll think up something else for you to do afterwards?"

"Ah, Greg, you're a star," Michelle said when she saw Jamie standing up at the sink with a big grin on his face. "I know I always say it but you'd be a great dad!"

Greg started to blush and went out the front to unlock the door.

Soon the day's customers started to come in and Isla sliced open a demi-baguette to start making a breakfast roll.

When Jamie got bored of playing in the sink he went out the front and helped Greg who was collecting the salt-and-pepper shakers to clean them. He handed them up to Greg to wipe, Greg handed them back when he was done, and Jamie put them on the tables again.

"I'd better up my game – it looks like I've got competition," Isla said, surveying them from behind the counter. She watched how naturally Greg took to the boy. Some adults when they interacted with children were stiff and awkward but Greg was as comfortable chatting to Jamie as he was to her. Michelle was right – he would make a great father. But it hadn't happened for them.

"Yeah, you'd better watch out – he's a great worker," Greg said, interrupting her thoughts.

She looked at little Jamie who was blushing.

71

"He's a sweetheart," she said to Michelle.

"Who – Greg or Jamie?" Michelle said with a grin.

"Jamie, of course," Isla said, feeling flustered.

"Ah, he is, he's my little man. I don't know what I'd do without him." She beamed with pride as she watched her son following Greg around.

The morning rush had just started to quiet down when the door opened and Réiltín and Jo came in.

Réiltín came up to where Isla was standing behind the counter.

"Why aren't you in school?" Isla asked, putting down the cloth she had in her hand.

"I had an orthodontic appointment." Réiltín flashed her braces at Isla. "I'm nearly there – he reckons six more months and my mouth gets to stop cohabitating with the Dublin-Donegal line."

"The train doesn't go to Donegal," Jo said, coming up beside her. "Hi, Isla."

"It's a joke, Mum!" Réiltín said with an exasperated sigh.

"Hey, Jo," Isla said.

"Look, I can't stay long," Jo said, "but the reason I'm here is because I've a huge favour to ask you."

"Go on."

"Well, I'm going to have to go into the office for a few hours on Saturday to catch up on some stuff and Ryan has a golfing tournament – so I was wondering if you had Saturday off and if you wouldn't mind coming over to stay with Réiltín for a few hours in the afternoon – but if you're busy don't worry about it."

"Mum, I keep telling you – I don't need a baby-sitter!"

"I know you don't, love, but I don't like you being on your own at home by yourself for the whole day."

"Sure, no worries," Isla said. "I've got Saturday off anyway. We might catch a movie – *The Fault in Our Stars* is out – what do you think, Réilt?"

"Fine." She rolled her eyes.

"Thank you so much, Isla, you're a lifesaver," Jo said. "Well, come on, you – we'd better go. I don't want you to be late for double science . . ." She looked down and smiled indulgently at her daughter.

"Because that would be the worst thing ever, Mum!" Réiltín groaned.

"Now, now, Miss Sarky! Right, we're off. Bye, Isla!"

"Bye, Isla!" Réiltín sang. "Enjoy work!"

"Have a good day at school! Hope you get loads of homework," Isla retorted.

Réiltín stuck out her tongue at Isla and went out the door after her mother.

Isla had just started wiping down a table when her phone bleeped in her pocket. She fished it out and, when she looked, an image of a swaddled newborn flashed up on the screen.

'Look who arrived early – I guess he was in a hurry to meet us – meet Jules Hanrahan. We're so in love already xx'

She put the cloth down on the table and took the phone in both hands. Vera had had her baby. Isla couldn't help but smile at the pink scrunched-up face and barely opened eyes. He was beautiful but she felt her stomach twist, the longing felt so acute. She couldn't keep feeling like this. This awful longing emptiness was killing her.

"What's wrong?" Greg asked, coming up beside her.

"My friend Vera had a baby boy this morning. We only just had her baby shower on Saturday!" She held out the phone for him to see his picture.

"Wow, he's gorgeous! So tiny."

She felt tears spring into her eyes and knew she was going to cry.

"Are you okay, Isla?" Greg knew that something was up with her.

"I'm fine, I just need to get the spray," she mumbled before running into the kitchen.

73

Once she was alone, she reached for a napkin and dabbed away the tears. She walked over to the sink and took a deep breath to compose herself. A robin with a beautiful rust-coloured breast caught her eye through the window. He was pecking along the concrete, making his way around the wheelie bins, scavenging for any food that had fallen out. Isla took off her rubber gloves and found a crust of bread. She opened the door carefully so as not to frighten him off and went outside to where he was still searching along the cold ground. Breaking the bread up into small pieces, she scattered them on the concrete for him. He started pecking at them in jerky movements. He ate the ones closest to him first, edging ever closer towards her until she had gained his trust enough for him to come within inches of her feet. She crouched down to him and he didn't flinch. She looked into his beady eye and she swore that he looked back into hers. He held her gaze for what felt like minutes, even though it could only have been seconds, and it had felt as though he was looking right through her. Right inside her head and her thoughts. He saw into the emptiness that seemed to be sitting inside her soul. She decided there and then that maybe she should pick up the phone and ring her doctor, see what she had to say about it.

Chapter 9

At the Doctor's

A few days later Isla was sitting in the waiting room to see the same doctor who had confirmed it when she had a urinary tract infection, prescribed her an antibiotic for a chest infection, and who had also told her that she was pregnant. Her heart was thumping wildly and she felt perspiration spread under her armpits. She actually couldn't believe that she was doing this; it felt like another person entirely had booked the appointment and was now sitting here in the waiting room. She had picked up the phone several times to make the appointment but found herself hanging up again before the call was answered. Now, as she sat in the waiting room, she couldn't help but wonder if she was insane thinking about having a baby on her own. Was it a ludicrous idea? Her mind kept throwing up different obstacles and problems that she was likely to encounter but her heart was singing a different tune. All she knew was that she wanted to be a mother so much. Though the circumstances weren't ideal, this was her only way to do it, but now that she was setting things in motion she was very apprehensive and was starting to doubt herself.

When it was her turn the doctor showed her into the surgery and took a seat opposite her.

"Good to see you, Isla. You haven't been in a while. You've been keeping well, I presume?"

"Yes, I have, thanks."

"So what can I do for you today?"

Isla took a deep breath. Her tongue felt thick in her mouth. "I-I-I've been thinking . . ." She paused and looked around at the posters on the wall.

The doctor was looking at her expectantly, her pen poised to take notes.

"About trying to have . . ." Isla found herself unable to say the word but at last managed, "a . . . baby."

The doctor put her pen back down on the keyboard so that it slotted in between the space bar and the bottom row of letters. She paused for a moment before she looked up at Isla thoughtfully and then said, "Okay . . . I see . . . and are you back together with your boyfriend? If I remember correctly, the last time you told me you had broken up with him?"

"No, I'm still single."

"Right, I see," the doctor said somewhat cautiously.

Isla was sure she was thinking that she didn't need to spell it out for her that somehow she would need male involvement.

Isla had been pregnant once before. That was Nevis's baby. He was in a band she used to follow. He was dark and intense like his music. He played bass. They had been together on and off for five years. She would stand at the side of the stage watching him come alive. He would lean over the guitar, his skin almost silver with sweat underneath the heavy yellow lights, with a cigarette hanging out from the side of his mouth. She knew what his skin would feel like under her fingertips when she was alone with him later that night. She knew it would feel sticky with sweat with a few odd hairs sprouting out.

This was the same doctor who had also later referred her to hospital when she had started cramping and bleeding that time in the supermarket. She was standing in a queue at the checkout when she started to feel the warm stickiness pooling between her legs and she knew. She lost the baby at eight weeks. And when she had called over to tell him that the baby was gone, like every good cliché she found him in bed with another girl. She recognised her as one of the groupies that followed his band around at their gigs. Isla calmly announced what had happened and then turned around and walked out of his apartment, pulling the door shut behind her. It was only in the hallway that she had allowed herself to dissolve into tears. He hadn't even bothered to come after her.

"I was hoping to do it alone," she said in a voice so low it came out as almost a whisper.

"So do you plan on using a donor then? Is that the route you're thinking of going down?" the doctor teased out gently.

Isla nodded.

A silence followed before eventually the doctor spoke again. "Okay, well, it certainly wouldn't be the most common thing that I'm presented with in the surgery, that's for sure!" She laughed nervously. "You've thought it out, Isla? I mean it's a big decision – huge even . . ."

Isla could see that she was doing her best to be tactful. "Yeah, I have. It's all I've thought about for the last while to be honest."

The screensaver flashed up on the computer screen. It was a picture of a hammock on a tropical beach somewhere.

"Okay . . . it's just – and I hope you don't take this the wrong way – but on a practical level, speaking not as your doctor but as a mother myself, you do realise that doing it on your own won't be easy, don't you?"

"I know, but it's what I want. I've given it a lot of thought."

"Okay, if it's what you want then I will have to refer you

on to a fertility clinic which will be able to help you in this regard. But please bear in mind, Isla, your age – you're almost thirty-nine – could make things more difficult. I don't want to sound negative but try not to get your hopes up too much, okay?"

She nodded.

"You also should be prepared financially as it can be expensive treatment, especially if it doesn't happen first time."

"Of course," she said, even though she really hadn't thought that end of it through very well.

"They will also make you take counselling first, to make sure it really is what you want – they have to by law."

"I know that."

"Okay, then, if you're sure, just let me type up this referral to the clinic."

She typed the letter, printed it, folded it in two and then handed it to her.

"Well, then, let me wish you the very best of luck!" She reached out her hand to Isla's and shook it warmly. "Hopefully, the next time I see you it will be to confirm your pregnancy."

Isla went outside and stood in the cool evening air with her letter. She still felt almost incredulous that she was doing this. It almost felt like it was someone else entirely and not her standing there in the middle of the street with this letter in her hand. She was not really sure what she should do next. Once she put that letter in the post-box, she would be a client of a fertility clinic and would be going down the route of choosing the most suitable sperm-donor to father her baby. It was not exactly what she had in mind when she had originally thought she might like to have a baby. She had decided not to tell anyone what she was doing, not even Jo. She knew she would probably try to talk her out of it. She hadn't decided whether or not she was going to be honest with people if the treatment was a success. What would she tell people? Would she tell them that she used a donor or that it was some random one-night stand? There was no point in stressing about that stuff now, she decided. She would worry about that further down the line.

She walked down the street until she reached the post office. She joined the queue for a stamp, and then she threw the letter through the slot in the post-box.

Chapter 10

Compare and Contrast

That Saturday afternoon, Isla almost felt claustrophobic as she stood just inside the entrance to the shopping centre where she was due to meet Réiltín. The mall was crowded and people were hitting against her legs with pointy-cornered paper bags.

A few minutes later she saw her niece coming towards her in the distance, her shoulders hunched forward as usual to hide her tall, willowy frame. Her auburn hair was tied up into a messy bun and she wore a headband with a large bow.

"Hi, Isla!" Réiltín threw her arms around her aunt in a hug. "Sorry, the bus was late." She linked her arm through Isla's and they walked down the mall towards the cinema.

"What time is it showing at?" Isla asked, squinting up at the board.

"You can't read that?" Réiltín asked. "Seriously, you really need to wear your glasses, Isla. The next one starts in ten minutes."

"You sound like your mother. Come on, if we're quick we'll have time to grab some contraband first."

They both got a crushed ice drink (red for Réiltín, blue for Isla) even though Isla knew that Jo would freak out about artificial colourings and e-numbers – unbeknownst to her, Isla had been buying them for Réiltín since she was four years old and they hadn't killed her yet. Then they got a large popcorn and mixed a large bag of Maltesers in through it like they always did and went inside to watch the film.

"That was so sad, wasn't it?" Réiltín said afterwards as they sat in the fast-food restaurant next door to the cinema.

"I know," Isla said. "How's my eyeliner holding up? I wasn't expecting it to be a weepie."

"It's fine, surprisingly. How's mine?"

"Grand. So what are we having?" Isla scanned down through the menu.

"I'm going for the burger," Réiltín said.

"So predictable," Isla teased.

"Well, I bet you're going to go for the Tuna Melt?"

"You're right," she sighed.

"Oh, I'm good!" Réiltín said, slapping the table triumphantly.

The waiter came and they ordered their food.

"So how's school?" Isla asked, sitting back.

"It's okay, I guess. Mum wants me to get grinds in Irish and Maths – I got an A in Art last week though! I wish I could just do art all day long. I hate all the other subjects."

"You're clever, you'll be fine."

They chatted until the waiter came with their food.

"How's that boy you like . . . what's his name again . . ." Isla asked as she cut her sandwich, "the one with the nice bum . . . did you ask him out yet?"

Réiltín started to blush. "His name is Rick but no way – I told you that I'd never ask a guy out!"

"Why not?"

"Because it's just too desperate. And imagine if he said no – I'd be so embarrassed! I don't think he even knows that I exist anyway," she sighed.

"Why do you say that?"

"Because he always flirts with the other girls. And who would want to be with me anyway?"

Réiltín placed her palms flat on the table, her fingers long and slender, and Isla couldn't help but notice the familiarity of those hands. Sometimes it just caught her from nowhere. If Isla was being completely honest, after she had donated her eggs and they found out that it had worked, she did worry that she would see parts of herself in the baby. When Réiltín was born and she got to meet her for the first time, she had studied her tiny scrunched-up face closely for similarities. She didn't really notice anything initially except for her long slender fingers. Isla got them from her mum, whereas Jo had their dad's broader hands. When Réiltín's baby chubbiness waned and her facial features started to be revealed, she could see some likenesses. She had her nose for a start. She had her hair too, the same auburn wildness that had driven Isla mad when she was younger trying to keep it under control. But she didn't think of her as hers – she saw her as Jo and Ryan's child from the start and she loved her as you would love any niece. Jo always said that she thought that Réiltín was the image of Ryan but Isla wondered if that was because it was what she wanted to see. As Réiltín grew up, Isla noticed that they shared some traits, such as the way that Réiltín was allergic to dust mites like Isla was. She would sneeze and sneeze repeatedly if she walked into a dusty room. Réiltín could draw too. And there was no one else in the whole world that Isla would rather spend her day with. Jo said it was because Isla was still stuck in the mindset of a teenager herself but Isla didn't see it like that. It was because Réiltín was a great kid and she enjoyed her company. She was funny and perceptive and, even when she was tiny girl, Isla could never fob her off. She was kind and Isla knew that she would do anything for her family or friends. Isla had seen her when her friends got caught up bitching about someone and she would stay quiet. She didn't allow herself to get drawn into things like that. Isla thought that she was the most beautiful person on this earth. It was her relationship with Réiltín that made her want a baby for herself.

"Hey, that's not true!" Isla snapped herself out of her thoughts before her niece asked her what was up.

"Yes, it is. I hate being this tall. I look like a man. I'm taller than all the boys in my year except for two of them and they're both over six foot two!"

"I'm telling you, one day you'll be glad that you're so tall."

"Bet you I won't be," she sighed. "The other girls are so much prettier anyway. I bet he fancies them."

"Don't be ridiculous! He'd be lucky to have you and if he doesn't notice you then he's not worth it."

After they had finished their food, they linked arms and strolled on through the mall. A shop window displaying a wire tree, decorated with pairs of tiny baby shoes hanging with ribbon from the branches, caught Isla's eye and she stopped to admire them.

"Oh my God, they are so cute!" Réiltín squealed.

"They are adorable, aren't they?" Isla watched through the glass as women with rounded tummies or with infants sleeping in prams lifted the clothes from the rails inside. She felt her stomach flip and that feeling of emptiness filled her once again. She linked Réiltín's arm and walked on.

When they reached the house, Isla saw that Jo was home. They strolled over the pebbled driveway and Réiltín opened the door.

Isla followed her down the hallway and into the kitchen.

"Hi, Mum!"

Jo swung around. "Oh, hi there, how did you two get on?"

"Great," said Réiltín.

"Will you stay for dinner, Isla?"

"Oh, we had a bite to eat after the cinema so I'm honestly not hungry."

"Oh, come on, join us anyway. I'm sure Réiltín will find room for more. I found a recipe for baked polenta vegetable lasagne so I thought we'd give it a try."

"*Eugggh*," Réiltín said. "We're not even vegetarians!"

"Now, love, it's full of nutrients. It's not just vegetarians who eat vegetables, you know!"

Isla had to stifle a laugh as Réiltín made a face behind her mother's back.

"Not too much of that, love – it's full of sugar," Jo admonished gently as Réiltín took some juice from the fridge.

"Is Dad not home yet?" Réiltín asked, ignoring her mother and filling a glass up to the top.

"No, they won their tournament so I think they're celebrating. So how was the movie?" Jo began to set the table.

"Good," Réiltín replied.

"How's your chest, love? I hope you took your inhaler?"

"Yes, Mum," Réiltín sighed.

They had only just sat down to eat when Isla's phone started to ring. She bent down, lifted her bag up onto her knee and rooted through it to find it. She eventually fished it out and switched it to silent but then she noticed that the letter that had come back from the fertility clinic the day before was lying on the floor at her feet. Isla had been a little taken aback when the letter had arrived, with an appointment for the following month, just days after she had posted off the referral.

Jo leaned over to pick it up but Isla reached down and snatched it out of her hand quickly.

"Oh sorry," Jo said, surprised by her reaction. "I was just trying to help."

"I . . . em . . . sorry, it's just some bank stuff," Isla said, stuffing it back into her bag again.

"I see," Jo said. "Must be some pretty important bank stuff!"

Isla looked down at her plate as she felt the heat creeping up her face.

Ryan came into the kitchen just as they were almost finished, his cheeks flushed. He bent and kissed Réiltín on the forehead and Jo on the cheek. Jo could smell the wine on his breath.

"So how are my two favourite ladies? Not forgetting you too, of course, Isla."

Jo smiled at the unusual display of affection from her husband. She knew it was the alcohol talking but it still felt good. These days she'd take whatever was on offer. "Sit down – I've kept a plate for you."

"So what did you two ladies get up to today?" he asked Isla and Réiltín.

"We went to the movies," Réiltín said.

"Oh yeah, what did you see?"

"*The Fault in Our Stars*," Réiltín replied.

"That was nice of you, Isla – thanks for taking her."

"Don't mention it. It was good, wasn't it, Réilt?"

Réiltín nodded. "But really sad."

Jo looked concerned. "Well, I hope it was suitable for Réiltín's age group?" she asked, turning to Isla.

"Don't worry, Mum, it was over twelves!" Réiltín said, cutting across her.

"That's okay then," said Jo.

"Oh, I forgot to tell you, Jo, that Vera had her baby – a little boy," Isla said. "They're naming him Jules. He was three weeks early – he arrived a couple of days after her baby shower!"

"Oh wow, I'm delighted for her, pass on my regards, won't you? Now the hard work starts!" Jo paused. "So how's work in the caff? You know I was just thinking the other day that you've been working there for over three years now . . . that's a long time for you!"

Isla could almost see Jo's thought process in the air in front of her: Vera = successful doctor; Isla = lowly café worker. She knew where Jo was trying to steer the conversation. She never missed an opportunity.

"I like it there – Greg is cool – he's a nice boss."

"Well, I think you're too talented for that place."

"It's all right, it pays the bills."

"Well, I think you're too talented to waste your life serving up plates of chips and tea for two. Isn't she, Ryan?"

Ryan nodded, obviously more to appease Jo than because of any strongly held belief that Isla was a wasted talent.

"Would you not have a look at courses, try and make something of your life?" Jo used the tongs to lift a pile of salad onto her plate. A stray leaf landed on the table between the bowl and her plate.

Jo said this to Isla a lot. She had never forgiven her for dropping out of school in fifth year. Jo was always an over-achiever and Isla had learnt early on that no matter how much she tried, she could never, and would never, live up to her, so she didn't try. Why bother when you were not going to succeed anyway?

Jo had studied law in university. It was one of the highest-pointed courses in the country so of course Jo had to do it because she liked a challenge. Isla knew that if you told Jo that she couldn't do something, then she would do it to prove you wrong and then she'd do it again just because you doubted her the first time. She was determined and Isla often wished that she had her balls.

Isla had always found it hard growing up in the shadow of an over-achiever. The teachers in school when Isla came into their class four years after they had taught Jo, would say "Your sister would have known the answer to that question, Isla" or "Your sister had no bother learning her tables when she was your age – you're just lazy, you know". The very worst day of the year was the day of her parent-teacher meetings. Her mother would always come home from them in a bad mood. She would stand in the kitchen with her eyes closed, massaging her temples in slow, circular movements and Isla would know that, yet again, she was in trouble. Jo's report would have been glowing, of course, but Isla's was always bad. Their mum had always said that Isla liked being difficult, that everyone was born with a certain disposition and Isla's was to be troublesome.

Isla had been born on the 27th of June 1976, one of the warmest days of the year, one of the warmest days ever recorded in Ireland. There was an extreme heat wave that summer. Their dad had said the air was hot and foetid. Everything and everyone stank. Dog-shit sat on the pavements scorched white by the sun. The rivers had dried up so shopping trolleys, broken buggies and bicycle wheels with fractured spokes lay beached in the sludge. Plants folded over on themselves, their leaves singed brown by the sun, wilting and dying of thirst. The reservoirs had started to dry up too so water was rationed and there was no water for baths or washing cars or watering plants and everywhere you went people tutted and said, 'Isn't it a terror? You'd think with all the rain we have in this country, from one end of the year to the other, that we'd have a drop of water left in the taps!'

As she prepared to leave the hospital with her, Isla's mother had only needed to dress her in a terrycloth nappy with a light sheet as a covering. It was too hot to wear the crocheted cardigans and booties that she'd had waiting for the baby. She sat into the backseat of the car with her baby in her arms and had exhaled heavily just as the news bulletin on the radio announced that it was going to hit thirty-two that day.

"Imagine, in Ireland!" her dad had said.

They drove the whole way home with the windows down and the blowers set to cool, to try and get some air circulating.

It wasn't long until they pulled up outside their house and, before her mother could even get out of the car, the neighbours who were out packing to head off to the beach for the day stopped tying their deckchairs to the roofs of their cars and stuffing cooler boxes into their boots for a few minutes and crowded around to see the new baby. Her mother finally managed to wrestle her out of their arms and brought her into the house to meet her older sister Jo who was being minded by her mother's sister Carole. They had called Jo over and told her that it was her new baby sister, Isla, and told her that the baby had brought her a doll. Jo hadn't been impressed and had stubbornly refused to take the doll no matter how much they tried to coax her. Their mother was upset by her reaction but their father had said to give it time, that it was a big adjustment for a four-year-old to realise that she was no longer the sole focus of her parents' affections.

But the cold shoulder had continued for the rest of the day and later, when her mother attempted to breastfeed Isla, Jo tried to pull her mother away. When that didn't work, she started to claw at her, digging in with her nails so that their mum had had no choice but to take the infant Isla upstairs to her bedroom. Jo stormed up the stairs after them and again tried to prise her mum away from her new baby sister. When she realised that the baby was physically attached to her, she threw a tantrum so bad that she hurled herself onto the landing and started screaming. She kicked the backs of her small heels against the pine floorboards, rolling back and forth and, before anyone could stop her, she tumbled off the top step and fell down the stairs. Their mother had screamed in horror while their dad frantically chased after her as Jo's small body fell all the way from the top step, right down the thirteen others below it before his eyes. She had finally come to a stop on the clear plastic runner in the middle of their hallway that their mum had bought to protect the orange shag-pile carpet. Isla was left on the bed as her mother rushed down to where Jo was splayed on the floor after knocking herself flat unconscious. They thought she was dead. Their father had called an ambulance and they prayed over her until it got there. Jo came around on the journey to the hospital but they kept her in overnight for observation as a precaution. She ended up with a small scar that cut diagonally through her right eyebrow. Their mother put Isla on the bottle after that.

For Isla's entire life their mother had said that she brought trouble, that it followed her around and lingered wherever she went. Just like what happened on the day she came home from hospital. Their mother used to blame it on the heat wave that she was born into. She reckoned that the extreme weather did funny things to people's heads. It brewed tempers and stewed restlessness. Like their neighbour Mrs McCarthy who left Mr McCarthy that August after thirty-six years of marriage – she just up and left one day, collected her pension in the post-office, stopped off to say a prayer in the church and never came home again. Just as the characters in a Shakespearian tragedy are mercurial with the heat, their mother had said, the same thing had happened to Mrs McCarthy.

Jo was born in the February of '72. But of course she wasn't a Leap Day baby – no, well-timed as always, she had missed that by three days. And nothing remarkable had happened weather-wise that year either; it wasn't exceptionally hot or cold, in fact it was "mild" their father had said.

The heat wave was her mother's explanation for everything that Isla did. She said that it had irreparably affected her. But Isla didn't mean to be troublesome – she wasn't doing it on purpose as her mother seemed to think – she just found school really difficult.

Jo, in her defence, seemed to be just as uncomfortable with the comparisons as Isla was. "Just ignore them, Isla," she would say. "Everyone knows that your teacher, Mrs Wallace, goes into the toilet to drink whiskey during class."

Having Jo there to show her up was like when you painted the skirting boards of a room and then all the other white

89

woodwork looked dull and worn by comparison and you ended up having to paint the window frames, ceilings and doors too. That was what it was like having Jo around. Isla would have been fine as she was but once Jo was there she always contrasted badly.

The only person who never compared them was their dad. He would pull Isla up onto his lap where he was sitting reading his broadsheet newspaper. "Come up here, *mo ghrá*, and tell me what you have been up to today?" he would say and Isla would climb up and point at the photos that sometimes accompanied the news pieces and ask him what they were about. There was the picture of the woman that her father didn't like because he called her "that Thatcher wan" and his face would grimace like even having her name on his lips tasted badly. There was the athlete Carl Lewis being presented with his fourth gold medal of the 1984 Olympics. Another photograph showed mounds of rubble lining a street after a bomb had ripped it apart in Belfast. There were men running out of buildings with masks over their faces: Chernobyl nuclear reactor number four had exploded.

There were a lot of pictures of babies with swollen stomachs. Bluebottle flies swarmed around their heads and their chocolate-brown eyes stared back at them from the pages.

"Why do they look like that, Dad?" she had asked.

"They live in Ethiopia, Isla, love. They've had no rain there in months and their crops can't grow so they've no food to eat. They're starving."

She had thought back guiltily to the uneaten sandwiches in her lunchbox at school earlier that day. "But can't we just give them some of ours?" she had asked.

"You'd think it would be that simple, wouldn't you?" he had said, nodding in agreement with her. "They should have you in talking sense to those government big-wigs! Oh, the world is a strange place, *mo ghrá*."

Isla was content like that. She didn't feel stupid. With her father she could say things without the fear of being laughed at. He had a way of making her questions sound interesting. If she told him said that her teachers said she was stupid, he would say "Never mind them – we all have our own talents and we just have to find them."

When she was a child, she would spend hours drawing and doodling, concentrating on getting it just right and rubbing out with her eraser if she had gone slightly wrong and going back to the start again. She knew that that was what her dad had meant when he had said that we each have our own talents. Isla could sketch people in better likeness than anyone in her class and she knew that she had found her own talent just like her dad had said she would.

Ironically, it was the only thing that Isla could think of that Jo wasn't good at. She could not draw. When Réiltín was small, she would ask Jo to draw her a picture of a cat or something and Isla could see Jo tensing up with the need to get it right and make it perfect like everything else she did in her life, but inevitably the cat would look more like a pig and then they would all explode with laughter.

Isla had taken Jo's advice a few years back and enrolled in a night course in animation but she had to drop out after a few weeks because she wasn't able for it. Looking back, she was stupid to have even thought that she could do something like that. The drawing part itself was fine, but after the first class she had known that she was in over her head. She wasn't able to keep up with everyone when it came to the theory side of things. She had naïvely thought animation was just drawing but there was a lot more to it than that. It was all 3D modelling software and storyboarding. Their tutor would give the class a project to research but Isla couldn't get her head around the books she was supposed to read, when it seemed so easy to everyone else. She would sit with hot palms and beads of sweat would break out across her back as she prayed that the tutor wasn't going to ask her for her opinion next. She would panic if she had to read out loud because she couldn't concentrate on the jumbling letters in front of her. She would go home exhausted from the class, with a pounding tension headache. She wasn't enjoying the course; it was just pressure and stress. She had lain awake in bed at night, imagining all kinds of horrible scenarios that could happen in the next week's class, like the one where she would go to draw but suddenly find that she had lost the ability and then the teacher would pronounce her stupid in front of everyone and tell her to go back to the café and stop dreaming stupid dreams. Isla felt as though the fun was gone once you added rules to something.

Anyway she was quite happy with the way her life was. She knew exactly how much money she would take home at the end of the week, plus a little extra surprise when they divided up the tip jar between them all. She knew what her rent cost, how much she needed to put aside for food and bills and then everything else was hers to spend as she wished. She would have hated to have what Jo had. The pressure of having a mortgage, bills, membership fees and all that increased the higher up the corporate ladder you went. She had seen Jo's bills and, although she knew that her sister earned a lot of money, it made her come out in a cold sweat at the thought of having all that responsibility. It was like a treadmill you couldn't get off because you had so many anchors tying you down. Isla liked to keep it simple. Her ESB and Gas contracts were as tied down as she could get. She even had a pay-as-you-go phone, which Jo laughed at because she said that it was probably costing her twice as much doing it that way – but at least Isla knew where she stood with it. The higher up you ascended in the world, the more anchors you gathered – that was the way Isla saw it.

Chapter 11

The Fertility Clinic

The buses always turned right onto King's Road. They stopped in front of the supermarket and then beside the library, before finally getting to the stop at the cinema where that day Isla was standing in the lashing rain underneath her umbrella. Finally she saw the bus approaching in the distance. As it pulled up, the wheels dipped into a large puddle at the side of the path and she had to jump backwards to avoid the splash. The hydraulic doors hissed as they parted. She climbed up and slotted her coins into the machine. Tearing off her ticket, she made her way down the swaying aisle and slotted into a seat behind a woman with a toddler. The child kneeled up on the seat, facing backwards, and stared at her. She tried smiling at him but his face remained expressionless.

The day had come for her first appointment in the fertility clinic. She had marked the appointment time on her calendar with a large black 'X' and then she had asked Greg for the time off in work.

"I hope there's nothing wrong, Isla?" he had asked over her shoulder as she lowered a tray of scones into the oven, the heat hitting her like a wall. "You've had a few appointments

93

lately – you're okay, aren't you?"

She shut the oven door and turned around to him. She could see the concern in his face.

"Nah, it's just a dentist appointment," she said.

"Oh well, in that case rather you than me!" The sides of his mouth had moved up into a grin.

It had crossed her mind that she could still just bin the appointment and forget about the whole thing and nobody need ever know what she had been contemplating – but then she had dreamt of the baby again and the longing felt more powerful than ever. She needed to hold him in her arms and she knew that this was the only way.

When she'd got out of bed that morning she'd thought she was going to be sick. She hadn't been able to stomach breakfast so she had just showered, dressed, put on her parka and left the house. She really wasn't sure if she was doing the right thing but it was like some unknown force was propelling her forward, making her take the next step. She had read about predestination a while ago, the belief that our lives are already predetermined and that, even when we make a decision, it is the decision we were always going to make anyway. And that was how she felt at that moment, like this was the path her life was to go down, this was where all the decisions and choices that she had made in the past had now led her and this was her fate. She was going along with it like a seed carried on the wind.

She scanned the numbers above the door and eventually she came upon the clinic. It was located in a redbrick Georgian townhouse on Fitzwilliam Square where people hurried up and down steps into the offices of architects and solicitors and language schools. Isla climbed the steps and went into a bright, modernly decorated reception area. Immediately the place made her feel nervous – everything about it oozed money and she wasn't sure she belonged there or even if she could afford it. She had heard that they offered payment plans and this was what she was relying on. The receptionist took her details, before showing her into the waiting room. She looked around her and noticed that all of the other seats were taken up with couples – she was the only singleton. Some spoke in whispered tones to each other while others sat silently, almost like strangers sitting beside each other. Glossy fashion magazines sat neatly on the coffee table in front of her. She declined the offer of tea or coffee. She rooted out an old *National Geographic* with well-thumbed pages from the bottom of the pile and flicked through it. She watched as the people before her were called until finally she was shown in to see the consultant, Dr Harvey.

Dr Harvey was a tall man and he greeted Isla with an almost vice-like handshake, gesturing for her to sit down at his desk. It was one of those eerily clean desks with nothing on it bar a photo frame of three red-haired children with white-blonde eyebrows. Isla noticed the eldest child, a boy, had the same sloping forehead as his father.

"So, Isla, you're very welcome. I'm going to start by asking you a few questions to allow me to learn some more about you and then I can give you more information about our services."

Isla nodded.

"So are you married or do you have a partner?"

"I'm single actually."

"Okay, I'm seeing more and more women just like you who are choosing to go down this route, because life hasn't presented them with the partner they thought they'd have at this stage of their lives, so they have to make the decision to go it alone. So just to reassure you, you are not the first woman and you certainly won't be the last woman that comes into my clinic like this."

She nodded anxiously.

He continued on reading down through his questionnaire. He stopped when he came to the questions about her menstrual cycle. She had told him that her cycle was irregular.

"How irregular?" he asked. He had an annoying habit of clearing his throat repeatedly.

"Well, I can't remember when I last had my period – maybe a few months back?"

He made a note of something on her file.

"And you're almost forty, right?"

"Well, I'm nearly thirty-nine actually."

"Okay, well, the first thing I need to do is to make sure you are fully aware of the implications of gamete donation."

"I already am, I –"

"Well, I still need to make sure. I wouldn't be doing my job properly otherwise." He cleared his throat again. "The first step in any donor programme is counselling. We need to be sure that you are aware of the legal and ethical issues of what you are undertaking." He paused for a moment. "We would also need to talk to you about your plans for caring for a child on your own."

She swallowed back a lump that seemed to have lodged in her throat. Suddenly it all seemed very real.

"There is another matter," he went on. "In the past donors could elect to be either anonymous or identifiable, but under the new Child and Family Relationships Act that will soon be enacted a national donor-conceived child register is being established and the right to anonymity will be removed. Whereas in the past, prior to this new law, anonymous donors were given explicit assurance of anonymity, when this legislation is changed we in this clinic will be obliged to seek personal information from the donor to allow for tracing. So under the new legislation children born using a donor will, at the age of consent, be entitled to the donor's identifying information if they so wish. Now this does not mean that you as a parent will automatically receive the donor's identifying information nor is the donor allowed to receive information about the identity of the recipient couple or the child – but any donor-conceived child will be entitled to the information down the line. So this is something that I would ask you to give a lot of thought to. Once the register comes into effect, the right to use an anonymous donor will no longer be allowed so you need to think about how comfortable you would feel if any resulting child from the treatment wanted to be able to get in touch with the donor in the future."

"Okay, I'll think about it."

"Also you must also be aware that the donor has no responsibility financially or otherwise for the child."

"Of course."

"And equally the donor has no paternal rights to a child born as a result of treatment using his sperm. The donor waives all rights to the child with the act of donation itself."

She nodded. She knew all this from when she had donated her eggs to Jo.

"Okay. Well, we'll start today by taking a sample of blood from you to make sure that everything is working as it should be. Obviously your age is the biggest factor working against us here. Sometimes I see women of your age and they have no problem conceiving but it's not always that way. The first blood test we will do will check for your AMH profile – these tests aren't cycle specific so we can do this today – and then you will also be required to give blood samples at Day 3 of your cycle to check your hormone levels, specifically follicle-stimulating hormone, luteinizing hormone, prolactin, oestradiol, T4 and TSH. Then on Day 21 we need another sample to check your progesterone levels, which will tell us if you have ovulated. You can do these at your GP's surgery and they will forward the results to me. These results will give us a better picture about your ovarian reserve – that is, the quantity of eggs you have left – and also if you are ovulating. Once we have the results of those back, then hopefully we will be in a position to progress to the next stage which would involve you filling out a donor-profile questionnaire where you would indicate your preferences for things like age, ethnicity, height, eye-colour, educational background, allergies *et cetera*."

"It sounds just like choosing off a takeaway menu," she said, laughing to lighten the mood.

"Hmmh. Well, usually we would try to select a donor with characteristics to match you or else match to characteristics that you would find acceptable. Then once we have you matched with a suitable donor we begin the insemination process. There are two methods we can use here: either intrauterine insemination or IUI for short, or in-vitro fertilisation also known as IVF. Usually, with both methods you will be required to undergo a course of drugs to stimulate egg production. With IUI the sperm are put in a thin tube, which is inserted into the uterus where we hope it will meet with your eggs and make an embryo. With IVF we harvest your eggs and, in the laboratory, fertilise them with the donor's sperm to make blastocytes. We will then grade these and if we are lucky and they are of a good quality, we will have several healthy embryos to implant – either a single transfer or, if we feel it merits it, a multiple transfer. However, in your case as a single woman, I would highly recommend nothing greater than a single transfer. Then we wait and hope it results in a successful pregnancy." He sat back in his leather chair and steepled his fingers together.

"I see," she said, already feeling overwhelmed with information.

"Have you any questions, Isla?"

"The donors – who are they usually?"

"Donors are ordinary, healthy men from a broad cross-section of society who are usually between the ages of eighteen and fifty. They only receive a small payment for donation so most of them are students. All donors are checked extensively before being accepted. They are also screened for genetic conditions such as a medical history of heritable diseases and infectious diseases such as sexually transmitted infections to ensure full patient safety."

"Will it work? I know you can't guarantee anything but what is the likelihood of success?"

"As with all treatments using your own eggs, the younger you are the greater your chances of success. For each treatment cycle, the success rate varies depending on the age of the woman. It varies obviously from person to person – I've seen forty-something-year-olds with healthier eggs than twenty-somethings – you could be one of the lucky ones. Have you anything else that you'd like to ask me?"

She shook her head.

"Okay, Isla, I'd like you to read over these information booklets first and then we can talk some more at your next appointment, all right?"

She nodded.

"Right then – when you go out the door, go into the next door on your left and a nurse with take your bloods."

"Okay," she said, taking the leaflets from him.

When she finished giving her blood sample, she went back outside into the bright reception area and walked down the steps. She was starting to feel excited.

She dreamt that the baby cried for the first time that night. He had never cried before and she didn't like it, because she wasn't able to settle him. His cheeks were red and his fists pummelled against her as she tried to soothe him. Her sheets were saturated with sweat when she woke up and she had to go into the shower to cool herself down. As she stood there underneath the flow of water, she couldn't get the image of his small fractious face from her head.

It had taken her a long time to settle back to sleep after the dream. She had tossed and turned until eventually her body had given in and let her rest. When she woke the next morning, she was left with a horrible aftertaste from the dream the night before. It had disturbed her. Was it trying to tell her something? Was the baby trying to say something to her? The dreams had always been pleasant before; he was always a happy, smiling baby. She was starting to wonder if the timing of the dream was a sign. Was it a warning? Was it trying to tell her that she shouldn't go ahead with having a baby? Was it a premonition of what was to come?

There used to be a photo of Isla and her mum hanging on the sitting-room wall in Lambay Grove but now it sat in a photo album in a cupboard somewhere in Jo's house. It was taken on her first day of school. They had only been in Lambay Grove for a few weeks at the time and her mother was heavily pregnant with her brother David in it. Isla was dressed in a wine uniform with green trim. The top button on her blouse was open but the collar was held together with a green elasticated tie. Her mum had brushed her hair up into pigtails. Neither of them was smiling in it. They were both staring at the camera stiffly like in a Victorian family portrait. They had the same eyes, Isla and her mother. Their eyes had the same intensity and were a shade between hazel and green. Jo had their dad's eyes, like the clearest blue of a winter sky. The photo was taken in front of the house and they were just standing beside each other like two people not related to each other, not a mother about to leave her daughter for her first day at school. Isla often wondered why her mother hadn't held her hand or put an arm around her shoulders. Why hadn't she crouched down beside her and hugged her close?

That would be Isla's biggest fear about having a child – that as a mother she would be like her mum. That it wouldn't come easily to her and history would repeat itself and she wouldn't do it right. She wasn't naïve – she knew that no parent was perfect – but the intention had to be there. You had to want to get it right most of the time. You had to care enough.

Chapter 12

An Argument

On Saturday morning Isla walked up the hill towards Jo's house and took in the view below her down to the sea. The house was in the centre of the arc that swept from Howth Head on the left to Killiney Hill on the right. If you folded a map of Dublin Bay in half, her house would be in the crease. The sunlight was shimmering and twinkling on the calm sea. She breathed in the salty air and let it fill up her lungs. The bitter wind roared loudly in her ears until they started to sting.

When Isla arrived, Jo was busy juicing. Isla sat up at the breakfast bar and watched as her sister tumbled a carton of blueberries into the machine followed by a fistful of seaweed. Isla had made up her mind to tell Jo. She needed to be able to talk to someone about it, to voice her worries and concerns, and Jo was only person she could trust.

"Want one?" she asked Isla, holding up a glass full of murky green liquid.

"No, thanks."

"It's full of antioxidants." She had an obsession with free radicals. Said they were responsible for so many diseases.

"I'm okay, thanks. So where's Réiltín?"

"She's bowling with some friends."

"I want to talk to you about something."

"You worry me when you say things like that."

"I went for some tests recently."

"Oh yeah?" She turned to examine Isla's face. "You're okay, aren't you? You're not sick?" Her forehead creased downwards in concern. "Please don't tell me there's something wrong – I don't think I could cope."

"No, no, it's nothing like that –"

"Oh, thank God!" She breathed out a huge sigh of relief. "Tests for what?"

"Fertility."

"*Fertility*?"

"I'm thinking of having a baby . . ." Isla said quietly.

"You're thinking of having a baby?" Jo said incredulously. "But how on earth are you going to have a baby? You're not even in a relationship!"

"No, I'm not, but there are ways around these things . . ."

"There are ways around these things?"

"Stop repeating everything I'm saying to you!"

"Sorry, it's just a shock, that's all. So you're thinking of using a donor then, is that what you're trying to tell me?"

"Yeah, it's not ideal but I think it's the only way for me, to be honest."

"But you can't just decide to do something like that on a whim!"

"I haven't decided to do it on a whim. You know this dream that I keep having about the baby? I don't know . . . it's like it's trying to tell me something . . ."

"Oh, that's a great reason to have a baby! Because you had 'a dream'! Jesus, Isla, can't you just come join the rest of us in the real world for once? I didn't know you even wanted to have a child!"

"Well, it's only something I've decided on lately."

"So it *is* a whim then!"

"No, it's not. I mean I've been thinking about it for a while but only made up my mind to go for it recently."

"But why would you want to do something like that on your own? You haven't thought it through properly. You can't just decide to have a child because it takes your fancy one day! You can't give them back, you know, when you've been up all night and they are screaming for no reason or when they're throwing a temper tantrum – you can't give them back when it gets hard, you know!"

"Give me some credit, please, Jo!"

"But you haven't got a clue about how hard being a parent is. If you want something to care for why don't you just get a puppy or kitten or something a bit low maintenance! This is just typical you!"

"Well, thanks for the vote of confidence."

"C'mon, Isla, you have to admit it's a crazy idea? You can barely take care of yourself. How do you plan on supporting a baby?"

"It's not just a financial matter – I can give a child so much love."

"And love is going to buy food and clothes, schoolbooks and after-school activities, is it?"

"I'll manage. It'll be tight but I could try and do some painting on the side – you know, when the baby is asleep – I could try and sell it at some of the markets or maybe I might be able to get a space in Merrion Square – you know, the way they have those artists on a Sunday?"

"Well, I'm sorry but if you haven't managed to do 'some painting' and sell it at the markets up until now, I can't see you suddenly finding the time to do it after you have a baby! And do you intend to haul a baby around the markets with you? And, anyway, how on earth do you think you could raise a child on such an unreliable source of income?" Her tone was condescending, almost contemptuous. "God, I can't believe you are even considering it, Isla – it's total madness!"

"Why can't you just be happy for me? A bit of support is all I want –"

"Because I have a child already, Isla! I know the commitment and patience that being a parent requires, not to mention the financial strain it will put on you!"

"Lots of mothers have to do it alone."

"Yeah, because they don't have a choice! But I bet if you asked any of them if they'd prefer to be raising their child with someone, they'd all give you a resounding yes! It's hard work as part of a couple – no one in their right mind would do it alone if they didn't have to."

"Why is it so different to when you wanted to have a child?"

"Well, because Ryan and I were together for a start! We had a stable and loving home. We had so much more to offer than you. What can you give a child? You live in a shoebox, in a dodgy area of the city. Your flat doesn't even have a lift for Christ sake! Would you drag a buggy up and down those stairs every day? You don't even earn enough to support yourself!"

"Yes, I do."

"Well, then, why did you have to borrow money off me to pay your rent earlier in the year?"

Isla had no argument for that.

"The whole point of having a child is that you have to put that person's needs before your own," Jo continued. "How can you take care of a child when you're not even grown-up enough to look after yourself? You hate commitment – you always say that you don't want to be tied down. You're being selfish even considering it. I'm sorry, Isla, but this is just typical you – you just jump straight in and never think about the consequences. You don't think things through properly."

"I'm not a child any more, Jo. I have thought it through and I want to have a baby."

"Yeah, well, good luck with that, Isla."

She placed the glass down so its bottom spun on the marble

counter top before coming to a stop. She walked out of the room, leaving Isla sitting alone in her kitchen.

After Isla left, Jo was fuming. She doubted Isla had even considered just how much responsibility you bore when you took another life into yours. The constant worry that weighed you down, the frightening news headlines that brought home just how vulnerable you were once you had a child. Not to mention the financial demands of feeding, clothing and educating a child. No, she knew that Isla would never have thought of the things that Jo, as a mother, needed to think of. Isla would never cope with that kind of responsibility. The constant stress of trying to balance motherhood with work demands, home-life and also with being a wife. Jo's head was constantly thinking. She was thinking about who would pick Réiltín up from hockey practice or whether they had lemongrass in the fridge for the curry that she would be making that evening. She was thinking about insurance renewals and whether her pension was too heavily weighted in favour of the property market. She was thinking of the money she needed to leave out to pay their cleaner, or making a mental note to ask her secretary to send flowers to one of their clients who recently slipped on ice and had broken her ankle. She was thinking about arranging for their landscaper to come and do a tidy-up of the flowerbeds. She was thinking about her book club which it was her turn to host and she was wondering if she could cheat and use store-bought pastry to make the canapés that she would be serving instead of making her own. Her head never stopped thinking. Jo prided herself on her organisational skills. Staying on top of everything like she did was her talent, like some people were sporty or artistic – this was her thing and she knew she was good at it. She was constantly thinking ahead of herself, because she knew that if she stopped thinking just for a second, the whole thing could fall apart. Jo knew that Isla wouldn't last five minutes with that kind of responsibility.

Chapter 13

Doubts

After their argument in the kitchen that evening, Jo and Isla went without talking for a week. Not since the period after their dad had died had they gone that long without speaking. It felt strange to Isla; she missed their early morning walks together on the beach. She would go to pick up the phone to call Jo but then she would remember their argument and maybe it was petty pride or stubbornness but she couldn't bring herself to ring her. Réiltín rang her every day to chat as usual but she obviously didn't know about the exchange that had taken place between her mother and Isla.

Réiltín had asked Isla the day before whether she would be at her hockey league final that afternoon and Isla, not wanting to let her down, had said that she would be. Isla had asked Greg if he would mind if she popped down to the school for a while and he'd told her to go ahead.

As Isla neared the pitch, she scanned the sidelines for Jo and Ryan. She spotted Jo dressed in a large black puffer jacket and Ryan in his work suit. She felt her heart rate quicken as she made her way over towards them.

"Hi, Isla," Jo said as she approached.

Isla could tell by her tone that she was taken aback to see her.

"Réiltín asked me to come," she mumbled quickly.

"Hi, Isla," Ryan said.

They all turned back to watch the match, only talking occasionally if the team scored or if the referee made a decision against them. They cheered as Réiltín on the wing took control of the ball from the opposition and dribbled it back to the defence to clear it away from the goal, maintaining their two-point lead with only two minutes to go. They all jumped ecstatically when the fulltime whistle sounded.

"I'll hang on for Réiltín to get changed if you want to head on back to work," Jo said to Ryan. They had come in separate cars.

"Okay, I'll see you later – tell our Little Star that I'm so proud of her," Ryan said and left.

Jo and Isla stood there awkwardly for a few moments before Isla said that she'd better go back to work herself.

"I'll walk you out," said Jo. "Réiltín will be a while yet."

They walked off the pitch sidelines.

"So, how've you been?" Jo asked.

"I'm good."

They walked along the tarmac surface of the schoolyard, passing by some other parents who waved at Jo. She waved back at them then looked at Isla.

"You're not still thinking of trying to have a baby, are you?" she said in a whisper.

Isla was taken aback with how forthright she was being. "Well . . . I'm just getting my blood tests done at the moment to check my hormone levels," she said quietly. "Once I have them I have to go back to the clinic to see what happens next."

"I had hoped you would have seen sense by now. Can't you see that it's complete madness, Isla?" Jo sounded weary. "What has got into you?"

"Jo, I want to have a baby, that's all it is, and unfortunately my circumstances dictate that this is the only way that it's going to happen for me. I really wish it didn't have to be this way but I'm heading towards forty and I can't afford to sit around waiting for Mr Right to arrive. If I want to be a mother, this is the only way that I can do it."

"But why all of a sudden? I've never once heard you mentioning the fact that you were feeling broody before. I don't understand what has changed and why you want it so badly that you're prepared to go it alone? It just seems like such a crazy, hare-brained notion!"

"Look, it's taken me a lot of time to pluck up the courage to do this. Please, can you not be supportive of me?" Isla's voice was raised.

"Keep your voice down, we don't want the whole school learning about your mad ideas," Jo hissed. "I'm your sister, Isla. I *am* being supportive – that's why I'm trying to make you see sense. I don't want you to make one of the biggest mistakes of your life because if you go ahead with this it's not just you who will suffer the fall-out – there's going to be a baby involved too. That's not fair, Isla."

"Why are you so against me having a baby, Jo?"

"I've already told you – you won't be able to cope with the responsibility. You've never been able to face things when life gets hard – you dropped out of school when you found it getting tough. You were no help when Dad died and who was left to sort everything out? Me, that's who! All our lives I've been picking up the pieces for you and I'm not going to stand by and watch an innocent child suffer, all because you took a notion to have a baby one day. But then again, I guess you've always been self-centred."

"I'm going to go now or else I'll say something that I regret. Bye, Jo." Isla walked off across the schoolyard and didn't look back.

The sky opened on her way back to the café. The rain spilled down, forming puddles on the pavement. She didn't have an umbrella with her so she kept her head down and picked her way through the puddles.

When she got back to the café it was quiet with most of the customers emptied out. It was Michelle's day off so Fran was in instead. He was just getting ready to go home when Isla came in and put her apron on. She went out to the kitchen and got stuck into clearing up. She felt the pressure of tears building behind her eyes. She hated fighting with people, especially Jo, but she had upset her.

"Did your niece win her match?" Greg asked as he began emptying out the salad trays.

"She did, by two points . . ." She couldn't hold back the tears any longer and they spilled down her face.

"That's great – hey, what's wrong with you?"

"It's nothing Greg, just family stuff, you know?" She wiped the tears away quickly with the backs of her hands.

He nodded. "Okay . . . well, I'm not going to pry but I'm here if you want to talk about it, you know that, don't you?"

"Thanks, Greg."

"Do you want to do something after work?"

"Sorry but I'm just not in the mood today. I'd prefer to be by myself if you don't mind?"

"Sure, no worries, I understand."

Greg stacked all the chairs up on the tables as Isla washed the floor and then they said goodbye as he locked up.

She decided to walk home the long way by the river. The path was a muddy trail bounded by the river on one side and the gates leading to the gardens of the houses backed onto it on the other. The earlier rain had cleared away to leave behind a bruised sky. She met a few dog walkers and joggers but otherwise was left alone with her racing mind. Maybe Jo was right, she thought. Maybe she wouldn't be able for the responsibility of having a baby. She had made some valid points. Isla knew she wasn't good under pressure; she did tend to run away from things. Would she do that to a baby? After their upbringing the last thing she wanted to do was to mess up a child's life. Yes, she wanted to have baby but was the way she had to do it just too much? Maybe she should just cancel the whole thing – when she thought about it, it was kind of crazy. Yet whenever she thought of having a child of her own and cradling a newborn in her arms, the picture in her head filled her with such an intense happiness, and she knew that that was what she wanted. When she saw what Jo had with Réiltín, she wanted that feeling for herself.

It had started to get dark by the time she reached the path that cut back up to the street where she lived. She came out through the turnstile and saw the glow of the streetlights had just come on, lighting the street in a sodium glow. She walked along until she reached the dry cleaner's, put her key in the door and climbed the stairs to her flat.

Chapter 14

Failure

The day had come for Isla's appointment with the clinic to discuss the results of her blood assays. She had gone to her doctor as instructed and given the necessary samples on the days that Dr Harvey had specified.

As she sat in the plush waiting room, she was nervous. She knew that this would be the deciding factor as to whether or not she was going to be able to have a baby. Her nerves weren't helped by the dreams. The night when the baby had been crying still left her feeling a bit uneasy. She had to admit that it had sowed a small seed of doubt in her mind.

Finally, she was called in to see Dr Harvey. She took a seat across the desk from him while he brought up her file on screen.

"Well, Isla, how've you been?"

He was staring at his large flat-screen computer as he spoke to her. His face gave nothing away.

"I've been good." She could hear the anxious edge to her own voice.

"Okay then, I won't keep you waiting any longer. We have the results of your blood assays back which, as I explained, is the first step to determine if you would be a suitable recipient

111

for donor sperm." He paused for a breath before continuing, "Now, there is no easy way for me to tell you this, Isla, but unfortunately the results were not as good as we would normally like them to be. One of the tests we did was to measure your AMH level. AMH stands for Anti-Mullerian Hormone and it is a hormone secreted by cells in developing egg sacs also known as follicles. Women are born with their lifetime supply of eggs, and these gradually decrease in both quality and quantity with age so the level of AMH in a woman's blood is generally a good indicator of her ovarian reserve. Unfortunately the results have come back to say that you have an AMH of 0.3 which is extremely low. We have had success using IVF with women with low AMH scores before so it's not an automatic disqualifier. However, you will recall the blood tests we did on Day 3 of your cycle where we measured your follicle-stimulating hormone – FSH? Well, FSH is produced by the pituitary gland at the base of the brain. When a woman goes into menopause she is running out of eggs in her ovaries. The brain senses that there is a low oestrogen environment and signals the pituitary to make more follicle-stimulating hormone. So more FSH is released from the pituitary in an attempt to stimulate the ovaries to produce a good follicle and some oestrogen hormone. In a menopausal woman, the pituitary is releasing high levels of FSH to try and stimulate the ovaries – even though there are no follicles or eggs left. The woman's body never gives up trying so FSH levels are permanently elevated. As women approach menopause their baseline FSH levels will tend to gradually increase over the years. When they run out of follicles capable of responding, their FSH will be continuously high and they stop having periods altogether. You had an FSH level of twenty-three on Day 3, which I'm sorry to have to tell you, is indicative of failing ovarian function."

"Failing? What does that mean?"

"I'm sorry to say, Isla, that the results would suggest that you are experiencing the early onset of menopause or premature ovarian failure as we term it medically. I'm afraid I couldn't recommend any artificial reproductive techniques for you. It would be medically remiss of me to allow you to go ahead when it is very unlikely that it would work. I'm so sorry that it's not better news."

"But I'm not yet thirty-nine! Surely I'm too young for the menopause?"

"For some reason this happens to about one per cent of women and it can come as a terrible shock when it does. You mentioned your periods had become very irregular, which would be a sign of it. Did you notice any hot flushes, night sweats?"

She nodded. She had been waking up to find her sheets saturated but she'd thought that she just had too many blankets on the bed or perhaps it was connected with the strange dreams she had been having. She never thought for a minute that it could be something like this.

"Can't I do IVF or something – isn't that what that is for?"

"Your body isn't responding to your own hormones therefore it is unlikely to respond to the drugs we would use as part of an IVF cycle either, and without eggs there can be no baby. I'm sorry, I do wish it was better news."

"So that's it – I have no more options?"

"The only other options open to you would be egg donation or embryo donation. It should be noted, however, that the number of available egg-donors falls far short compared with the number of sperm-donors available – supply falls far below demand. Also using an egg-donor might not even be an option that you are willing to consider if having a genetic link to the child is important to you? Again, I'm sorry to be telling you this."

"Right . . . I see . . . okay . . . I'd better go then . . ."

Suddenly she felt awkward and embarrassed. She wanted to be far away from this man and his impossibly orderly office. She went to stand up and leave the room but realised that she had forgotten her bag so she turned back around for it but banged her knee against the chair in her rush to escape. The pain shot through her leg and she was mortified by her clumsiness.

"Sorry . . . I'm going . . ."

Dr Harvey flashed her a sympathetic but strained smile.

She picked up her bag and said goodbye again.

Taking the stairs down to the ground floor, she went outside into the fresh air. She took the steps leading from the Georgian building down to the pavement two at a time and, when she reached the footpath, she stopped and rested her back up against the railings thickly painted with years of glossy white paint. She hadn't been expecting that at all. She felt winded. She watched the traffic pass by on the road in front of her. Her head was spinning. *Whir, whir, whir . . .* car after car went by, each with its own people going about doing their own things, fretting over their own problems or worries that the rest of the world knew nothing about. That was it for her now, she thought. She was at the end of the road before the journey had even started. There was no way she was going on a crusade to have a baby at all costs and setting down the arduous path of trying to get a donor embryo – the genetic link was important to her. Disappointment was there but so too were shock and anger. She felt cheated that her body had done this to her without giving her a chance to do something about it. If she had known about it earlier, she could have tried to have a baby earlier. If she had been unsure about having a baby before then, suddenly it seemed like the one thing that she wanted most in the world.

She didn't go back to the café afterwards. Instead she texted Greg to say that she wasn't feeling too well. She knew he would hold the fort for her. It started to rain so she pulled up the hood of her parka. The cars turned on their wipers. Puddles were starting to form at the side of the road. She walked along the chewing-gum-strewn pavements, stepping over the cracks.

Chapter 15

Everything Happens for a Reason

Isla went into work early the next morning well before the café was due to open. She had felt bad about not returning after her appointment the day before and wanted to try and make it up to Greg. She hadn't been able to sleep anyway. She had spent the night tossing and turning and thinking about what might have been. As she came down St John's Street towards the café she knew that Greg would already be in the kitchen getting ready for the day ahead and she found herself wanting to see him. He was the one person she wanted to be near right then.

As she gave him a hand to make the day's scones by mixing flour, butter and sugar together with her hands, she found there was comfort in just being in his calming presence. He didn't ask her why she hadn't returned after her appointment the day before or why she was in an hour before she was meant to start; it was like he could just sense that she needed to be there. She worked faster than usual, kneading forcefully until the mixture turned doughy. Then she cut the dough up and put the tray in the oven. She went out the front to get ready to open up by lifting the chairs down from the tables.

Greg turned the sign from 'closed' to 'open' and soon customers began to trickle in through the door. She found it hard to concentrate on her tasks that morning. She found herself watching women with babies even more closely than usual. It stung. She greeted Mrs O'Shea and Mrs Price and set to making their breakfast for them but she made a pot of coffee instead of tea. Mrs Price came back up to the counter and handed it back to her and she had to make it again. She was insulted that Isla had got their order wrong. Then Isla accidently short-changed another customer and had to apologise profusely.

"Your head's all over the place today, Isla, love," Greg said when the rush had died down. His clear blue eyes were sympathetic.

"Sorry, Greg, I've just got some stuff on my mind."

"Did you get on okay in the doctor's yesterday?" She had used the doctor as her excuse. "I hope you don't mind me asking but is everything okay?"

"I'll be fine," she said. "But sometimes life is a bit shit, isn't it?"

"Look, why don't we go for a drink tonight? You sound like you could use some cheering up," he coaxed.

"Yeah, all right, we'll go for one."

At five o'clock her phone rang as they were cleaning up for the day. She reached inside her apron pocket and, when she took it out, saw that it was Réiltín.

"Isla?" She sounded panicked.

"Yeah? Is everything all right?"

"I think I just got my period."

"Are you okay?"

"I think so but it's a bit . . . weird . . ."

"Where are you?"

"At home. I've none of those, y'know, *things* and I'm too embarrassed to buy them on my own . . ."

"Well, did you call your mum?"

"No, she's still at work – anyway I don't want to tell her yet. She'll just tell Dad and make a big deal about it all, probably say something cringey about how I'm a young woman now and then she'll probably want to do 'the talk' again."

"I hear you. I'll come over and I'll run into the pharmacy on the way, okay?"

"Thanks, Isla."

Isla knew that the last thing Réiltín wanted was a fuss but she couldn't help thinking that it was a big day. Her little niece was growing up and it made her kind of sad.

She went out the back and found Greg humming along to the radio as he cleaned the oven.

"Greg, I'm so sorry to do this again for the second day in a row but would it be okay if I headed off now? Something's come up with my niece Réiltín." She saw his face drop and watched the disappointment wash down over it. "Oh, I'm sorry, Greg – I totally forgot we were supposed to be going for a drink after work, but it's an emergency. We'll do it again soon, yeah?"

"Sure, Isla, you go on. I'll see you in the morning."

Isla went into the pharmacy on the way home and bought a packet of pads before walking on to Sandymount. She climbed the stone steps to Jo's seafront house and, before she could even knock on the door, Réiltín had opened it to let her in. Oscar bounded down the hall behind Réiltín, wagging his tail furiously at Isla.

"Well done, you!" Isla said. "That's a big moment – don't worry, I won't say anything cringey like welcome to womanhood but still it's great news. At least someone in this family's reproductive system is in good working order."

"What?"

"Never mind. Here you go," Isla said, giving her the pads. "Do you want a demo?"

"Are you serious, Isla?"

She could see Réiltín was having second thoughts about having confided in her but then, when she burst out laughing, Réiltín laughed too.

She went into the bathroom and Isla slid down onto Jo's thick wool carpet with her back resting against the wall and talked to her through the door.

"So are you going to tell your mum later?"

"No – and don't you tell her yet either."

"Okay, whatever you want but tell her soon – you know what she's like – she might be upset that you didn't tell her first."

Réiltín and Isla were in the kitchen when Jo came home from work a while later. Isla and Jo hadn't been in contact since the day of the hockey match.

"Isla? I wasn't expecting to see you here?" Jo placed two bags of groceries onto her white marble counter-top. There was a definite coolness in her tone.

"Oh, I just said I'd drop in to say hi."

"I see." She started to move around the kitchen, putting away the groceries.

Réiltín got up off the stool and started to give her a hand.

"Did you get much homework?" Jo asked her.

"A bit."

"Well, why don't you go upstairs and make a start on it and I can fix us something to eat?"

Réiltín did as she was told and Jo started leafing through the pages of a cookery book.

Soon the noise of a repetitive drumbeat layered with a whiny voice filtered down from Réiltín's bedroom.

"I don't know how she concentrates on anything with that racket," Jo said.

"I got my results back yesterday," Isla said.

"What results?" Jo raised her head from the page and gave Isla a withering look before looking back down again to turn the pages of the book.

"From the fertility clinic."

Jo stopped flicking through the pages.

"They said that I'm in early menopause," Isla continued. "My ovarian reserve is too low and it's unlikely to be a success.

"Oh, Isla, I'm so sorry, I really am."

Isla nodded. "It was such a shock. I thought I had years to go before I'd hit the menopause."

"Gosh, so would I have! Had you any signs?"

"Well, yeah, in hindsight I can see things, like my periods were so irregular and I was waking up with night sweats but I never thought it was because of something like that. You don't think it has something to do with, well, y'know . . . all those drugs and hormones I had to take?"

"Oh, for god's sake don't be ridiculous, Isla!" Jo flashed her a burning look before trying a softer tone. "Look, I'm sorry, but maybe it's not meant to be. How would you have managed anyway? You earn a pittance – you can barely afford the rent on your flat as it is and you've no partner!"

"Yeah, I know, you're probably right but it's still hard to accept that that is it," Isla said quietly.

"Come on, Isla, I know it was difficult for you to hear that and I'm sure you're disappointed but don't you think it would have been too much to do it on your own? Some days I really struggle to get it right and I have Ryan to support me! I don't know how people do it alone. Look, I'm sorry, I know it wasn't what you wanted but it's probably for the best, Isla. As the saying goes 'everything happens for a reason'."

"Yeah, maybe. It's hard to get my head around it though . . . I really wanted to have a baby."

"I know you did – life can be unfair sometimes," Jo said soothingly. "Will you stay for dinner?"

Her tone sounded to Isla as though she thought the offer of dinner was a fair consolation for her disappointment.

"No, I ate a big lunch so I won't, thanks. Look, I'd better

head on. I'll just run up the stairs and say bye to Réiltín before I go."

After she had said goodbye to her niece, Isla left and walked down the quiet leafy streets where Jo lived, through the city until she reached shops with neon signs out front advertising Cash for Gold and Western Union money transfers. There was an Afro Caribbean store as well as a Polski *sklep*. The last fifteen years had seen the area transformed into a melting pot of cultures. Soon she was at her door.

The smell of the chemicals that always hung around the hall hit her nostrils, sharp and pungent, as she climbed the narrow stairs. The faded blue carpet was worn away to threads on the crease of each step, just like the knees of a well-worn pair of jeans. At the top she opened the door leading into her flat, took off her coat and threw it onto the couch. Then she unlaced her boots and kicked them off so that they fell down like wounded casualties just in front of the TV.

As she'd walked home she'd been trying to figure out which she was more upset about: Jo's constant lack of belief in her abilities or the fact that she couldn't have a child of her own? She had always just assumed that having children would happen for her one day but now here she was and her 'one day' was gone. It had sailed past her on a foggy sea without so much as flashing a signal to warn her as she was left stranded on the shore.

She had always thought that she would meet the right person and that it would just happen the same way that it seemed to do for everyone else. But since Nevis, she had been too afraid to open herself up to anybody new. She could never forget that sense of betrayal, the devastating hurt. And now it seemed she had missed her chance. Of course there was her thing with Greg but she was too afraid to let that develop any further. Now the reason why she hadn't fallen pregnant with Greg started to make sense to her. It hadn't happened yet because it would never happen for her.

That night the baby was gurgling and smiling. She could hear the throaty sounds as clearly as a brook babbles on a summer's day. They started low and guttural and then sprang up into high-pitched shrieks of laughter as he experimented with the range of his voice. Soft *aaaaa* sounds blended with sharper *eeeee's* and back again.

Chapter 16

Transparent

As Isla came down St John's Street on the morning of June 27th, she noticed a red balloon stuck on the outside of the café door. It was bobbing delicately in the wind. Her mouth broke into a wide smile. When she pushed the door open, she saw more balloons decorating the counter inside. It was her thirty-ninth birthday.

"Happy birthday, Isla!" Greg came towards her and gave her a hug.

"Aw, thanks, Greg."

"So how are you feeling?"

"Depressed."

"Hey, come on, cheer up," he said, putting an arm around her shoulders.

She went out the back to hang up her coat. Michelle wasn't in yet.

Réiltín came running through the door a few minutes after they had opened. "Happy birthday, Isla!" She threw her arms around her aunt.

Jo came in after her and put her arms around her too. "Happy birthday, Isla! Here, these are for you." She handed her a beautiful bouquet of yellow roses.

"Thank you, Jo, they're lovely."

"I made you this –" Réiltín said, thrusting a gift into her hands. "Well, I made the frame and Mum got the photo."

Isla untied the ribbon and opened up the wrapping, which Réiltín had decorated herself.

"I made the frame in art class." It had been decorated in purple sequins. "I know purple is your favourite colour," she added proudly.

It was a photo of Jo and Isla taken in the garden of the house in Lambay Grove. Isla reckoned she was only about six or seven when it was taken and Jo must have been around ten. Jo's arm was slung around Isla's shoulders and Isla was grinning up at the camera while Jo was looking at Isla. They were both wearing matching white cotton sundresses and the bridge of Isla's nose was covered in tiny freckles. She was squinting at the camera as usual.

"It's beautiful," Isla said, touched by how thoughtful Jo was. "I remember that day . . ."

"I found it when I was clearing out some of Mum's old stuff." There was a slight charge of awkwardness between them at the mention of their mother. "We have so few photos of us as kids so I thought you might like to have it."

"Thanks, Jo – it's really nice."

"Well, we'd better go – we don't want you to be late for school," Jo said to Réiltín.

"Bye, Jo, and thanks again. It's a lovely gift."

"Bye, Isla!" Réiltín sang going out the door. "And remember: you have only another three-hundred and sixty-four days to go until you're forty!"

After they were gone Isla stood with the photo between her hands and stared down at it. It was taken in August; she remembered it because, just afterwards, when they had gone back inside to the house, her mum had got really mad with her.

She had told her to bring down her schoolbooks from the previous year so that they could take them to sell in the second-hand bookshop. As usual Isla was getting all of Jo's hand-me-downs. Jo's books were always perfect. Jo minded her things. She never doodled on the pages or wrote her name over and over again along the margins. She didn't draw people or dogs or houses or witches on broomsticks at Halloween. There were no diagonal creases from where she practised folding perfect triangles by turning down the corners of all the pages. They were covered, of course, in the Superfresco wallpaper. Every year they had taken a leftover roll from the garage and used it to cover the new school books. At one stage it had looked like they might even get secondary school out of it too.

Their mum had gone berserk when she saw Isla's books because she said that they wouldn't be able to sell them in the second-hand bookshop, that no one would want them in that state and that they didn't have money to throw around. Then she had taken each of her tatty books and fired them one by one against the wall until they landed on the floor splayed out on their spines or pages first, lying creased on the floor. Jo had turned to her and Isla had looked back at her and they both started to cry because their mother was frightening them. Isla had said that she was sorry but then her mother had turned to her and roared: "Why can you never be easy? Jo is an easy child, I know David *would* have been an easy child but *you* –"

She never did finish what she was going to say. That was the first and last time Isla had ever heard her mention David's name – David, their infant brother who had died when he was only seven weeks old. Their mother put him into his crib for a nap and, when he hadn't woken up for his feed, she went to check on him and found him lying there still and purple-tinged. He was still warm but not warm enough.

'Cot Death' they called it back then. Nowadays it had a

proper title: 'Sudden Infant Death Syndrome'. It wasn't as common today.

For the rest of their childhood it was like he was an angel child standing atop a pedestal, looking down on them all from afar. They could never aspire to get near David's pedestal – not even their dad could.

On the day of David's funeral their Auntie Carole had stayed in the house with Isla and Jo while their parents went to the funeral. Jo was crying loudly and Isla didn't really understand why she was crying. She thought that maybe it was because everyone else was allowed to go to the church except them. Carole had kept rubbing Jo's shoulder and telling her that it would be okay, that he was far too good for this world and that was why he had to go to heaven but then Carole had started crying too and Isla didn't know what to do then because she had never seen a grown-up cry before. She remembered not being sure if she was supposed to cry like they were doing or not. She had tried but she wasn't able to pretend to do it. Jo and Carole didn't notice when she slipped out the back door to go exploring. That was one of her favourite things to do since they had moved to Lambay Grove. Jo used to say that Isla was nosy but their dad said she had an inquisitive mind and that the world needed inquisitive people. He would pull her up on his knee and say "Sure we'd all still be thinking that the world was flat if that Christopher Columbus fella hadn't thought to go off exploring in that boat of his, wha'?" or "If Fleming hadn't noticed that those fungus yokes had killed off the bacteria we wouldn't have had antibiotics".

Isla loved looking inside everyone's house on their street. She loved how they all smelt differently, like the Walshes' house always smelt of chips and fried food – not just on Fridays like in their house, but every day. The smell would meet you as soon as you stepped inside the front door. But the

McGuirks' smelled of polish. She loved their little quirks too, like how the Waldrons always took their shoes off and left them paired neatly on a shelf just inside the door or the O'Rourkes had so many children that the eldest boy Eric slept on the sofa in the sitting room after everyone went to bed and his pillow and duvet were left folded on the side arm until the next night when it was time to make up his bed again.

But her favourite of all the houses in their cul-de-sac was Mrs Peabody's. She lived on her own and would answer the door to Isla like she was an important guest that she had been expecting. She would usher her into the 'good room', serve her up homemade cake and talk to her in a different way than all the other grown-ups spoke to her. Isla didn't know what age Mrs Peabody was but she knew that she was a lot older than her mum. Her white hair was neatly clipped into the same beehive style every day.

Rows of shelving ran around the walls on which sat heavy glass jars full of seashells preserved with glycerine. They were like the shelves in the science lab in the secondary school that she would go to in her later years with its jars of preserved rabbits and frogs and its wooden benches carved with pointed compasses. Mrs Peabody had come from Cornwall and said the shells reminded her of her childhood spent collecting them on the blonde sand. She told Isla she had lost her great love who had fought on the Western Front in the Battle of Normandy. Isla didn't know how she had ended up in Lambay Grove. Her shells were stuck in time and in some ways Isla thought she wanted to be stuck in that time too.

On the day of the funeral Isla came out of their house and saw Mr Taylor who lived in Number 5 standing on his doorstep holding a pair of tan-coloured lady's nylon tights. He was reaching into them and tossing out pieces of torn bread for the birds. He saw her watching him and called over to her and asked if she wanted to give him a hand. She knew that no one on their street liked Mr Taylor and she didn't know why because he seemed all right to her. The women would gossip: "I can't quite put my finger on it but there is something very odd about that man." Whenever the neighbours had people over for Christmas drinks or communion parties he was never invited. Isla used to think it was because his paint was blistering off his walls like giant yellow scabs and he never cut his grass. Everyone else kept their grass trimmed so the estate looked tidy but his house always stood out with its meadow of knee-high weeds. Her father would sigh as they passed his garden as if it personally pained him that Mr Taylor didn't have the same pride in his home that he and the rest of their neighbours did.

When they were finished feeding the birds, he asked her if she wanted to come inside for a glass of red lemonade. She really wanted to see the inside of his house for herself. The other children had told her stories about how they sometimes peeped over Mr Taylor's window ledges and saw captured children in a cage, just like in the story of Hansel and Gretel. Sometimes when Isla saw him leave the house, she would run up and peer through his letterbox to see if she could see any children, but all she could see was a long, dark hallway beyond. She nodded her head eagerly and stepped inside the door behind him. She followed him down the hall and went and sat down in the kitchen. She stared around the room, which was the mirror image of her own but with less furniture. There was no sign of cages anywhere. A *hsssssss* filled the air as Mr Taylor twisted the top on the lemonade bottle and the bubbles rushed to the top.

"So where are your mammy and daddy gone today?" he asked. "I saw them going off in the car earlier on."

"The baby died," Isla said.

"The new one?" he asked as he took two glasses down from the press above the fridge.

"Uh-huh. Mammy wouldn't let me and Jo go to the church so Jo's at home crying now."

One of the glasses slipped from his hand and banged against the counter below. He reached for it quickly to stop it from falling on the floor.

"You should have brought her over here with you – she could have had some lemonade too."

She had nodded to agree with him but really she was glad that Jo wasn't there because she knew she would never have let her go into Mr Taylor's house. She knew she would have taken her by the hand and led her away from him and she wouldn't have had the chance to look around his house.

There was a loud knock on the door then but Mr Taylor made no move to answer it.

"There's someone at your door, Mr Taylor," Isla said.

"It's probably the bloody Jehovah's Witnesses."

"What are jovah's witnesses?"

"*Je-ho-vah*," he corrected.

Then the knocking turned into banging and a voice shouted, "Taylor, I know you're in there! Taylor!"

"Maybe you should answer your door?" Isla said. "It might be your friend wondering where you are?"

The letterbox flapped open then and the voice roared through it. "Taylor – open the fucking door this minute or I'm calling the Guards! I'm warning you, Taylor!"

"That's Daddy!" Isla hopped up off the chair and ran out to the hall.

Mr Taylor followed her out with heavy, methodical steps and took his time unlocking the door. He had to twist the key in the lock and push over the two bolts too. Finally he opened it and Isla saw her dad was standing on the step with his face bright red. The bulging blue vein near his forehead was sticking out too and she knew that that only happened when he was losing his temper.

"What the hell are you doing here, Isla?"

She knew he was mad with her and she didn't like it because he was never mad with her.

"I was helping Mr Taylor feed the birds and then we were going to have lemonade –"

"Get out of here this minute, young lady! We're going home. Everyone is out looking for you. Of all days you could pick to disappear . . ."

She said bye to Mr Taylor. He was smiling at her but it wasn't a nice smile, which she thought was strange because smiles were meant to be nice. His bottom lip stayed straight instead of curving upwards to meet his top lip and you could see the tops of his yellowing teeth sticking up like tombstones.

Her dad brought her home and the house was now full of people. Some of them she knew like her aunties and uncles and neighbours but most of the people in the room she didn't know.

Then Auntie Carole came running out from the kitchen and said, "Oh thank God – thank God you're okay. Where did you go to, Isla? You had me worried sick!" Her Scottish accent was stronger than her mum's but it was even stronger then and Isla knew by her voice that Carole was really mad at her but was trying to hide it.

Her mother came into the room then and stood just inside the door. Isla remembered her make-up was all smudged and she wondered why she didn't try to clean it. Her eyes looked around the room and then they stopped on her. Isla knew she was going to say something but no sound could be heard. It felt like forever until they waited for her to speak.

Then it came: "Of all days, Isla . . ." She paused. "Of all the days you could pick to do this!" Her voice choked. "Just for one day could you not behave yourself? Would that be too much to ask? We put your baby brother in a wooden box in the cold ground today and you decide that this is the day to just disappear! Why does *everything* have to be a drama with you?"

It felt like everyone in the whole room was staring at her through narrowed eyes. She felt their eyes burning into her, like everyone in the room hated her just like her mum did. She turned, ran out of the room, up the stairs and into the bedroom that she shared with Jo. She closed the door behind her and it was only then that she noticed Jo was lying back on her bed with two red eyes.

"Where did you go to, Isla? Everyone was looking for you."

"I went into Mr Taylor's house but it's okay because I didn't see any cages."

"You have to promise me, Isla, that you'll never go there again, do you hear me? Gareth Waldron said that Mr Taylor used to talk to the little girl that lived in our house before us and that's why her family had to move away."

Her name was Mandy, the girl who used to talk to Mr Taylor. Isla knew that because her name was scribbled on the Holly Hobbie wallpaper on the inside of her bed in purple crayon. When they first moved in, her mum had wanted to change the wallpaper but Isla had begged her not to, so she had left it there. She lay back onto the bed and traced her fingers over the loops and curves of her writing.

"You stepped on a crack coming home from school on Wednesday," she said.

Jo would always go to great lengths to avoid the cracks – she said you'd get seven years bad luck if you stood on one. She was really careful, almost to the point that it looked like she was playing hopscotch going down the street with her pigtails swinging out as she jumped. Isla tried to avoid them too but sometimes she would land on one or else she would clear one but then accidently land on another with the side of her foot or heel. David had died on Wednesday.

Isla was disturbed by how quickly a good memory could always be tainted by a bad one in her head. That photograph was a metaphor for her whole childhood really: for every good memory there was an ugly one waiting to push it out again.

Greg came over then and looked at the photograph over her shoulder. "That's a cute one, isn't it?"

"Yeah. I think I was about six or seven when it was taken."

"Here, this is for you –" He handed her an envelope and then he fished a small box wrapped in purple tissue paper out of his pocket. "Happy birthday."

"Oh Greg – you really shouldn't have –" Her hands flew up towards her mouth.

"I just saw it and thought you might like it . . ." His eyes flicked down towards the ground.

Isla untied the silver ribbon that the parcel was tied with and lifted back the lid of the box. Inside was a bracelet with alternating pearls and green stones.

"I chose pearls because they're your birthstone – I kept the receipt so you can take it back if you don't like it."

"No, it's beautiful! Thank you, Greg." She was almost speechless by how kind he was.

"Where are your manners by the way – did no one ever teach you to open the card first?" he said with a laugh.

"Oh sorry, Greg." She opened the envelope and felt the familiar thud of her heart. She took out the card and pretended to read it. It was joined writing. There was no chance of her being able to pick out any words. It was all a mess of loops and scrolls. They were all jumbled together, running into one another on the white card.

He was looking at her expectantly.

"Sorry, Greg, I left my glasses at home."

"You can't read, can you?"

She felt everything stop. Her ears filled with blood until they rang. "Yes, I can!" she said indignantly.

"Why don't you get help?" he was saying in the softest voice.

"I don't know what you're even talking about, Greg!"

"Why are you so damned stubborn?"

"I'm not."

"Why can't you let yourself be happy?"

"I am happy."

"Well, maybe you are but you could be happier. You deserve more, Isla," he said softly.

"Look, Greg, if this is because of us then I'm sorry but I can't change how I feel."

"It's not just that – look at you – I've seen your paintings – you have such a talent and you work here with me. You don't value yourself, you won't push yourself out of your comfort zone." He positioned himself in front of her and took her hand firmly in his. "Let me help you, Isla, please." A dark curl fell over his eyes and he pushed it back out of the way.

"I can't, Greg, I'm sorry," she whispered.

He let go of her hand. "Well, the way I see it is that you have had your finger on the self-destruct button for your whole life. If you don't want to help yourself, there isn't much more I can do for you." He walked past her into the kitchen.

That evening Jo moved around the kitchen getting the dinner ready. Ryan hadn't yet come home. He was late. She decided to go upstairs to Réiltín and see if she wanted to join her downstairs for a while. She longed for her daughter's company. A parenting book that she had read recently had said that if you felt your teenager was growing distant, it was important to keep the lines of communication open so she climbed the stairs and knocked softly on her daughter's bedroom door. She took a deep breath and entered.

"The dinner is almost ready so I thought you might like to take a break for a little while and come downstairs until it's ready?"

"No, Mum, I can't. I've too much to do." Réiltín didn't raise her head from her laptop.

"Oh . . . okay then . . . well, it'll be ready in another ten minutes."

She went back downstairs. She wished Réiltín wouldn't

keep pushing her away like that. She tried phoning Ryan to see where he was but he didn't pick up. She began to grow worried; he always rang if he was going to be late home.

When the dinner was ready she called up to Réiltín but, when she didn't appear, she was forced to climb the stairs again to tell her.

Réiltín followed her down and sat at the table.

"Where's Dad?" she asked, grabbing a slice of garlic bread from the dish Jo had put in the centre of the table.

"I'm not sure," Jo said, serving up the pasta bake. "I'm sure he'll be home soon."

Jo made conversation with her daughter, asking about her homework, her hockey training, how her friends were doing. Réiltín just replied with one-word answers. Finally she heard Ryan's key in the door and relief flooded through her.

"I was worried about you," she said when he appeared in the doorway of their kitchen.

"Worried? Jo, I was working late," he said tersely, putting his laptop bag down on the floor.

"I know, I know, I was being ridiculous – I was imagining all sorts. So maybe you could ring me next time, yeah? Just so I don't worry?"

"Jesus, Jo, I'm an hour later than usual! Why don't you put a GPS tracking device on me or something!" He sighed heavily.

"Sorry, my mind was running away with itself," she mumbled, feeling embarrassed.

He sat down at the table and he and Réiltín exchanged a look. Jo knew that look and she hated it. Like they were a team and she was the outsider.

"Would anyone like to go the movies at the weekend?" she asked, trying to change the subject.

Nobody answered her and she felt silly then.

"Right, I'll take that as a no then, shall I?" she said, helping herself to another small wedge of the bake.

They ate the rest of the meal in silence.

Chapter 17

Sticks and Stones

Isla let herself in the door and climbed up the stairs with a heaviness that she didn't usually feel. Once inside the flat, she stared around the small living area, the narrow kitchenette and the well-worn sofa with the throws she had knitted for it. This was it, she thought, this was all she had managed to do with her life by the age of thirty-nine. She didn't have a partner, she didn't have a child and now it was too late for that. And she couldn't read. She kept thinking about what Greg had said to her. She felt so embarrassed that he had been able to see through her charade. What if he told the others? What if she went in to work tomorrow and everyone knew that she couldn't read? Her stomach churned at the thought of facing everyone in the morning but something deep down told her that he wouldn't do that. What had surprised her the most was that he hadn't laughed or joked like she had always expected people would do if they ever found out. In fact, he had seemed concerned about her which nearly made her feel worse about it all.

Isla was supposed to wear glasses but she usually never wore them because she needed to have an excuse to cover up the fact that she couldn't read properly. Whenever anyone asked her to read something, she told them that she had forgotten her glasses or had left them at home or that she couldn't find them. She had an array of carefully prepared excuses for every scenario. That was the reason she did a job where you didn't really need to be able to read; once you were able to talk to people you could get around almost everything. Not even Jo knew. She wasn't sure how she had managed to hide it from her over the years. Sometimes she saw ads on TV for help lines for people with reading difficulties and she thought about ringing the number but then she chickened out again. She had been managing fine as she was, or so she had thought.

In school, Isla had never had a brilliant relationship with her teachers but her teacher in fourth class, Mrs Wallace, seemed to hate her particularly. She would hiss at her and the spittle would fly from her mouth in every direction as Isla squirmed in front of her. She moved her onto a table on her own then because she said that Isla was holding the rest of her table back with her stupidity. Isla had had to sit alone at a table facing sideways so that on her right was the blackboard and on her left were the rest of the thirty-eight girls in her class. The other girls took to calling her 'Isla the Island'. Isla would sit at her own table island and when her teacher would ask her to read the words on the blackboard she would scrunch up her eyes and try really hard but she could only see a blurry jumble of letters. 'O' would bounce before her and 'a' would turn into 'e', sixes grew into eights and back again. The letters and numbers would become so shaky that she was unsure about which one it was. Inside her head she would be praying for them to stop moving. She would try to make out the shape of the letter but by the time she would figure one out and try to do the next one, she would have forgotten the first letter and her teacher would get mad and roar 'You stupid girl! Don't you dare insult me by scrunching up your face like that in my class! If you can't be bothered learning then I can't be bothered to teach you!" Then she would fire all the coloured chalk pieces that usually rested in the dusty pit at the bottom of the blackboard at Isla. They would come raining down around her like bullets. One after the other they would come, some hitting her on the head, some missing her and landing on the floor, others crashing off the desk.

It was a routine eye test that revealed she had very bad eyesight and that was why she would squint. Her mother had taken her to the optician's and she had to pick from a range of terrible glasses that were in bright colours "specially for children", as the optician had told her mum. Isla wanted a purple pair but her mother said they would clash with her hair and instead picked out a bottle-green pair for her. Isla had hated them. "Oh, don't you look lovely, chicken!" the assistant in the optician's had said. "Doesn't she look as cute as a button in them?" Isla knew by her forced niceness that she looked hideous. She was ten years old – she didn't want to look "as cute as a button".

She went into school the next day and as soon as she walked into her classroom they started saying: "What's on your face, Isla the Island?"

She had said nothing and kept walking over to her solitary table.

"Oh look, *Isla the Island* is now *Isla the Alien!*"

"Specky-four-eyes!"

Then someone started singing the 'Star Trekkin'' song and they all joined in.

With the chorus of thirty-eight girls singing, Isla had kept looking down at the floor. The pressure of tears was building up in her eyes until she couldn't hold them back any more and they came spilling out and rolling down along her face until she couldn't see through the glasses anyway.

The next day, as soon as Jo said goodbye to her in the

schoolyard, she had taken the glasses off. She didn't dare let Jo see her doing it because she knew she would tell their mum if she didn't wear them. She would put them on again for the walk home, as soon as they were beyond the schoolyard. She wouldn't wear them in class even though Mrs Wallace would scream at her for squinting at the board.

"Where are your glasses, Isla Forde?" she would roar at her.

"I forgot to bring them this morning," Isla would lie.

"You see, didn't I tell you she was a stupid girl?" the teacher would announce to the rest of the class.

Not wearing her glasses probably isolated her even more than she realised. She fell behind the rest of the class because she could never read what was on the blackboard. She retreated into her own world and started sketching in the margins around the text.

She took a pizza out of the freezer and put it in the oven and then she poured herself a glass of wine.

"Happy birthday, Isla," she said out loud so her words filled the small room. "Haven't you done well for yourself?"

Chapter 18

La Vita è Bella

When Isla woke up the next morning she could feel her head thumping before she had even attempted to open her eyes. Her mouth was dry and it tasted awful. She delicately manoeuvred herself into a sitting position, while at the same time trying to minimise the pain that was thumping through her head. She finally dared to peel her eyes open. The room seemed to be spinning. She put her feet over the side of the bed and stumbled onto the floor but had to sit back down again because she thought that she was going to fall over. She had drunk the whole bottle of wine herself and she was paying for it now.

She tried to get up again and managed to pull herself up slowly. She made her way into the kitchen and pulled out the drawer to see if she had any Paracetamol. She rooted around amongst spools of thread, keys that she didn't know where their locks were and a box that had opened spilling coloured paperclips all over the drawer. Eventually she had found the white blister pack and popped two tablets, swallowing them down with a drink of water. She felt a nauseous hunger growing inside her stomach and she needed something to settle it fast so she opened the press to find some bread. There was only the heel left so she pushed it down into the toaster.

As she sat on the sofa eating her buttered toast she heard the doorbell go. Groaning, she dragged herself up and went down the stairs to answer it.

"Oh, it's you," she said, pulling open the door to see Réiltín standing there.

"I was trying to ring you! Want to hang out? Dad is playing golf and Mum is working from home so she said I could come over to you for a few hours."

"Oh sorry, I didn't turn my phone on yet. Come on up." Isla climbed back up the stairs with Réiltín following behind her. Her head thumped with every step.

They sank into the sofa beside each other. The curtains were still drawn on the grey day beyond the window.

"Want to watch a movie?" Isla asked.

"Can I choose?" Réiltín said, jumping up and going over to Isla's DVD tower.

"Go on then."

"What's this like?" Réiltín asked, holding up the cover of *Pulp Fiction*.

"Your mum would kill me."

"Maybe this one?"

It was *No Country for Old Men*. Isla shook her head. "Try again."

"How about this one?" She was holding up the cover of *Life is Beautiful*.

"Good choice," Isla said, taking it from her and putting into the player.

Isla dragged the duvet from her bed and put a bag of popcorn in the microwave and then they both settled down to watch the movie. She had lost track of the number of times that she had watched it but it was Réiltín's first time to see it and Isla was enjoying seeing her emotions unfold as the film played.

She looked over at Réiltín as the film was ending and saw she had tears streaming down her face.

"That's just so sad," Réiltín cried as Guido, who was being led off by the Nazi soldier to be executed, passed by his son Joshua one last time, still keeping up the charade that it was all just a game.

"Hey," Isla said, taking her in her arms, "I know – I was like that the first time I saw it too. That's why I love it so much."

She wiped away her niece's tears and stroked her auburn hair with its shades of gold and electric blue streaks. As she allowed herself to look at her face, she studied its familiar outline. She didn't usually allow herself to dwell on it but now she couldn't help thinking back to how she came to be. It seemed ironic considering the situation she now found herself in, and lately she couldn't help thinking back to that time in their lives.

As Isla looked down at her niece, it suddenly hit her. When she had donated her eggs to Jo and Ryan there were two embryos created – one that grew into Réiltín and another one that they had hoped would be a future brother or sister for her. They had never used it. But what if the other embryo was still in storage? She could have a child of her own, just like Réiltín, if the embryo was still there. As she stroked her niece's hair, she couldn't help feeling the excitement start to bubble up inside her. She felt as though her mind was buzzing and alive like someone had switched on a thousand light switches inside her head and the synapses were fired up. Her mind started to drift off as she let herself wonder if it could still happen and the sense of loss from the last few weeks instantly lifted. What if her chances weren't really over, as she had thought? Yes, it was a long shot – she would need to talk to Jo and Ryan to make sure that they still had the embryo – the embryo that was created using her egg. Even if they let her have it there was no guarantee that the treatment would work but still it was a glimmer of hope in what had been a dark void over the last few weeks. There was another way for her to have a baby. She knew that it wasn't the most straightforward of ways but there was still a chance. There was another way of doing it.

The buzzer sounded shortly after and she knew that it was Jo arriving to pick up Réiltín.

"What's wrong with you?" Jo asked, coming into the room and observing Réiltín's red eyes. "Did something happen?" She automatically looked over at Isla for answers.

"No, Mum – it's just this film we were watching – it's the saddest movie I've ever seen."

"Well, maybe it wasn't entirely suitable then." Jo looked over at Isla reproachfully. "What was it?"

"*Life is Beautiful*," Isla said.

"Never heard of it."

"Do you want to stay for a coffee?" Isla reached up to take down two mugs from the cupboard above the cooker.

She found herself unable to look Jo in the eye; she was afraid that she would read her thoughts. Now, in the actual presence of her sister, she felt guilty just thinking about it. Could she really ask her sister for her embryo? Even though it was made using her eggs? She knew it was a long shot but she also knew that she had to try it. Suddenly the dreams all clicked into place. She felt that this was what it had been trying to tell her: the baby had been there all along but she hadn't realised it. If she wanted to have a baby – which she did, badly – well, then, this was her only hope.

"No, I can't, we're having friends over for dinner. What's wrong with you, Isla? You're looking very peaky – are you feeling okay?"

"Oh, I . . . eh . . . just had a late night last night." Her heart was hammering inside her chest.

Jo pursed her lips in disapproval before turning to Réiltín. "Come on, love, your father will be waiting for us."

Chapter 19

A Question

After Jo had brought Réiltín home, Isla didn't sleep that night. Her mind was too awake, too wired. Her head was buzzing thinking about that one remaining embryo. She kept imagining the baby in her head. She knew she needed to ask Jo – it was her last chance and she couldn't move on and accept that she had done everything possible to have a child of her own unless she did. She had lain awake imagining the conversation with Jo and how it would go. Would Jo be shocked or would she want to help her just like Isla had helped them all those years ago? What if she asked Jo and she said she had destroyed it, what then?

She made up her mind to go over to Jo that morning; there was no sense in delaying it any longer. She needed to know whether they still had the embryo or whether she was getting her hopes up for no reason.

She jumped into the shower and let the water rush around her. She quickly dried herself off and got dressed. She didn't bother doing her eye make-up. She was anxious to get over to see Jo as quickly as she could. Réiltín had said that her dad was taking her to a hockey match so Jo would be alone.

When she got to Jo's house she let herself in with her key and called out to Jo as she walked down her Victorian tiled hallway. "Jo? It's me."

"I'm in the kitchen!"

Jo was sitting at the table, still in her dressing gown, with her glasses on as she read the Sunday papers. Oscar rushed out from his bed to greet Isla and she tickled him behind his ears. Jo had the French doors opened out onto the garden and the smell of salty sea air filled the room.

"Want a coffee?" Jo asked.

"Yeah, go on. I thought you didn't drink coffee?"

"Well, I don't usually but it's a Sunday morning treat to myself." Jo got up from the chair and stood in front of the doors and surveyed the lawn. The breeze played with the delicate silk fabric of her robe. "Isn't it glorious out? The hydrangeas have just started to bloom – they're late this year. It's so lovely to see that summer has arrived at last."

Isla sat down and Jo placed two coasters on the table while they waited for the coffee to brew in the machine that she had integrated into the presses. When it was ready, she pressed a button so that it filled the two mugs.

"So how've you been?" she said, placing them down on top of the coasters as she sat at the table across from Isla.

"I'm good." Isla tried to keep the nervousness from her voice. It felt as though the words were building up pressure inside of her, that they were waiting to escape her head and become real on the air around them.

"Well, I'm glad to hear it. So you're okay about . . . everything then?"

Isla knew what she meant. Jo didn't want to raise the subject again.

"I'm still finding it hard to accept that I will never have a child of my own. Very hard. For the last few weeks it's almost been like I have been grieving that that part of my life may never happen."

"Of course it has, Isla." Her voice was soothing. "I'm sorry you've had to go through this." She reached across and squeezed her younger sister's hand.

"But I've been doing some thinking . . ."

"Go on?"

Suddenly with Jo here before her, it didn't seem as certain a possibility as it seemed in her head earlier on.

"Well, last night I remembered something – something that may just be my last chance." She took a deep breath. "I have something that I want to ask you, Jo . . ." Her heart was pounding through her chest. She could hear the blood ringing in her ears.

"Go on . . ."

"Remember when you were trying to have Réiltín?"

"Yes . . ." Jo's tone was cautious. Measured.

"There was a second embryo created, wasn't there?"

Jo nodded.

"Well, I hope you don't mind me asking but what did you do with it?"

"Why do you want to know?"

"Well, I know it sounds a bit crazy but I was wondering if . . . well . . . if you still had it, if you would be prepared to give it to me . . . I mean, I know you'd need to talk to Ryan first but . . ."

"I'm sorry?"

"The second embryo that was made but wasn't implanted – I still really want to have a baby and if you still have it that's my only option, Jo."

"I can't give you our embryo!" Jo spluttered. "Jesus Christ, Isla!" She stood up from her chair and took off her glasses. She began pacing around the room.

"So you do still have it then?"

"Yes, but *you* can't have it! I'm just waiting for one of those hidden cameras to pop out and tell me that this is all a joke! You must be out of your mind coming over here to ask me that!"

"But you're not ever going to use it!"

"And you know why! Because I nearly died having Réiltín!"

"Well, then, surely it's not that big an ask?"

"Well, from where I'm standing, it's pretty huge! Jesus, Isla, I can't believe you just asked me for it! What on earth goes on inside your head?"

"Come on, Jo, it's not that outlandish – it's my only chance to have a child of my own."

"Well, we haven't decided what we want to do with it yet . . ."

"But it's not as if you can have another baby, Jo!"

"Stop it, Isla! Look, it's absolutely absurd – the child would be a genetic brother or sister for Réiltín. Surely even you can see that that is just too complicated? I'm sorry, Isla, I can't do it. I don't feel comfortable even discussing it!"

"But you felt comfortable enough to take my eggs."

Jo's eyes met hers and she stopped dead on the kitchen floor. "Look, I appreciate so much what you did for me. You know that I do – I wouldn't have Réiltín if it wasn't for you but what you're asking me to do now – it isn't fair."

"Please, you're my last chance, Jo. If you turn me down then I can never have a child of my own . . ."

"I'm sorry, Isla, but there is just no way that I can give you that embryo. The answer is no."

At that moment the wind blew a gust of wind into the kitchen, blowing over the pages of the newspaper and sending a chill through the room.

Isla pulled Jo's door shut behind her and walked over the dove-grey pavement. The traffic crept on the road alongside her but Isla was unaware of it because her mind kept on replaying the conversation she had just had with Jo. She knew that what she had asked for was a big deal but she still hadn't expected her reaction to be so full of vitriol. She had obviously underestimated the strength of Jo's feelings about the embryo. It was only occurring to her that perhaps Jo had pushed out of her head what they had done all those years ago. In her head had it all been left firmly in the past as soon as Réiltín had been placed into her arms? Perhaps time had allowed her to forget the origins of her daughter. Maybe the years had layered distance, and lacquered some of those thorny memories. As Isla walked along, she wondered how she had got it so wrong? She had just hoped that, because she had helped Jo once, she would be willing to help her in return but it seemed that she had sorely misjudged it. Isla wondered if she had re-opened those thoughts, the ones that Jo had long suppressed into the darkest corners of her mind, where she had thought they would stay forever? Was Isla like the pike that clouded up the riverbed?

But she wasn't going to let it go that easily; she couldn't. It was all that she could think about. The urges were calling to her, they were screaming at her to *do* something. Sometimes when she watched a mother with her child in the café, it felt like a piece of twine was wrapped around her insides, around her heart, and someone was pulling either end of it so tightly that she couldn't breathe. She didn't just want to have a baby; she *needed* to have a baby. And Jo didn't seem to understand it.

Jo was stunned after Isla had left. She sat at the table, head in hands, unable to process what her sister had just asked her. Sometimes she felt as though she didn't know her own sister at all. She knew that she and Isla were very different people; they were born to the same parents, they were fed the same food, they wore the same clothes – Isla wore all of Jo's hand-me-downs – and they went to the same schools, yet they still turned out like two completely unrelated beings. She had to wonder what on earth went on inside Isla's head for her to ask a question like that.

When she heard Ryan and Réiltín come in through the

door a while later, she couldn't even get up off the chair to greet them like she normally would. Réiltín went straight upstairs to the shower while Ryan strolled into the kitchen to fill himself a glass of water.

"How was the match?" Jo asked distractedly.

"Great, they won. Was that Isla I just passed in the car? How is she?"

"She . . . you'll never guess what she just asked me for?"

"What?"

Jo lowered her voice to a whisper. "The embryo – the one in storage – she wants to use it – she wants to have a baby!"

"Isla wants to have a baby?"

Ryan seemed to be as shocked as she was.

"She's already been to a fertility clinic and had tests done. Apparently she's in premature menopause and has no egg reserve left of her own so her only hope is to use a donor."

"This *is* Isla we're talking about, isn't it?"

She nodded. "Yes, this *is* Isla. Who else do we know that would be crazy enough to think of something like that!"

"What did you say to her?"

"I told her there was no way I could give it to her."

"You did?"

"Well, of course I did – I mean it's ludicrous!"

"But it was conceived using her eggs."

"And *your* sperm! It would be a genetic brother or sister for Réiltín! Ryan, it's complete madness!"

"Well, I suppose I can see where she's coming from . . ."

"*What?*"

"I just think, to be fair to her, she donated her eggs to us without even a second thought –"

"That's because Isla never thinks about anything!" She got up, tore off a sheet of kitchen roll and mopped up the water droplets that Ryan had trailed along the marble counter top until it was shiny once more.

"Well, she must really want to have a baby then, I guess."

He lifted an apple from the fruit bowl, turned and walked out of the room, leaving Jo sitting in their kitchen stewing.

It annoyed Jo that Isla thought that it was her right to have a child. Like it was her right to buy food to eat or to have a home to shelter in. Isla thought she could just decide whimsically that she felt like becoming a mother because she was almost forty. Knowing Isla, that was probably the only factor in her decision-making, thought Jo wryly.

Jo disagreed with people who believed it was their automatic right to have a child and that people were entitled to procreate as they wished. One of the newspapers had run a poll recently about whether there should be a limit imposed on the number of children people living on social welfare should be allowed to have. People had erupted over it, saying that it was human nature and money should never be involved in a decision to have children. Jo had listened to a radio show discussing the issue that evening and, as the debate wore on, she found her shoulders getting ever tenser until she was almost going to throw something at the radio. It was all these leftie liberals who were to blame for it. They were constantly spouting nonsense like that in the media and she disagreed with it wholeheartedly. People placed too much emphasis on the 'human nature' side of things. It irked her that there were children's lives being destroyed every day in the name of 'human nature' and the 'right' to have children. Jo often wondered why, then, if nature was such a powerful force, were there children being harmed mentally and physically at the hands of their own parents? She believed that while nature gave us the physical things like what our hair would look like, how tall we would grow, whether we would be prone to certain diseases or were going to have our bones curled by arthritis in our old age, that it was *nurture* which gave us the people that we loved. It was nurturing which gave the bonds and relationships and how far one would go for the loved ones in one's life. That was what made a person, thought Jo.

148

It was not what they looked like; it wasn't their physical attributes. Every child needed to be nurtured. In the Victorian days, who was it that formed the bonds with the children? It wasn't the parents to whom the children were presented for half an hour before bedtime every evening, it was the nannies that cuddled them, tucked them up in bed and ultimately were mothers in all but name to these children. They were the ones that stayed in the minds of the children when they became adults themselves. She believed that the mind began as a blank slate and the person that we would grow into was determined by our experiences and not the genes that we were born with. *Tabula rasa.*

It was a privilege to have a child, she thought, and if you were so blessed as to have one, then you should thank your lucky stars every day for the rest of your life because it didn't happen like that for everybody. She of all people knew that. If nature was allowed to take its course, she knew that she and Ryan would still be childless. If nature was allowed to take its course, Réiltín would have died but because of technological advances through the ages there were machines that could keep her alive until she had been strong enough to fight back herself. After a long journey to get their Little Star, they felt blessed to have her in their lives and, from the first time that they were allowed to hold her, she had lit up their world. Jo knew that nurture was what was truly important. Nurture was what really mattered.

Jo would never forget what Isla did for her, the dark hole, that hellish place that she brought her out from. For the rest of her life she would be indebted to her younger sister but what she was asking of her now was too much, even for her.

Chapter 20

Secrets

Over the next few days life went on as normal as Isla tried to acknowledge the fact that she was never going to become a mother. She went to work. She served up mugs of tea and plates of food and collected them again afterwards. She stacked the dishwasher and unloaded it again when it had completed its cycle. Then, in the evening, as the day's customers started to trickle out, she started to get ready for the next day.

She was trying to tell herself that she just had to accept that this was the plan that life had made for her and there was nothing that she could do about it. It seemed that everywhere she went, though, she was confronted with babies. She was supposed to call over to Vera to meet her new baby but her heart broke just thinking about it. She felt so empty. The yearning was like a gnawing hole inside her, eating its way through her, but now she knew that there was nothing that she could do to satisfy it. She had to make a conscious effort to stop and catch herself whenever she started to get upset by it because she knew it was futile – it wouldn't change anything.

The rain had stopped and the sky was now washed clean. The

clouds had started to part, permitting slanted sunbeams to rush in through the gaps. Isla took a deep breath, climbed the three steps leading up to Vera's house and pressed the doorbell. She waited a minute and was just about to press it again when Vera answered the door. She was wearing a tracksuit and she had a muslin cloth slung over her shoulder. Isla didn't think she had ever seen her wearing a tracksuit before.

"Hey, you," Isla said, hugging her warmly. "Congratulations!"

She followed Vera inside and into the living room where she led her over to a Moses basket in the corner. They both peered in at Jules who was sleeping soundly, his two fists balled on either side of his head.

"He's beautiful," Isla whispered. "I won't disturb him."

Vera cleared packets of wipes and nappies from the sofa and Isla sat down. Isla noticed that the usually immaculate room was littered with baby paraphernalia of all sorts. There was a pile of soiled vests, tiny babygros and bibs in the middle of the floor. Muslin cloths were draped over chairs. A breast pump lay upended and bottle lids were scattered all over the coffee table.

"So how's it all going?"

"It's okay. I'm tired but I expected that. I know it sounds ridiculous, considering I spent so much time being pregnant and thinking of this little baby, but I don't think I gave any time to thinking about how we would actually care for the baby. I never knew someone so small could create so much work."

"You'll be fine, Vera. It's a huge adjustment. I doubt anyone can ever imagine what it's going to be like when the baby is born. I don't think anyone can ever be truly ready."

When Jules woke a few moments later with a small mewing cry, Vera hopped up and lifted him out.

"Do you want a hold?"

"I'd love to."

Vera placed her baby in Isla's arms while she went into the kitchen and made a pot of coffee. As Isla breathed him in, he smelt of powder and warm milk. Tears sprang into her eyes.

"Oh my goodness, what's wrong, Isla?" Vera said when she came back into the living room holding a tray.

"I'm sorry, Vera, it's nothing."

"Well, it can't be just nothing if it has you in tears!" She made room for the tray on the coffee table and set it down. Then she reached for a muslin cloth to give to Isla before realising what she was doing and instead reached for a tissue from a box on the coffee table. "Sorry – baby brain!"

"It's just silly, stupid stuff – sorry, I'm so embarrassed," Isla said, dabbing at her eyes.

"What is it, Isla?"

"Well, I went for some tests recently – fertility tests."

"And?"

"And, it seems I'm going through early menopause."

"Oh, Isla, I'm so sorry about that." Vera bent down and hugged her.

"Hey, you're squashing the baby!" Isla said, laughing through her tears.

Vera sat down and gazed at Isla. "Were you hoping to have a child?"

"That's the funny thing – I'm not even really in a relationship but recently . . . oh, I don't know . . . it's like it was all I could think about . . . I had this crackpot-crazy idea to go it alone, y'know?"

"You mean you were going to use a *donor*?"

Isla nodded.

"Wow! Go, you! I was reading an article about it in one of the medical journals recently actually – there was a name for it, oh, what was it again . . . oh yeah . . . *Single Mothers by Choice* is what the women in the article called themselves. I have to say I really admire women that do that because they haven't met the right guy or whatever."

"Well, it's not going to happen for me now so I just need to push the idea out of my head again as ridiculously as it came into my head in the first place."

"Oh, Isla, I'm so sorry to hear that, I really am." Vera reached out and placed her hand over Isla's and gave it a squeeze.

Isla went quiet for a minute before continuing. "I always swore I would never speak about this but do you remember when I told you that Ryan and Jo were having difficulty conceiving a baby?"

"Yeah, I remember – they had to go through several rounds of IVF to have Réiltín."

"Well, I helped them actually."

"What do you mean?"

"I donated my eggs to Jo."

"Oh my god!" Vera's hands flew up to her mouth. "So you . . . it's *you* who is Réiltín's biological mother?"

Isla nodded. "Genetically, I am, yes, but I don't think of her like that –"

"God, that was very generous of you, Isla." Vera exhaled loudly and started fiddling with the cross on her chain.

"To be honest, it wasn't a big deal at the time." Isla shrugged her shoulders. "She was going through an awful time and I wanted to help her."

"I don't know if I could do that. It'd be like having another child out there, y'know? I think I'd keep looking at it wondering if it looked like me or something!"

"I suppose if I'm honest, sometimes I do. I recognise certain mannerisms or something she does will feel really familiar, almost like déjà vu, but I don't think of her as my child."

"Does Réiltín know?"

"No, of course not. And please don't tell anyone at all about it. No one knows except Jo, Ryan and me."

"I won't."

Isla leant forward and lowered her voice. "There was another

153

embryo left over from the treatment and Jo still has it in storage."

"Okaaaaay . . ."

"I asked her for it."

"What? You ask her for the embryo?" Vera spluttered and dribbled a small bit of coffee down her chin. She wiped it quickly with the back of her hand. "Sorry."

"Well, why not?"

"Oh God, because . . . I don't know . . . it's an *embryo*, Isla!"

"But it was conceived using my eggs! And Jo is never going to be using it. You know she had a hysterectomy."

"But isn't it all a bit mixed up? I mean firstly you donated your eggs to her and she had a baby but then you want the embryo back that was made using Ryan's sperm?"

"Maybe, but I really want to have a baby and this might be the only way that I can. There's an egg or an embryo or whatever that is genetically mine hanging out in a lab somewhere – doesn't it make sense to use it?" The baby started to cry and Isla held him out to Vera. "I think he wants his mammy."

Vera lifted him out of Isla's arms and planted a kiss on his forehead. He snuggled into her chest and started to nuzzle for her breast.

"I suppose . . . how did she react?"

"Not good. We had a huge row actually."

"Oh, Isla, I'm sorry. Is this really the only way that you can have a baby? Isn't there another way?"

"This is it – last chance saloon."

"Well, maybe she'll calm down in a few days?" Vera said hopefully but Isla knew that she thought she was crazy asking Jo for the embryo.

"I'm not so sure. Maybe though."

The baby was growing angry and red-faced, his mouth opening for a feed, rooting for Vera's breast. Vera pulled down her track-suit zip, fumbled about inside and pulled a breast out. She looked distracted as she struggled to latch him on but he kept turning his head the wrong way and just grew more fractious.

"Look, I'd better go," Isla said. "He looks hungry."

"But you've only just got here!" Vera protested.

"I know, but I have to meet someone."

Vera looked at her doubtfully. "Okay . . . well, it was nice to see you. Thanks for calling, Isla."

They got up and walked out to the door.

Isla stood down onto the step. Jules was screaming in protest now. "He's gorgeous, Vera. Take care of yourself."

"You too, Isla, and I just want to say, what you did for Jo, not just anybody would do that. It is one of the most generous gestures I've ever heard of."

Chapter 21

A Slap

Several days went past without Jo or Isla making contact with each other. Usually when something didn't work out for Isla or it required a degree of effort to be made, she would walk away from it but she knew that she wasn't ready to give up on the chance to have a baby yet. As long as there was an embryo there, there was still a chance – she just had to make Jo see it. Even though she had never been persistent with anything in her life before, she knew that she had to give it another shot. Isla knew Jo better than anyone and she wasn't hopeful that she would change her mind but she couldn't give up now. She decided she would call over to Jo again and try to talk to her, even though she was dreading facing her. If it was anything else, she would have left it alone but it was just too important to her and she wasn't ready to let it go just yet.

When Jo pulled back the heavy wooden door a few days later, her welcome for Isla was less than enthusiastic. She swung around on her heel and walked briskly down the tiled hallway and into the kitchen. Isla followed after her, walking past the artwork which hung in the hallway, including the painting that she had done for them when they had first bought their house because she had been too broke to buy them a proper gift. Isla instantly knew by Jo's actions that she hadn't softened over the last few days. Absence had not made the heart grow fonder. Isla took off her jacket and hung it over the back of one of the chairs around the table. The house felt cool.

"Catching up on some work?" she asked, nodding towards the orderly piles of paper that covered the kitchen table.

"Just trying to get a bit done while Réiltín is at rehearsals," Jo replied brusquely in a tone that implied Isla was disturbing her. "Can I get you a coffee?"

"Yeah, that'd be lovely." Isla took off her parka and hung it over the back of a chair. "Is Ryan not home yet?"

"No, he's working late."

Isla waited while Jo busied herself with the hissing machine. Eventually a mug was set down in front of her on the table. Jo didn't make a mug for herself or offer biscuits like she usually would. She stayed standing, making Isla wish that she hadn't sat down. It was obvious by Jo's manner that she wasn't in the mood for sisterly niceties; she wanted Isla to get straight to business.

Isla took a deep breath, knowing that this conversation was doomed before it had even begun. "So did you get a chance to think about things any more?"

"Oh, Isla, for God's sake! I thought we were finished with that! I've already told you my decision. I'm sorry but there's no way that I can give you that embryo."

"But it was made using my egg – it's half of me!"

"And half of Ryan!"

"Is that what this is about – you think it's going to be like me having a child with Ryan?"

"Well, in a way, yes! But there are just so many other issues with it."

"Like what? Give me one of them."

"Well, for starters, I think it could increase the chances of

157

Réiltín discovering how she was conceived. What if she notices? What if she saw that the baby looked like her and she noticed that they were related? It's not just an embryo, Isla – it's her brother or sister!"

"Isn't that a bit far-fetched? She wouldn't notice and, even if they did look alike, she'd just think that any similarities were because they were cousins."

"Well, another reason is because it would be half Ryan's child as well and that's not fair on him. It's not just my decision – it would be Ryan's too."

"Come on, we both know that Ryan will go with whatever you decide like he always does."

"You're putting me in an awful position, Isla, don't you see that?" Jo began to pace around the kitchen.

Isla felt anger awaken inside herself. She had to fight for this. "How can you say that? I gave you my eggs and you made two embryos, one of which grew into Réiltín and the other is sitting in a lab somewhere! That's what I'm asking you for – an embryo that is already a part of me, which you are never going to use. When I donated my eggs to you, I just wanted you to be happy. I would have done anything to help you and bring you out of that awful place you were in. I would have done whatever it took to fix the problem because you're my sister and I just wanted to see you happy again. I didn't have to think twice about it – it was the easiest decision I've ever made. Why can't you do that for me?"

"Because it's not the same thing. You didn't go through the nightmare of trying to get pregnant only to be told that it just wasn't going to happen!"

"Oh, so I haven't earned my infertility stripes, is that what you mean?"

"Look, you're in a very different place to where we were, Isla. You just decided on a whim: 'Oh I'm nearly forty, maybe I should think about having a baby!'"

"I don't think it's that different actually. Okay, I know I've only been trying to get pregnant for a short while but still I feel all those same desires that you did."

"Yeah, well, I'm still not going to change my mind."

"So that's it then? You're going to make a huge decision that affects my ability to have a child, a decision that changes the whole outcome of my life because you're not comfortable with it?"

"I'm sorry, Isla, I really am. Look, you could try and get a donor embryo? I could put you in touch with Dr Collins and see what he says? I'm sure we could arrange something for you."

"I don't want a donor embryo!" Her voice was climbing higher and she could hear there was an emotional edge to it. "There is a child out there who is genetically half mine and that's the one I want. I don't want anyone else's eggs or embryos. I just want that one, Jo. That one. That's all that I want."

"Why do you always have to be so difficult? Why can you never just do things without any trouble? Ever since you were born, every single thing that you have ever done has had a drama associated with it."

And there it was, Isla thought. The age-old low blow was thrown in: whenever Isla expresses her opinion or gets upset about something, just whack her over the head with it.

"I'm not causing a drama – I just want a baby. There's an embryo in storage somewhere that is half mine –"

"It's not 'half yours' – stop saying that – you know you gave up all rights to that egg with the act of donation. You spoke to the counsellor, you signed the forms – you knew the drill!"

"Well, it is, Jo, whether you like it or not – it's half mine and I really, really want to have a child of my own."

"You're putting me in a very unfair position, Isla. It's not fair of you to ask me to do that."

"It's a gift, just like I gave you a gift."

Jo took off her glasses and rubbed her eyes. "I'm sorry, Isla – but I can't."

"Are you going to deny me that opportunity when I helped you to conceive a baby – does that sit easily with you?"

"Of course I'm not trying to deny you anything but why does it have to be *that* baby?"

"Because *that* baby is the only chance I have to have a biological child of my own."

"But why are you so fixed on having your own egg? I didn't have my own!"

"Is that what this is about? You don't want me to be able to have a genetic child because you are not Réiltín's biological mother? You don't want your younger sister getting one up on you?"

Jo's hand shot out and the next thing Isla felt was a sharp stinging, which spread its way out across her cheek. "She *is* my daughter, no matter how she was conceived! She *is* my child!"

Isla stood there momentarily dazed. She raised her hand up to her cheek, which was tender to the touch.

"I think you should go now," Jo said, handing her her parka.

A stunned Isla took the coat from her and walked down the hall towards the front door. She placed her hand on the doorknob before stopping and turning around to face Jo who was standing in the kitchen doorframe watching her leave.

"What you're doing to me, Jo . . . you know it's not right . . ."

Then she pulled open the door and walked out into the fresh air.

After Isla had gone, Jo opened the fridge and poured herself a large glass of Pinot Grigio. And then cried. She hated the way that Isla did that to her. She pushed her to her outermost limits until suddenly she snapped out of sheer frustration.

Whenever Jo looked at friends of hers or at the other girls in the office, their relationships with their sisters seemed to be so much more loving and supportive of each other. They were friends first and foremost and sisters second.

With her and Isla it was an endless clash. They could not be more different as people and yet when she thought back to their childhood, they had once been really close. They would lie curled up together in bed every night. They had clung to each other whenever their mum was having a bad day. No one else would ever understand what they went through together, the greys and blacks of their childhood, but sometimes the yellows too. Jo just wished they were closer; she wished they weren't such polar opposites. They were like opposing poles on the magnetic spectrum, irresistibly drawn together on one side, yet pushing each other apart on the other.

When Ryan came home that evening a pale-faced Jo was sitting in silence on the sofa with no TV on. She was more than halfway through a bottle of wine.

"What's wrong? Is everything okay? Where's Réiltín?"

"At rehearsals. She's getting a lift home." She looked at him. "You'll never guess what just happened."

"What?"

"Isla came over and starting going on about that bloody embryo again. She's not going to let it go. I'm so angry with her. Look at what she's started!"

Ryan linked his fingers together and moved his arms up over his head to stretch. His knuckles cracked. Jo shuddered.

"What happened?" he asked.

"She just doesn't get it, she doesn't seem to realise how dangerous all of this is. I'm so mad with her right now."

"So she's serious then?"

"She doesn't get that it is half *your* child – you would have a genetic connection to the child, as would Réiltín."

Ryan shrugged his shoulders. "I know it might be a bit weird but it sounds like she is desperate to have a baby, and I

161

really think, after everything she has done for us, if we can help her we should at least try."

Jo glared at him in disbelief. "How come no one else can see the enormity of what she is asking? The whole thing is absolute madness. Sometimes I wonder how Isla and I are even related, let alone sisters!"

"I suppose it depends on how you look at it. I know it's our embryo but I'm sure she also feels some ownership towards it . . ."

"Isla knows that she signed away all rights to that embryo when she signed the paperwork. Why doesn't she realise that a contract is a contract?"

"Isla isn't a solicitor, Jo. She goes with her heart."

"Well, you don't need to be a solicitor to know that the whole point of signing an agreement in the first place was so that a situation like this wouldn't arise. I know I shouldn't be surprised – I mean this is the kind of thing that Isla does all the time but, still, this is a new low even for her. Do you really think we should give it to her?"

"Well, all I'm saying is that maybe it's not as crazy a suggestion as you think it is."

Jo opened her mouth incredulously.

"Hear me out," he said. "I've been thinking about it and, since we're not going to use it, it's just sitting there in storage somewhere. Maybe we should give it to Isla. Wouldn't it be better for everyone if it was used?"

"But I thought you said that you'd support my decision, whatever I decided?"

"I did and I will, but I've been thinking about it and I don't see why we wouldn't give it to her. And I didn't realise that we're still paying an annual storage fee to the clinic!"

"Is that what this comes down to? You don't want to waste money on it! It's our *baby*, Ryan!"

"It's not a baby, Jo, it's an embryo! And it will never be a baby unless Isla gives it life!"

"An embryo that is a brother or sister to Réiltín – a child that would be genetically related to you! Why can't you see that?"

"Well, of course I can see that – I know it's complicated – but we'd –"

"Ryan –"

He put his hand up to stop her. "Just let me finish, please. Isla gave us a gift that you cannot put any price on. Imagine if Réiltín wasn't in our lives? It's unthinkable! Isla gave us that. She allowed us to become parents, to experience the joy and wonder of watching our child come into the world, the amazement when the bonds start to form and you realise that you would do anything to keep it safe from harm and you look back on the rest of your life before that moment and think it was all a bit of a waste really up until that point. That you weren't really living before. I just think there is nothing too big that we could ever give her back in return for that but giving her that embryo would be a good start."

"You know that I would never take what Isla did away from her – I can never thank her enough –"

"But you could – you could give her the embryo."

"But it's not just a simple case of playing swapsies. She gave me an egg, so I give her back an embryo and we're quits! Even Stevens! It's not that simple any more!"

"But why isn't it? I don't see why it can't be that simple. What is so different from Isla giving you an egg and you giving her an embryo – which I don't need to point out to you was made using the eggs she gave us in the first place!"

"Well, for starters Isla isn't in any position to have a child! She's single, she barely earns enough money to keep herself, she's totally unreliable. She doesn't have the first clue about what it takes to raise a child."

"Does any parent really? Looking back to when Réiltín was born, we didn't have a clue either."

"But that was different – we had a stable and loving home.

Isla is on her own – a child needs two parents."

"Come on, Jo, it's the twenty-first century – things have moved on a lot. Plenty of people raise children alone nowadays."

"Well, I can't allow a baby – a baby whose fate rests in my hands – to have a life like that and then have to watch as that child grows up in an unstable home. I think I would always feel a responsibility for that child. I could never forgive myself for something like that."

"But why do you think it would be like that? Why do you have such a negative view of your own sister? You see what she's like with Réiltín – I think she'd be an incredible mother actually."

"She just wants to do the fun stuff with Réiltín. I watch them together, Isla matching Réiltín with her childlikeness and irresponsibility. She can sit there and play computer games with her, or giggle over something on her Facebook page. They can go shopping for impractical clothes because Isla doesn't have to worry about Réiltín feeling chilly because she is wearing a light T-shirt in the middle of winter or worse that she might catch a cold and exacerbate her asthma. And I know Isla lets her eat junk food when I'm not around. Food that is full of artificial colourings and God knows what else, when she knows that I am trying to instil healthy eating habits. She doesn't have to worry about affording school fees or extra home tuition so she can make her grades. Isla doesn't have to worry about getting out of a meeting in time to make the hockey game that she is playing in. She doesn't have to police Réiltín's mobile phone and be treated with disdain for doing so. She doesn't have to worry that she is making friends with the wrong sorts or watch with her heart sitting in her mouth as she starts seeing a boy. She isn't the one whose heart is racing and checking her phone when she said she would be home by nine and it's ten and there is no sign of her or phone call to say why she is late. She didn't have the worry that comes with a baby born thirteen weeks too soon. I overhear their phone conversations – I know what goes on. Did you know that Réiltín told her first that she got her period before she told me?"

"How do you know that?"

"I just do – she denied it of course when I asked her about it. I wish she would come to me about stuff more but I'm trying to deal with having a teenager for the first time and I'm not sure which side I am meant to be on and every time I try Réiltín shuts me out. Isla gets all the good bits. She gets to do all the fun things and be 'cool Aunt Isla' and I can never be that person because Réiltín doesn't need another friend, she *needs* her mother. I don't want to be this stuffy, uptight woman but it's like that is the role I have been assigned and I can't get out of it. It's like Réiltín has given me the job of bad cop and Isla takes the starring role. Would Isla be there doing the night feeds or worrying because the child didn't eat enough at dinner time? Oh, I think the novelty would wear off pretty fast indeed, Ryan!"

"I think you're underestimating her actually."

"You see – there you go again taking her side!"

"I'm not taking sides – I'm trying to be the middle man here and see it from both perspectives."

"But you're not the middle man – can't you see that? It would be your child as well – you would have a child out there who is every bit a part of you as much as Réiltín is!"

"Is that why you hate the idea of it so much?"

"It's part of it – there are so many things about it that don't sit well with me."

"But you've always held the belief that the genetics don't matter. I don't understand how you can change your whole stance on the nature versus nurture debate."

"I haven't changed anything – this is just how I'm feeling. So when that child is born, are you telling me that you won't feel anything for it like you felt for Réiltín?"

"Look, Jo, I know that it might be a bit strange watching a child growing up knowing that genetically it is half mine but I do know one thing for definite: I wouldn't think of it as *my* child."

"But how do you know that, Ryan?"

"Remember the moment that the pregnancy test turned positive for Réiltín?"

Jo nodded. She would never forget it.

"Well, we knew instantly she was *our* baby and we didn't care about the route we had to take to conceive her and it will be the same with Isla. The moment Isla's test stick turns positive then it's going to be *her* baby."

"But nobody knows how they're going to react to something like this. What if it just happened – you started to bond with the baby? And you'd be bound to be a large part of the baby's life, given how much time Isla spends over here. What if she saw you or the child saw you as the only male role model in its life and you unwittingly took on the role and formed the bonds of a father? Or what if Isla started struggling financially or found motherhood too trying, what then? Would we have to pick up the pieces out of a sense of duty because it was our embryo in the first place? Would the fate of that baby still be our responsibility? You don't think about these things."

"Come on, you know she'd never be like that – as I said, I reckon she'd be a great mother."

"Or what if, down the line, when the child starts asking about its father she tells it that you're the genetic father. Is the child going to see you as its dad then and want to form a relationship with you?"

"We'd have a relationship anyway."

"Yeah, as an uncle but not as a dad! You haven't thought it through properly, Ryan – you're just thinking in the here and now as usual. You haven't thought about the future or the child's future or what might be coming down the tracks for us if we allow Isla to have that embryo."

"Do you always have to be so analytical? I can't see why you wouldn't do a good turn for someone who has given us the greatest gift we could have ever hoped for. And even if she never had given us anything, she's your sister. Surely, if you're in a position to help her, you would? You don't do altruism very well."

"But that's not what this is about. It's so much more than just giving her an embryo like . . . oh, I don't know . . . say giving her a spare juicer or something because I couldn't be bothered recycling it. There is so much more to it than that. Like have you even thought about Réiltín? Have you thought about how something like this could affect her?"

"How would any of this affect her?"

"Well, it increases the chances of her finding out about her own origins. Imagine if Isla let it slip or if she found some of the paperwork or something?"

"Come on, Jo, that's a ridiculous argument."

"I don't think it's that crazy actually. Look, we agreed we're never going to tell her about Isla's involvement in her conception. We made the decision that she doesn't ever need to know and we all made a promise that we would do our best to ensure that she never finds out. We're her parents, end of story. I don't want her to have any doubts or insecurities about her origin. What if she starts asking how Isla is having a baby without having a partner? She knows that Isla is single. What if she assumes that Isla had a one-night stand? Will she get the wrong message about casual sex? She's fourteen – she knows how babies are made, she's not stupid – she'll be asking all sorts of questions. What if it comes out about the embryo and she learns about her own origins?"

"She won't. I'm sure Isla would invent an imaginary boyfriend for a few weeks if you asked her to. She knows how important it is to you that Réiltín never finds out about our agreement."

"Well, there are just too many unknowns for my liking. It's too much to ask."

"So you keep saying but I still can't see it."

"It's a child – you can't just give it away willy-nilly without thinking things through properly."

"The only way it will ever be a child is if we give the embryo to Isla and let her bring it to life. Until that point it will always be just a bunch of cells sitting in that vat of liquid nitrogen in the clinic."

"Why do you have to be so clinical, Ryan?"

"But it's the truth, Jo. Don't you think we owe it to that embryo to at least have a chance at life? What's the alternative? You keep renewing the storage licence every year and it never has life? Who wins there? Or do you intend to destroy it?"

"You know I would have loved to have another child after Réiltín but that wasn't to be. And anyway I feel I've outrun my luck – I have a beautiful daughter that I never thought I'd have. But at the same time it's Réiltín's potential brother or sister and I can't bring myself to destroy it. I just feel awful even thinking about it . . ." Her voice trailed off.

"So make things easy on yourself then. Let her have the embryo. You don't have to have any guilt about destroying it then and Isla gets to experience motherhood for herself. Surely even you can see that that is the best option for everyone here? It's win-win!"

"What do you mean 'even you'?"

"Oh, come on, stop twisting my words, Jo! You know what I mean!"

"No, I don't actually. It seems like since Isla brought this whole crazy idea up, you have a problem with me. I didn't do anything wrong here, that's what I don't get. I didn't start any of this. If Isla doesn't like my response when she asked me for something, then that's hardly my fault, is it? She always has to cause trouble. She's been doing it her whole life. I thought at this stage we could both be mature adults but it seems not."

"So you've made your mind up then?"

"I have and I won't change it."

"You do know that you could lose your sister over this?"

"She wouldn't do that – I mean, I know she'll be angry with me for a while but she'll come round when she starts seeing things from my perspective."

"Oh yes, you mean when she starts seeing things from the 'right' perspective?"

She knew that he was being catty but she chose to ignore his sarcasm. "Why do you always take Isla's side on everything?"

"Stop overreacting – of course I don't."

"Yes, you do. You would rather side with her than with your own wife."

"That's not true."

"I always ask myself why you'd feel more loyalty to her than you do to me – and then I think, '*Oh wait, is it because she gave him a baby when his own wife couldn't*' – is that it?"

Ryan was rendered momentarily speechless. "That's not fair, Jo."

"When you take her side over your own wife's, then I'm sorry but I think there is something wrong with that!"

"I don't do that!"

"You do, Ryan! Ever since Réiltín was born you've been doing it." Jo hissed angrily. "You put Isla up on a pedestal – she can do no wrong. You completely idolise her! It's because you see her as the mother of your child, isn't it?"

He wouldn't meet her eye.

"I'm right, aren't I? I will never compare to her in your eyes because my body wasn't up to the job of giving you a child!"

"I do feel grateful to her and I don't see what's wrong with that!" he finally snapped. "You really know how to push my buttons, Jo! Why do you always get so bitchy when you've been drinking? God, a few glasses of wine and you start hurling out the insults!"

169

He got up and stormed out of the room.
She emptied the last of the bottle into her glass.

Ryan slept in the spare room that night. Lately the distance between them felt like a gulf. Jo felt herself get angry once again with Isla. She had brought all of this unnecessary hassle into her life. She had started the whole bloody thing. Jo couldn't remember the last time that she and Ryan had even kissed properly, with tongues darting to search and explore one another. If he kissed her like that now she didn't think she'd know what to do. She was mortified just thinking about it. She knew that she should try to talk to him but the thought of putting herself out there like that, that feeling of vulnerability and sense of doubt, was too overwhelming. Did he even want them to be close again?

When they had first started going out together, they'd had sex everywhere they could, every second that they could. It felt so strange now, to think about it. She could still remember the tingle she felt when his skin brushed hers, the touch of his fingertips as they traced patterns from the top of her back down to the bottom, until she felt goose pimples rise up on her skin. They would pass each other in the kitchen and he would pull her close into him. They only had to be in the same room to be turned on by one another. Where had that passion and excitement gone? The sad thing was that she hadn't really noticed it happening. It seemed to just ebb away over the years until one day she woke up and realised that they seemed to be sitting on opposite sides of a deep void.

Chapter 22

A Listening Ear

Isla walked home in a daze. It had gone even worse than she had expected. She really hadn't anticipated Jo reacting like that. She knew that Jo wasn't keen on donating the embryo to her but Isla now realised that she had clearly misjudged the strength of her feelings on it. She couldn't believe that her own sister had just slapped her across the face.

Isla didn't see what other avenues were open to her. She didn't have the money or the time to go down the long road of egg donation or embryo donation, without any guarantee of success. And, besides, her baby was already there, albeit in a container of liquid nitrogen somewhere.

She kept walking until she found herself on Greg's doorstep. She hadn't realised that that was where she was going until she found her finger reaching up to press his bell.

Suddenly she felt a huge wave of guilt flood through her. What was she doing coming here? He had done so much for her and it wasn't fair to continuously ask him to be her crutch every time things were going wrong for her, but somehow her feet had led her here.

She took her hand down, shoved it back inside her pocket

and turned away from the door. She walked back down the narrow path and out through the small iron gate.

"Isla? What are you doing here?"

He was coming down the path towards her with a bag of groceries in his hand. He was casually dressed wearing a T-shirt, jeans with a rip at the knee and flip-flops.

"Sorry, Greg – I was just – I shouldn't have come here."

"Hey, what's wrong? What happened to your face?"

She automatically raised her hand to touch her face. The skin was tender underneath her fingertips. She had never seen Jo lose it like that before.

"It's a long story," she sighed.

He put an arm around her. "I've got all evening. Come on inside. I was going to make a big bowl of macaroni and cheese for my dinner – it's the food of champions. You can't say no to that."

"Comfort food at its best. Go on so."

She followed him back up the path and he put his key in the lock to open the door. She followed him past the bike and into the small kitchen at the back of the house. He flicked the switch on the kettle and then began unpacking the groceries. The narrow kitchen was functional but dated, a row of six small cupboards ending with a stand-alone gas cooker. The other wall had a small table pushed in against it, which was where Isla had sat down. Greg put a pot of water on a ring and, when it boiled, made a pot of tea for the two of them. He took out a pint of milk from the fridge, sat down beside her at the table and poured out the tea.

"So are you going to tell me what's going on?"

She took the carton of milk he had left out and added a few drops to her tea. She put it down again and looked at Greg directly. "I want to have a baby," she said as tears filled her eyes.

"Really, Isla? But me and you . . . you know I'd love to have a baby with you!" His face exploded into a huge grin.

172

She raised her hand up to stop him. "It's complicated. Very complicated. I'm going through the menopause – I know it's crazy – I've only just turned thirty-nine. You know all those times I needed to take a half-day for different appointments? Well, I was actually going to a fertility clinic for tests and it appears that I'm experiencing an early menopause."

"I see . . . so, eh . . . I guess that's why we . . . eh . . . why . . . eh, you and me . . . why you didn't get pregnant then?"

Isla nodded.

"I'm sorry, Isla. I didn't realise that you wanted it that much but we can get help if that's what you want – my friend and his wife went through it so I know it's not easy but I'd be happy to do it with you – actually, I'd be more than happy, I'd be thrilled."

"It's not that simple. They have advised me not to get treatment because it's very unlikely to work."

"Oh . . . I see."

"Greg, I'm going to tell you something but you have to promise me that you will never say it to anyone else?"

"You know you can trust me."

"Fifteen years ago I donated eggs to my sister Jo, because she couldn't have a baby using her own eggs. Well, by using my eggs and her husband's sperm, the clinic made two embryos. One of those embryos was put into Jo, which resulted in my niece Réiltín."

He looked gobsmacked. "I see . . . wow . . . that's a pretty big deal alright!"

"Well, Jo has an embryo left over from her treatment all those years ago. I asked her if she would be prepared to let me use it but she flat out said no."

"I'm sorry, Isla, I'm not up to speed with how these things work – so that embryo would be half your baby, is that right?"

"Well, that's the big dilemma. Legally, when I gave Jo those eggs, I signed away all my rights to them but I still thought that as my sister she'd want to help me out, y'know?"

"And who would the father be?"

"Well, genetically it would be Jo's husband Ryan." Then she added quickly, "But I'd be raising the baby on my own."

"I see."

He went quiet and Isla sensed that he wasn't saying everything that he wanted to say.

"You think it's mad, don't you?"

"Well, it's certainly not straightforward."

The water was bubbling in the pot.

"One sec," he said. "Just let me throw in the pasta." He quickly attended to it and sat back down again at the table. "Sorry," he said. "Look, Isla, this isn't my business but I guess I can see where your sister is coming from. Wouldn't it be like you had a baby with her husband? That'd be strange for anyone!"

"I know it's strange but I honestly wouldn't see it like that. It's weird but when Réiltín was born I knew she was my niece and I never thought about her as the daughter that I could have had – if that makes sense? And I know that if Jo gave me that embryo that I wouldn't see it as Ryan's – it would be *my* baby."

"But how would *he* feel about it? And Jo?"

"I don't know, Greg. Look, I know it's weird and not what anyone would choose. But, you see, it's my only remaining chance."

"It's complicated, that's for sure," Greg said thoughtfully. "Which is the 'real' parent – the person a child shares their genes with or the person who raises the child?"

"And what do you think?"

"I just don't know, Isla. There's no easy answer to that one. My friend Kenneth was raised by his aunt and uncle because his mother had him so young and she wasn't able to look after him properly and to this day he still thinks of his real mother as a cousin or something, even though he sees her all the time. And then, of course, there are so many people who were adopted and, even if they meet their biological parents in later life, they still think of the people who raised them as their parents."

"So what do you think I should do?"

"Well, what can you do? If your sister has said no to you then you really don't have any other options left, do you? Unless you're thinking of going down the legal route?"

Isla sighed. "I've thought about it but I really don't want to do that. Jo is a solicitor, she knows everyone in the business. She'd have the best legal team – I wouldn't stand a chance against her. Plus it would probably be all over the news. A case like that would attract the media and I just don't think I'd be able for it."

"I guess then it all depends on how badly you want to have this baby."

"I'm pretty desperate, to be honest. I wish it was simple and me and you could just have a baby together – it would be a hell of a lot easier, that's for sure."

"I wish we could too," he said with a bittersweet edge to his voice.

She shrugged her shoulders. "Well, what can I do?"

Isla woke the next day in Greg's bed, having dreamt of the baby again. She took her hand out from underneath the warmth of the duvet and reached out to check the bed beside her but of course the baby wasn't there and instead her hand hit off Greg's bare chest. He was still sleeping soundly, his mouth half-open, making a gentle snoring sound. She took a moment to look at his face while he slept, lost in a peaceful world somewhere.

The dream came back to her again. It seemed like just minutes ago that the baby was laughing; he was reaching his pudgy fists upwards and reaching out for strands of her hair as she had leant in to kiss him. He laughed heartily whenever he caught hold of a fistful and she had leant in further and tickled him on the part of his stomach that was lovely and round. "You're my baby," she said. He laughed some more at that, like it was the funniest thing that he'd ever heard. "Yes, you are, you are. You're my baby." Then parts of him began to fade and reappear. It was his left leg first and when she reached out to touch it there was nothing there. Then it was back again just like it had always been there but then his left arm was gone. Parts of him kept disappearing and reappearing but he was never whole. "Come back!" she called. "You can't be playing games like that on me!"

When Greg woke up, he opened his eyes and smiled at her. A smile that said so much. A smile she wished she could take for herself, to be her smile whenever she opened her eyes in the morning. But there was something stopping her from reaching out to it. She knew that that feeling could be hers to keep if she wanted it but there was something stubbornly insistent within her that wouldn't allow it.

"Did you sleep okay?" he asked her.

"Yeah, I did."

"You were tossing and turning all night."

"Oh, sorry, was I? I hope I didn't keep you awake?"

"Don't worry about it. You know that I'll support you, Isla – whatever it is you decide or your sister decides or whatever happens – you know that I'll support you, don't you?"

"Why are you so nice to me?"

"No, I'm not."

"Yes, you are."

"Well, I love you, Isla – don't worry, I know you don't feel the same way and that's fine but it doesn't mean that I'll stop caring about you."

"You see what I mean? That's what I'm talking about." She paused. "You're right, by the way," she sighed.

"Right about what?"

"The reading. I've struggled with it every day since I was six years old."

"Oh, Isla, I'm sorry. Why didn't you ever say something?"

"Because I'm thirty-nine years old. It's ridiculous."

"You have nothing to be embarrassed about – there are lots of adults in the same position as you. But don't let it ruin your life any longer. There are groups out there that help people like you. Why don't I look one up for you?"

"Maybe," she sighed.

"Isla, you owe it to yourself to learn to read properly. It must have been awful for you trying to keep it a secret for all these years. I was thinking back on all your excuses since I've known you and, I have to give it to you, you're fairly crafty."

"I just can't face going to see a complete stranger and telling them about it."

"But they'll have helped people just like you before."

"But what if I'm the worst one that they've ever seen?"

"You won't be."

"How do you know that I won't be?"

"Because it's a support group – they want to help you – that's the reason they exist!"

"I can't face it, Greg. I know it sounds mad but school wasn't a very happy place for me and I think it will dredge up too many bad memories and anxiety."

"So that's it? You're going to let this ruin the rest of your life because you're too afraid to get help?"

"I'm sorry. I know it seems hard for you to understand but I couldn't face it."

"You're so stubborn, Isla, do you know that?" Greg breathed a frustrated sigh.

Chapter 23

Rebellion

The witching hour was what they called it. It was the time at night where a person could feel like they were the only one in the world who was still awake. It was the time when babies wouldn't settle and dreams fused with reality in the unconsciousness of sleep. It was where Isla now found herself lying in a pool of sweat after waking from an awful nightmare. She had dreamt that she had walked into a square room with white walls. She had stood looking around at them for a moment but when she went to get out again the door had vanished. A smooth wall, just like the other three, was now in the place where the door had been. Then a window appeared so she had walked over to it but, when she got up to it, she saw that it wasn't a window any more – it was a mirror and, when she looked into it, it wasn't her reflection looking back at her. Instead it was Jo. She started to scream, '*Jo, Jo, help me! I can't get out. Jo, please, help me, I'm trapped in here!*' Jo's face started to crease in concern but she still didn't do anything to help her so Isla had started calling out louder to her. '*Jo, help me, please! I can't find my way out!*' Then Jo had opened her mouth and Isla could see that her teeth were black and rotten all the way down to her gums. Isla shouted, *'Jo, look at your teeth!'* but then Jo started to laugh at her and the more Isla screamed for help, the more she just laughed.

As she lay there shivering her phone rang shrilly and cut through the darkness of the night. Isla fumbled a hand around the top of her locker and eventually located it. She was almost going to hang up without answering it when something deep within her, some kind of instinct, told her to check who it was. She looked at the screen and saw Réiltín's name lighting it up. A sense of panic washed through her. She quickly pressed the answer button.

"Réiltín, is everything okay?"

"I'm outside your door – can you let me in?"

"What's wrong, what's after happening?"

"Please, Isla, just let me in."

She could hear the wheeze in her chest, the shallowness of her breath. Her asthma always got worse when she was upset about something.

"I'll be down in a sec."

She jumped out of bed and threw on her dressing gown. She took the stairs two at a time. She pulled open the door and saw her standing on the path underneath the orange glow of the sodium street lamps. She was almost unrecognisable in the short dress with heavy black biker boots underneath. Thick black eyeliner mixed with mascara sat smudged underneath her eyes. Isla knew that there was no way that Jo would have let her out of the house dressed like that.

"Thanks, Isla," she mumbled.

Isla let her walk up the stairs ahead of her. She noticed that she was unsteady.

"Have you been drinking?" she asked, shocked.

She nodded. "Please don't tell my mum."

"Are you going to get sick?"

She shook her head.

179

"Does your mum know where you've been?"

"Of course not. Do you think she'd let me go to a party?"

"I didn't think so. So where does she think you are then?"

"In Fiona's house." She plonked down onto the sofa.

Isla nodded. "So are you going to tell me what happened?" she said, sitting down in the chair beside her.

"You know Darren from my class?'

Isla nodded – she had heard Réiltín mention his name before.

"Well, he was having a party – his parents are gone away for the weekend and Rick asked me to go with him. You have to promise you won't tell Mum . . ."

"Go on –"

"Well, we were drinking vodka and I started to feel sick so he said he'd come outside for some air with me. Then he started kissing me but I felt really dizzy and was afraid I'd get sick on him so I pushed him away and he got mad with me and said horrible things and then he stormed off and when I went back inside he was kissing Doireann Walsh."

"Oh, sweetheart! That's awful. Are you okay?"

"Yeah, my head hurts though."

"That's what's known in the business as a hangover! You'll just have to sleep it off. You can stay here – there's no point going home now and starting World War Three."

"Thanks, Isla," she mumbled. "Please don't tell Mum."

"Don't worry, I'm not going to say anything this time but you have to promise me there'll be no more wild drinking night-time adventures, okay? You're not old enough yet to steal my thunder!"

Isla gave her some fresh pyjamas and tucked her up in her bed. Réiltín fell asleep almost instantly and Isla sat on the edge of the duvet and stroked her hair. Then she climbed into bed beside her.

For a while she lay awake, listening to the gentle rhythm of Réiltín's breathing. This wasn't like Réiltín. She knew that all teenagers rebelled at some point but it wasn't like her to lie to Jo about her whereabouts. When had she even learnt how to lie? When she was a child if you asked her if she had done something like eaten a packet of sweets that she wasn't supposed to eat, she would burst out crying with guilt. She wondered if things were tense at home because of the situation between herself and Jo and she felt a wave of guilt wash over her. She and Jo still weren't back in contact and Réiltín was bound to have picked up on it, considering how close they used to be.

When Réiltín woke the next morning, she came into the kitchen where Isla was already up. Her auburn hair was wild and black eye make-up was smudged beneath her eyes. She was pale and sheepish.

"Morning," Isla said through a mouthful of toast. "Do you want some breakfast?"

"I couldn't look at food right now."

"That bad?"

"I feel terrible. I'm never drinking again."

"I'm glad to hear that. Even I wasn't doing that at your age."

"Look, Isla, I just want to say . . . well, thanks for letting me stay here and not telling my mum. I'm so glad I have you." She walked over and threw her arms around her neck.

"Well, you know that's what aunties are for – we do the cool things that mums can't!"

"You're more than an aunt – you're like a second mother to me."

Isla was cringing inside at her innocence.

"Sometimes I don't know how you and Mum are even sisters. You're total opposites!" Réiltín was saying now.

"We're not that different really." She was trying to keep her voice casual in case Réiltín detected something in her tone. "I know you don't always understand where your mum is coming from but you're her world. She just wants the best for you. You're her Little Star. It's not such a bad thing really. Everyone should have a mum who loves them as much as your mum loves you."

"I suppose so." She sighed heavily. "I better go home. Mum has already been ringing my mobile and if I don't answer she'll probably drive over to Fiona's or something." She paused. "You know what she's like."

Isla had to try really hard to keep the smile from her face. "Yeah. Give her a ring now and tell her that you're on your way."

Réiltín groaned and made her way into the bedroom while Isla cleared up after breakfast.

"So what did you tell her?" Isla asked as soon as Réiltín came back into the room.

"I said I was asleep when the phone rang earlier but I'm on my way home now."

"You better go and get changed then."

Réiltín retuned a few minutes later in the outfit she had worn when she was supposed to be going to Fiona's house, her face washed clean and her hair brushed. She stuffed the tiny dress back into the bag.

"I'll walk you home," Isla said when Réiltín was ready to go.

They chatted as they walked along, passing the Cash for Gold shop, the launderette, the taxi rank and the bargain store that traded on Isla's street. Soon the shops became the up-market boutiques and fancy cafés that populated Réiltín's area.

"Aren't you coming in?" Réiltín asked when they had reached Sandymount Heights.

"Nah, I better head on. Your mum would be wondering why we're coming in together anyway."

"I could just say that I met you on the road if she says anything."

"She's not stupid, Réilt!"

"But we haven't seen you in ages – Mum will want to see you!"

"I'm sorry, I'm supposed to be meeting someone," she lied.

"What's going on, Isla?"

Réiltín was looking at her with her green eyes with their flecks of hazel and Isla had to look away.

"Nothing."

"Well, then, why aren't you coming in to see Mum?"

Isla knew that Réiltín was testing her. "Okay then, if it makes you feel better, then I will." The last thing she wanted was for Réiltín to get a sense of what was going on between them.

Isla followed Réiltín through to the back of the house and into the kitchen. She saw Oscar dozing in his basket in the corner, his paws twitching as he dreamt.

"Oh hi, love. How was the sleepover?" Jo asked, hugging her daughter in close. She didn't notice Isla lingering in the doorway behind her.

"It was good – I'm wrecked though."

Isla was amazed at how easily the lies seemed to fall off her lips.

"Hmmh, I bet you are. You probably were up chatting half the night. I remember those nights myself and we never slept a wink." Jo leant in and kissed Réiltín on the head.

Isla felt like an intruder, spying on a private moment between mother and daughter. There was a closeness like no other in that embrace. She felt the string tightening around her heart.

Jo straightened up then and her eyes landed on Isla. "Oh – Isla – hi."

"I – I thought I'd drop over to see you."

"Sure, yes."

Réiltín yawned loudly. "I think I'll go get some sleep, Mum. I'm wrecked."

"Oh to be fourteen again!" Jo admonished gently.

They listened to Réiltín's footsteps on the stairs growing fainter until it was just the two of them alone together.

The silence between them was awkward and strained.

"So how've you been?" Isla asked finally.

"Okay, I guess. Busy in work but nothing unusual about that," she replied brusquely. "How've you been?"

"Okay too," Isla said. "Trying to get my head around it all . . . you know?"

Jo wouldn't meet her eyes.

"Please, Jo . . ."

"Don't start, Isla!"

"Jo, I'm begging of you. I will never ask you for anything else ever again. Please, can you let me have that embryo? I'm actually begging here."

"I've already explained my reasons to you!" Jo said in an exasperated tone, the same kind you would use for a child who kept asking why they couldn't have more sweets.

"So that's it – you're refusing to give me an embryo, which my egg helped to create, even though you know that it is my only hope of having a child of my own and it is all because it 'doesn't sit easily' with you?"

"Why do I have to keep telling you – it's not that simple! It's not black and white, Isla! There are so many reasons. You never do anything the right way. You won't commit to anyone. Why should you be able to waltz in and have a baby?"

"I could say the same thing to you. Aren't you forgetting how you had your baby? And for all I know it could be all those fertility drugs that I took for you that has me in this position! All that 'shutting my cycle down' crap, 'down-regulating' or whatever fancy name the doctors called it, and all those hormones can't have been good for my body!"

"There have been studies done to show that they don't have a long-term effect on the person."

"Really? All these medications are only a recent thing. Who's to say that they won't discover in a few years that actually they have made millions of women infertile just like me?"

"Come on, Isla, there is no scientific proof about any of that!"

"Not yet!" Isla sighed heavily. "Jo, I just don't understand why you're so against me using the embryo if you're never going to use it."

"I just can't do it. I'm sorry, Isla."

"Imagine if I said to you that it 'doesn't sit easily' with me seeing Réiltín every day and knowing that genetically she is my child?"

"Stop it, Isla, stop it right now – you're crossing a line here!"

"Or what? It's the truth!"

"Mum was right about you – you always have to cause trouble. You turn everything into one big long drama. All your life you've only ever thought about yourself. How must it have felt to be you growing up?" How wonderful it must feel to be free from everyone else's expectations, she thought bitterly to herself.

"What do you mean by that?"

"To grow up with no limits, no boundaries or expectations weighing you down! Unlike me!"

"You're talking crap, Jo. No one expected you to do anything."

"Didn't they?"

"No, they didn't!"

"And who brought you to school and held your hand when you were too shy to go past the other kids in the school yard? Who made your lunch and dinner too most days? I had to look after you – that's the role I was given simply because I was born first. I had to be the good girl – sensible and reliable because no one else was going to do it! I had to protect you."

"No, you didn't – no one asked you to!"

"Well, somebody had to!"

"Dad would have! You didn't have to do all of that – no one forced you to – you chose it."

"You think I wanted that? Dad had so much on his plate trying to hold down his job in the recession of the eighties, deal with Mum and all that went with that and then look after us. Someone had to help him. You were lucky, you were assigned the fun role – you got to be wild and carefree. You didn't have to care about what anyone thought, you were free from restraints – you could do whatever *you* wanted! You don't know what it's like having to think about other people's needs before your own the whole time, thinking about what everyone else wants except what you yourself would like."

"You make it sound like you had such a hard life. It wasn't just you that was affected, Jo – I had to deal with Mum too, you know."

"You don't know the half of it. There is stuff about our childhood that you don't even know because I shielded you from it."

"What do you want me to say? Thank you for being my protector? C'mon, Jo, that's life. Some people get a bum deal, some don't – yes, our childhood was shit but we just have to suck it up."

"No, Isla, I'm tired of sucking it up. I'm tired of always being the safety net for you. Worrying about you and hoping you're not going to end up in another mess or, worse still, that I'm going to get a call to tell me that you're in trouble somewhere."

"What has all this got to do with me having a baby?"

"Because the point I am trying to make here is that you're not able for the responsibility. And that's what would happen if you had that embryo. I would end up picking up the pieces for you yet again. You've been running away from it your whole entire life. Even the day I got made managing partner, you got so drunk on the free champagne at the party the firm had thrown for me that I had to leave my own party early. Just for once it would have been nice to enjoy 'my night' without having to worry about somebody else. When Dad died you just flaked out on me – as usual I was left to sort everything out. I washed his clothes, ironed them, put them into bags and brought them down to the St Vincent de Paul. I sorted through all of his belongings. I was the one who had to put the house up for sale. Well, I'm sick of carrying the can for you! When are you going to grow up and take responsibility and be an adult?"

"What's going on, Mum?" It was Réiltín.

They both swung around to the doorway.

"What's wrong, Little Star?" Jo asked, panicked.

"I just wanted a glass of juice and then I come in and you two are going at it."

"I never heard you come in."

"Well, I didn't know I had to knock before coming into my own kitchen," Réiltín replied sarcastically before continuing over to the fridge.

Jo flashed Isla a burning look and Isla knew that she was seething.

"I'd better go." Isla grabbed her bag and left.

Chapter 24

6 Lambay Grove

Even though they were sisters, Jo firmly believed that she and Isla were completely different people. Although they were raised under the same roof, she felt that they'd had completely different upbringings. Being the elder sister always came with the burden of expectation. An expectation of responsibility. Jo had learned early on that her mother's patience was in limited supply in the presence of a wayward younger sister and she'd had to take on the role of peacekeeper.

Jo had spent most of her childhood trying her best to please her parents. She had tried so hard to be good. She did her best in school; she always did whatever it was that her mum and dad asked her to do. She kept her bedroom tidy, even when Isla scattered toys and clothes around it. She would watch Isla out on the road to make sure she wasn't getting up to mischief, as she was wont to. She never gave their mum a cause for trouble because she had just wanted her to go back to the way she had been before things went all wrong.

Everything had been going fine until they had moved to 6 Lambay Grove or at least that was the way it had seemed to the eight-year-old Jo.

Their mum was pregnant again and they had needed more space. She also wanted to live closer to the sea. She was craving salty air and briny wind. Having grown up on the Isle of Skye in Scotland, she missed it. She missed the feel of it against her skin and the taste of it on her tongue. Jo still remembered Mrs Dunphy, the estate agent who had shown them around the house. She wore a matching candy-pink trouser suit, pink stiletto heels, pink handbag, pink nail polish and fuchsia lipstick. She extolled the virtues of all its 'mod-cons', which in 1980 amounted to a washing machine and built-in wardrobes. When they had got outside to the garden, her mum had said that you couldn't swing a cat in it which Jo had thought was a very funny thing to say as she imagined a cat being swung around by its tail. Mrs Dunphy ignored her mother, turned to their dad instead and started making a big fuss over the garage where you could drive your car inside on cold nights.

"Imagine that, Daph!" her dad had said, turning back to her mum, clearly won over. "Imagine not having to de-ice the car on a frosty morning!"

Jo had watched as her mum lit up one of her slender More cigarettes and inhaled deeply, pulling the smoke back between her teeth. Seconds fell in a long pause until she exhaled a long plume into the air in front of them.

In the car as they drove away, their dad had turned to their mum. "Well, Daph, what did you think of it?" he asked eagerly. "Is it the house for us?"

"She looked like Barbie's grandmother."

Jo and Isla had started to giggle from the backseat. Jo could see her dad looking back at them in his rear-view mirror.

"I'm talking about the house, not her," he said, "but I thought that she looked quite nice actually."

Jo could detect a wounded tone to his voice.

"Well, there is no accounting for some people's taste," her mum had said, crossing her arms purposefully over her bump before turning her head away to stare out of the window.

Their dad had sucked in sharply through his teeth and his fingers tightened around the polyester fur of the steering-wheel cover.

They obviously came to an agreement because they bought the house and the baby was born three months after they moved in. Their mum's sister Carole came over from where she lived in Fife in Scotland to give her a hand. Jo remembered it seemed like she had just gone home when their dad was asking her to come back over again because the baby had died.

Jo had one clear memory of David: she was lying with her cheek pressed against the carpeted floor of their living room. The sun was coming in through the net curtains and making a holey pattern on the floor beside her. She was spreading her fingers out, letting their tips cover the circles. She was watching him lying back on a powder-blue rug, kicking out his little feet, balling his hands into fists and putting them into his dribbly mouth. He gurgled and squealed. But she wasn't sure if the memory could be trusted. She didn't know how reliable it was – maybe she'd just seen the image in an old photo or maybe it was someone else's baby that she was recollecting. She did remember her mum crying though. Her tears for him lasted a lot longer than the time he was with them. She used to sit at their kitchen table chain-smoking all day long until the ash grew heavy and fell off the tip of the cigarette by itself and landed into the ashtray waiting beneath. She never had to check for it – it was like she always knew the ashtray would be there, ready for the fall. She would smoke the cigarette right down to the butt until she must have felt the heat on her fingertips. Eventually she would stub it out and light another one straightaway.

Jo had minded Isla while their mum sat in her room and cried every day. Their childhood forced them to be united because, if they weren't, they would never have survived.

Their dad had tried his best but it never seemed to be enough for their mother.

Whenever they saw his canary-yellow car coming around the corner to their cul-de-sac after his day's work in the factory, they would run down to meet the car and jump in. She'd sit in the passenger seat and Isla would sit on their dad's knee and steer the car home. Sometimes he'd jerk her arms left and right and they'd zigzag the whole way up the road to their house with the two of them screaming in that childish mix of pretend-fear and excitement.

As soon as he came in the door, though, he would go straight over to their mum. He would give her a kiss on the cheek and ask her how her day had been but she would barely acknowledge him. Then he would go and start to make their dinner while their mum stayed staring off into whatever world she was living in after David died.

Time went on in their cul-de-sac. Their mum went through the motions of life. She could be really hit and miss as a mother. Sometimes it seemed as though the darkness had lifted its lid a little and she would be full on, like it was her resolution to try harder. She would overcompensate by insisting on walking them to school even though they were past the age of needing her to accompany them. Sometimes it was plain embarrassing like when she would wear her dressing gown instead of her coat or slippers on her feet instead of shoes. She would wear wellies in the summertime and shorts in the wintertime. They would watch her walk out in the middle of traffic and bang on a car window for a light for her cigarette and if they wouldn't give her one she'd weave her way through the other cars until someone would. Jo felt guilty even thinking it but she used to wish their mum could just be normal like the rest of the mothers. She wished she could have made more of an effort to fit in. She just wanted her to be like the ones that plaited their daughters' hair every morning, made their lunches and put them into Tupperware boxes, and parted with a kiss on the cheek. She wished her mum could have long conversations over the garden hedges of Lambay Grove like the other mothers as she pegged out washing. That's all she wanted but her mum wasn't friendly with the other women. Jo used to think that it was because they didn't understand her accent and she would have to slow down and repeat what she was trying to say. But everyone said that she was a different woman after the baby died. She left with David.

One time their mum was waiting at the school gate with a buggy and Jo had been so excited when she saw it. She thought they were baby-sitting a neighbour's baby but, when she had got closer, she'd seen there was no baby in the buggy. Jo had got really angry with her that time and wouldn't walk home with them so Isla and her mum walked on with the empty buggy. Isla had kept turning around to look back at her trailing behind them in the distance. Jo could still remember what she did then: she pointed her index finger to the side of her head and moved it around in a circular motion but Isla just looked back at her in confusion. Isla had turned away then because she was trying to keep up with their mother who was pulling her along by the wrist.

Then there were other times when their mother would be too tired to even lift her head off the pillow to get them ready for school so Jo would step in and butter bread for Isla's lunch, put it in her lunchbox and hold her hand as they walked to school. Jo always allowed Isla to have jam sandwiches and lots of biscuits as a snack instead of fruit like the other children in her class. Jo would make the dinner too but it was nearly always potatoes and baked beans. When convenience food arrived on the shelves, calling to housewives with the promise of no more drudgery at mealtimes, Jo was the one who brought the brightly coloured boxes home for them to try. Findus crispy pancakes, diarrhoea brown, oozing out through the goldfish-coloured breadcrumb coating put in a regular appearance. Jo could still see their half-moon shape sitting on her plate with the syrupy beans creeping closer until she was almost gagging but she had to eat them because she thought their dad liked them. Their dad, who Jo only found out in later years wasn't a crispy-pancake fan either, ate them too and complimented Jo on the lovely dinner, so the crispy pancakes kept on coming.

One day Jo and Isla came home from school to find that their mum wasn't at home. The back door was open and they searched the entire house but she definitely wasn't there. Jo had checked around to see if she could find her handbag but it was gone too. Although it was unusual for her to leave the house, they assumed she had gone to the shop to buy more cigarettes or something but when she hadn't come back by four o'clock, Jo called their dad in work. When he came home at five she still wasn't back even though it was dark outside. Eventually at nine o'clock that night the phone rang and Jo and Isla raced each other down the hallway to answer it. It was Auntie Carole calling and she asked to speak to their dad. She said their mother had shown up on her doorstep in Fife without any bags and she thought that they should know in case she hadn't told them where she was going. Their father, to save face and not wanting to admit to Carole just how bad things were between him and their mum at that stage, said of course she had told him. Carole said she needed a rest and that she was planning on staying for a few days.

A few days came and went and then it was a couple of weeks. A couple of weeks ended up being three months. Jo and Isla had stopped asking where she was and started to get on with their lives without her. They walked to and from school together every day. They ate cream crackers piled with butter and watched TV after school until their dad came home from work. Sometimes Mrs Peabody would drop them in an apple tart and say that it was for after their tea but they would eat the whole thing before their dad got home.

Then he announced one day that their mum was coming

home. Jo looked at Isla and Isla looked at Jo but they said nothing.

"Well, aren't you pair excited? I said your mum is coming home!" he asked, confused by their deflated reaction.

They had been told she was coming home four times already and she hadn't materialised. This was the fifth time.

"You said that the last time and she never came," Jo said.

"I know, love, I know, but she really is this time. She's booked her ferry and everything. She's sailing into Larne at five to eleven on Monday morning! We're going to drive up there and bring her home."

Their dad had spent the rest of the weekend wallpapering. He had seen an ad on TV for the new Superfresco wallpaper and had said to Jo and Isla "Do you think your mum would like that, girls?"

They had shrugged their shoulders because their mum didn't seem to like anything. When they came home from school he had already finished the sitting room and he was standing back admiring his work with his hands on his hips humming a tune. By Sunday evening he had Superfrescoed the whole house. Every wall was covered in it: kitchen, bedrooms, even the bathrooms weren't spared.

They picked their mum up in Larne. Jo was given a Sindy Doll because their mum didn't like Barbies and she gave Isla a colouring book but there were no pencils or crayons with it. Isla had started to cry but Jo told her not to be silly because she had lots of colours in her pencil case at home anyway and at least they had their mum back.

When they got home to their house, their dad had unlocked the door and proudly shown their mother the wallpaper but she just said "Oh" and went upstairs with her case.

Jo watched her dad's shoulders sink downwards and then she had gone upstairs to their room.

She heard Isla coming up the stairs after her a few minutes later.

"I think Dad just said the 'F' word."

"No, he didn't, he would never say that." Jo closed the book shut that was resting against her knees and sighed heavily.

"Well, I heard him say it."

"You're lying, Isla. You always hear things wrong. He probably said something that rhymed with it like 'book' or 'duck'," she said, looking proud of herself.

"Well, I'm telling you that he said 'fuck'."

Jo's mouth had opened wide and she slammed the book down on top of her locker. She jumped up from the bed. "I'm telling Mum what you just said!"

She wouldn't really have told on Isla. Their mother probably wouldn't have cared anyway. She would have just shrugged her shoulders.

Jo stormed out of the room and off down the stairs, leaving Isla on her own to think over the argument. Isla had then reached up and run her fingers over the new Superfresco wallpaper. The Holly Hobbie paper had finally been replaced. Their dad had chosen a bubbly cloud pattern for their room. It was raised and spongy against her skin and begging to be picked. She started off by tearing away a small cloud between her bed and the wall, then another bigger one and another and another. She couldn't help it. Soon there was a huge bald patch on the wallpaper and she knew she was going to be in big trouble. Sometimes she couldn't stop herself as a child when she knew something was going to get her into trouble but still would go ahead and do it anyway. She had tried lining up her teddies along the wall but they weren't tall enough to cover it so she piled up her pillows and sat the teddies on top of them but the problem was she knew she would never be able to move her construction. Jo had came up later to tell her that dinner was ready (potato waffles, eggs and beans) and she asked her why her teddies and pillows were stacked up on top of each other and Isla said that they weren't. So she came over and pulled all her efforts of concealment away.

Jo's face dropped when she saw the wallpaper. "Oh no, Isla!" Her hands had flown up towards her mouth.

"Dad's going to be really sad, isn't he?" Isla had seen the look on his face when her mum just said "Oh" after his weekend wallpapering session and she knew that this was going to add salt to the wound.

Jo nodded, too afraid to speak, not because their dad would be mad – their dad rarely got mad – but because, even though they were so young, they both knew that something like that could push him right over the edge. If he saw the hole in the wallpaper what would he do? If he had said the 'F' word when their mum just said "Oh", they were worried that he would leave them like Trevor Quinn's father left his family. They just lived with their mum and she did everything, all the jobs that the dads on their street normally did and the mothers' ones too. She made the dinner, cut the grass, took out the bins, she changed the fuse in the plug when the Christmas lights blew. Their dad had joked one time when they had a mouse that they should get Mrs Quinn to come and catch it, but their mum still didn't laugh.

"We have to hide the hole," Jo eventually said.

"I did hide it but you ruined it."

"Dad would have noticed that in two seconds flat. We'll have to rearrange the furniture a bit."

So they did. They dragged a chest of drawers over to cover the hole in the wallpaper and they moved Isla's bed so that it joined Jo's because there was nowhere else in the room for it to go.

When their dad was reading *James and the Giant Peach* to them that night, he had asked why they had moved the room around and why their beds were joined together. Jo had said it was because they wanted to be able to cuddle when they went to sleep. Their dad had smiled contentedly and said,

"I'm so proud of my two little girls."

Every night Isla would move over into Jo's bed and curl her small form into the mould of her older sister. Jo would drape her arm around her and they would sleep soundly like that all night long.

Jo didn't know why Isla had to ruin the wallpaper but sometimes it seemed like she just couldn't stop herself. Jo really wished she hadn't done it because their dad was nice and she knew he would be really hurt. She was worried that her dad would think that they were on their mum's side and she didn't want to be on anyone's side. If she had to take a side – but she really didn't want to – but if you made her, well, then, she would actually have taken their dad's because he always tried so hard to make their mum happy but she never could be happy. Sometimes Jo just wanted her to give him a smile, just a simple smile even if it were fake, just so he could feel okay about himself.

Jo and Isla stayed like that with their single beds joined together until Jo went off to university and then Isla had the two beds to herself. The chest of drawers only moved after Jo bought her first house and she needed to take it with her to have some furniture to tide her over for a while. She had actually forgotten all about the bald patch but, when her dad saw it, he had just laughed.

In the months after their mum had come back, Jo and their father had both focused on Isla because she was the youngest and, besides, it was easier to cope when they had something to occupy them. Their dad would come in the door from work and ask Jo how Isla was doing that day and Jo would give him a rundown of the day, about what Isla had got up to, whether she had been upset or not, but no one ever asked how Jo herself was doing. Looking back, it had seemed as though Isla was always up on his knee with both of their heads hidden behind his newspaper. Jo would be in the kitchen making the dinner and there they would be sitting together, giggling conspiratorially in his armchair. Jo would have liked to be pulled up onto her dad's knee too occasionally but there never seemed to be a time when Isla wasn't on it.

Jo finished secondary school, moved out of home and went to university. She joined societies, made a small circle of like-minded friends. She graduated with first class honours and her dad and Isla cheered for her at the ceremony. She joined one of the big five law firms and did her training. She worked her way up and through sheer hard work she was eventually made managing partner. Her work gave her a sense of self and it was a relief not to feel like the spare wheel, like the interloper that she had always felt like at home. She never really felt like she belonged in her family, like there was a slot for her.

Meanwhile Isla had announced in fifth year that she wanted to leave school. Jo had told their dad that it was the wrong decision. She knew that Isla had no back-up plan or alternative career option mapped out but she couldn't believe it when he didn't put up much of an argument to stop her. He just said it was her choice. Isla was like a small rowing boat floating around the edge of a stormy bay. Some days she was taken out on the tide and they wouldn't hear from her for days on end while other days she would change direction and the wind would carry her home.

Jo knew that their mum had been grieving but after David died she checked out on them. Her skin had turned from the golden bronze of the summer sun to the grey bark of the ash tree almost overnight. Grey like the endless cigarettes that she smoked that clouded up the kitchen air. Jo could still see her sitting there with her two elbows resting on the surface of the pine table, staring off into the middle distance with a cloud of smoke thickening around her head. It would catch in her throat and make it scratchy until she would eventually cough. She wouldn't even get up to open a window so Jo would have to do it for her. Isla didn't have a memory of the way things were before, but Jo did. Before, her hair was plaited every morning going to school and Isla's was tied up in two tiny pigtails on each side of her head. They had proper lunches and dinners. But when David died their mum stopped doing all of those things. She didn't bother to clean the house any more either so Jo used to do it for her. She knew that they weren't neglected or anything but the little details that make a childhood special were gone. Yes, the woman may have given birth to them, but she really let them down too. As Jo had always said, nurture trumped nature every time.

Chapter 25

Fizzy Orange

The air was heavy. Pensive. Mischievous and restless. The wads of heavy clouds overhead were bullet-grey. The gusts started. Leaves swirled and blossoms fell. They danced upwards, sucked into a vortex before scattering to the ground again. As she walked into work the ends of Isla's scarf danced on the air in front of her before falling downwards again. The grass was bent forward as the gales rippled through the park. All around the wind made a *Sssshissssssh* as it talked through the leaves. *Sssshissssh*, it said in a whisper. She noticed a man chasing sheets of white paper as they twirled on a gust before him.

She turned the corner onto St John's Street and pushed open the door to the café. It was early so she knew that it would be just her and Greg in.

"Hi there," she said softly.

He didn't reply.

"Look, Greg, I'm sorry about the other night – I really am."

"It makes no difference to me, Isla," he said with a nonchalance that he didn't really pull off.

"Greg, please, don't be like this –"

"What is it that you want, Isla?"

"What do you mean?"

"Maybe you could explain it because I just don't get you. I mean, I'm trying my best to help you but you just won't help yourself! Do you know how infuriating that is? Why won't you allow yourself to be happy? Do you want me to treat you badly, is that what you want? Would you like me then? Because if that's what you want, it's not going to happen. Call me old-fashioned but I wasn't raised that way. I want to help you, Isla – I love you – yes, I do. I'm not going to stand by and watch you destroy your life."

"I'm sorry, Greg," her voice was a whisper, "I'm sorry I can't be the person that you want me to be."

A frustrated Greg threw the tea towel that he was holding in his hand down onto the counter. "You see what I mean? You just won't help yourself!"

"What's going on in here?" Michelle asked, coming into the kitchen and unwinding her scarf from around her neck. She looked from one to the other and back again for an answer.

Isla felt the heat creeping up her face.

"The head on you, Greg, and the price of cabbage!" Michelle went on.

"Leave it out!" Greg snapped, grabbing his apron and heading out the front.

"What's got into him?" Michelle looked at Isla in bewilderment.

"It's nothing," Isla sighed.

"Well, it doesn't sound like nothing to me!" Michelle said, keen to have the last word before following Greg out the front.

The atmosphere was strained for the rest of the day. They all got on with the day's work and only talked when necessary. After Michelle had gone, Greg and Isla worked around each other without speaking.

"You're going to have to start charging him rent or at least for a contribution to the electricity," Isla said in an effort to break the ice. She was nodding in the direction of the only customer left. 'The Writer', as they had christened him, was sitting in his usual spot in the corner with his fingers busily clacking away on his laptop. He usually scraped coppers together for a cup of coffee and then sat sipping it for hours long after it had gone cold.

"Ah, he's okay. You never know, he might just be the next Stephen King and we can say we knew him when he was starting out."

Isla went out to the kitchen and started tidying up. When she came back out the front, The Writer was gone and the café was now empty.

"Look, Isla, I'm sorry about earlier." Greg stopped sweeping and leant on the handle of the brush. "I shouldn't have gone off at you like that."

"I'm sorry too, Greg."

"It's dead in here – how about we close up a bit early and do something?"

"Like what? Catch a movie?"

"Nah. Do you know where I'd love to go on a day like today?"

"Where?"

"The beach."

"*The beach*? But it's freezing out!"

"I know, but there's something about good brisk walk with the wind stripping your skin and catching your breath to make you feel alive."

"Okay, the beach it is then. What about Donabate? There's a lovely beach there."

After they locked up the café, they walked the short distance to Greg's place to get his car. Isla hopped in and Greg drove them through the city up along the coast of North County Dublin. The wind was howling and the crosswinds shook the small car as they travelled along the motorway. They soon exited it and followed the signs for Donabate, passing fields of polytunnels, golf links and haphazard caravan parks. Eventually they pulled up outside a hotel, which Isla couldn't help thinking looked familiar although she didn't know why. Greg silenced the engine and they struggled to open the car doors against the force of the easterly wind. The wind cut against their faces and sucked their breath away as they stepped out of the car. They walked down through the dunes to get onto the flat, hard sand. It was stained black in places where people had lit a fire. Stringy brown seaweed was draped across the strand with bits of decaying driftwood. Besides a man out walking his dog, they were the only ones on the beach. He nodded hello at them from underneath the hood of his windbreaker. They both raised their hands in a half-wave back to him. Isla couldn't shake the feeling of déjà vu, of having been there before and it was starting to annoy her. She looked over at the circular Martello Tower in the distance and then it hit her. She had been there before.

"I think I came to this beach with my mum once, just me and her," Isla said. "I remember my legs ached from all the walking. I don't know why we came here. I don't know how we even got here – Mum didn't drive so we must have got the train. See that Martello Tower?" She pointed over to it. "That's how I remember – I kept running around it until it made me dizzy."

"Your mum is dead, isn't she?" Greg probed gently.

She nodded and looked down at the wind skimming ripples across the surface of a rock pool at her feet.

"I've never heard you talk about her before. How did she die?"

"She killed herself twenty-nine years ago."

Isla left Greg on the sand while she climbed up towards the tower. When she reached it, she put the palms of her hands out to touch its stone and closed her eyes. She could still remember how it felt, the feel of the jagged rock underneath her fingertips. She remembered the eventual dizziness from circling round and round it. If she closed her eyes, she could still feel the cool February sun on her face and see the orangey-red colour on the inside of her eyelids.

Her legs were aching. They had walked and walked. She felt every pebble through the thin soles of her rubber-soled shoes and they were starting to hurt her now. The road seemed never-ending.

"I'm tired, Mum."

"We're nearly there now."

She had said that three times already and they weren't.

"Where are we going, Mum?"

"The beach."

"But I don't have my swimming togs with me."

"It's too cold to go swimming today, Isla."

"Then why are we going there?"

"To see the sea. I need to see the sea."

"When we see the sea do we have to walk all the way back again?"

"No, Isla."

She said it so wearily that it frightened Isla and she didn't dare ask her again.

A song came into her head then, a rhyme that Jo had taught her, "*A sailor went to sea, sea, sea to see what he could see, see, see but all that he could see, see, see was the bottom of the deep blue sea, sea, sea!*"

She started singing it out loud as they walked "*A sailor went to sea, sea, sea . . .*" She found if she sang it loudly enough she couldn't feel the pain in her legs or the stones pushing against the soles of her shoes.

Eventually a hotel came into view and her mum said that they were nearly there. She believed her that time because she had said it without Isla having to complain first. They walked down a steep slope and were on the beach. The salty air hit her nostrils. She liked that smell, she decided.

Isla had seen the tower and started to make her way across the dunes to climb up towards it. She ran around its circumference, still singing her song, until her head started to spin. She had to stop running and stand still for a moment to let it settle. When it eventually stopped, she saw her mum was wading far into the water fully dressed. What was she doing?

Isla climbed down from the tower and made her way over the rocks and onto the beach towards her. She started calling out to her but her words were lost on the wind. Her mother kept on walking deeper into the water. Then a woman ran over and went into the water after her mum – she reached her quicker than Isla. She talked to her mum for a minute and then she took off her coat and put it over her mum's shoulders, even though the woman's cardigan underneath had loads of tiny little holes but it was meant to be like that. She guided her mother out of the water and back onto the sand. Then she was following the woman and her mum into the hotel. The woman sat her mum down at a table in the corner overlooking the car park and then ordered a pot of tea for her and a scone with marmalade for Isla. She had got a coffee for herself. Isla wanted jam because she didn't like marmalade. She didn't like the bits of orange peel and she told her that but the woman ignored her and kept on talking softly to her mother. They sat there for ages, her mother and this woman talking very quietly. Isla couldn't hear what they were saying and she started to get restless, fidgety.

She went up to the bar and ran her fingers back and forth along the brass rail that was running along the front of the bar until it was covered in her greasy fingerprints and she got bored of doing that too. Then she started climbing up the stairs and bouncing back down each step again on her bum. She picked up all the salt and sugar sachets and tidied them up into their little white ceramic bowls. The people at the tables around them changed over several times. The barman smiled at her and asked if she wanted a mineral. She had nodded that she did and he gestured to a barstool and she climbed up on to it. He lined up three glass bottles along the bar in front of her.

"We have Cidona, Fanta or TK Red Lemonade? Which one would you like?"

She couldn't decide, so she did a dip like she saw Jo doing sometimes with the other girls on the road. "*Dip, dip,*" she pointed her index finger, "*eeeny meeny, miney moe . . .*" Her finger landed on the Fanta and she drank her fizzy orange through a straw, delighted with herself. They rarely had minerals at home and she couldn't wait to tell Jo when she saw her later.

Then the woman from the beach came up and said that her dad was in the car park and he was going to drive her and her mum home. Isla looked out at the dusky night and saw the glare of his yellow headlights through the window. They were the same colour as her fizzy orange.

Her mother was sent away to a psychiatric unit after that and their dad had to take time off work to mind them. Isla remembered talking to him about it once and he had said that "she wasn't well in the head", that her "nerves" were at her – that was the word people used to use for someone who was suffering with mental illness back then. Heaven forbid you should use the correct term.

Isla could remember going to visit her at the home but she was frightened by the behaviour of some of the patients. She and Jo would follow their father through the reception area, which led into a large communal living room. She could still remember the knot of anxiety as it closed around her chest and the way her heart would start to race as soon as she went through the door. They would have to pass some of the other residents, sitting in armchairs, to reach their mother's room down the end of the corridor.

"I know what you're doing! Don't think I don't! I know what you're at!" one man kept shouting at them whenever they walked past.

Their dad would hurry them along and tell them not to take any notice of him, that he didn't know what he was saying, but she would cling to her father until they were past him. She would have just started to calm down again by the time they reached her mother's room. Going into that room would cause her to be even more frightened because their mum barely seemed to notice them. Isla could still see her room now: it was rectangular in shape with a single bed, a wardrobe, a wash-hand basin and a window overlooking the car park. The walls were painted a sickly peach colour: it was the same colour as the 'bittersweet' in her Crayola crayons at home. One week their dad brought photos of them all but, when they had gone back to see her the following Sunday, they were all still lying in a pile on the top of her locker. They hadn't even been moved so he placed them around the room on her locker and windowsill and on the shelves but she just said, "You forgot to bring one of David".

The second time she tried to do it was when she was back home and their dad had taken them off to the beach one day. "We'll give your mum a rest," he had said and Jo and Isla giddily ran up the stairs to grab their swimming togs. They'd had a great day jumping over the waves and poking at crabs with sticks. When the sun started to go down for the evening, they climbed back over the dunes and their dad bought them an ice cream from a shop with netted buckets and spades hanging outside. They sat outside on a wooden picnic bench eating their ice creams and watching the sun set in an apricot sky. Then when they were finished, the three of them piled back into the car with sand stuck to their clothes and lining the creases of their bodies.

The first thing they saw when they arrived home and went into the kitchen was that the tap was running and there was orangey-red blood smeared all along the kitchen sink. It was watery just like they had been painting and were in the middle of washing out their brushes. It was only when they rounded the corner that they saw their mum lying slumped on the floor. Their dad had shouted at Jo to dial 999 so she ran out to the hallway and Isla ran after her because she didn't want to be left in that room with her mum. Jo had picked up the receiver and put a shaking finger in the hole for nine and pulled it around to dial the number. It seemed like an eternity as they waited for the panel to return each time to dial the next number before finally it connected. Isla was crying so loudly that Jo had to tell her to be quiet because she couldn't hear the operator. Then the man on the phone asked her for directions and she wasn't sure how to get to their house so she had called their dad and he shouted at her "Just give it to me for the love of God!" He grabbed the receiver out of her hand and directed them to their house. Isla had known that he didn't mean it – he never shouted at them usually – but he was just as panicked as they were.

The ambulance came and all the neighbours gathered in the street, gawking at the scene as their mother's trolley was loaded into the back, but nobody said anything to them. Their dad went off in the ambulance with her and Jo declined the offers from Mrs Peabody and Mrs McGuirk to come over to their houses for tea. She led Isla back inside and turned on the TV for her. *He-Man* was on and Isla watched that while Jo cleaned up the kitchen.

Their dad came home after midnight and said that they'd saved her. That she was doing okay but she would need to stay in the hospital for a few days. Jo couldn't look him in the eye. That night she cuddled Isla even closer in her bed.

Isla's bare legs touched her older sister's and she felt her ribcage lift and fall gently behind her as she breathed.

"Why did she do it?" she asked Jo.

"Because she doesn't want to be here. She doesn't want to

208

be with us," Jo had replied.

Isla hardly closed her eyes that night because every time that she did she saw their mum and the colour red.

It was her third time lucky that she finally succeeded. It had been quite peaceful actually, compared to the times before it. Well, as peaceful as it can be when your mum takes her own life. Their dad had found her slumped down in the bath on Good Friday when they came back from the Stations of the Cross in the church. Isla had come into the bathroom after him and saw that her hair was fanned out in the water around her. An empty bottle of vodka lay on the floor beside the tub. He had screamed at her to get out then. The doctors said she would have gone quickly, probably in her sleep.

After she died Isla had felt a strange mixture of overwhelming sadness for the mother that she hadn't ever really got to know but also relief. She was ashamed to say it but she was relieved that she no longer had to carry around the constant weight of wondering whether it was them or her? It just seemed like none of them could get near to her, not even their dad. She often found herself wondering if she really hated them all that much. When she was alive, when the girls in school were talking about their mothers, Isla would get a knot of anxiety deep inside of her because she felt embarrassed by the pathetic relationship that she had with hers. Isla never asked friends over to her house because she didn't want anyone to see how crazy her mum was. At least now whenever someone asked her about her mother she could say that she passed away and they never wanted to know any more. They were too afraid of upsetting her, so the conversation came to a swift end. It drew a neat line under it.

She knew that Jo's feelings were a lot more complicated, however, probably because she was the elder of the two of them. Jo was still very angry with their mother. She couldn't imagine how awful losing David must have been for her mum but she had people who needed her – it wasn't just her decision to make – the decision to exit the here and now because her grief was overpowering. It wasn't her right to abdicate from her life. As a mother herself, Jo didn't know how her mother could rationalise it in her head that it was okay to do something like that. Did she need to leave those imprints on her living children's minds for the rest of their lives?

In some ways Isla thought it was probably harder for Jo than it was for her because she had memories of a different mother. Isla only knew the woman she had been continually locking horns with from a very young age but Jo said that the one before David died was caring and loving and she had to deal with wondering where she had gone to. She was left trying to reconcile two versions of the same person, like a plate that had been smashed in two and the pieces never quite fitted back together again. When David died it was like someone had pulled the rug out from underneath their whole family, leaving a mess of broken fragments behind. Isla used to go and visit her grave but she hadn't been in years. She imagined it overgrown with weeds and the headstone thick with moss.

When Isla and Greg got back into the car afterwards, she felt exhausted. Greg seemed to sense her need to be quiet so he flicked on the radio and they listened to some eighties easy-listening station the whole way home. Eventually he pulled up on the path beside her flat. He silenced the engine and turned towards her.

"Are you sure you're okay, Isla? I'm so sorry – the last thing I wanted to do was upset you. I would never have brought you there if I had known . . ."

"Don't worry," she sighed. "I'll be fine. Just sometimes it sneaks up on you, y'know?"

"Well, I'm always here for you if you need me – you know that, don't you?"

"Will you come up for a cuppa?"

"Sure, I'd like that."

She opened the door and he followed her upstairs.

"You can take off your coat, you know," she said eventually.

"Sorry, I'm not used to being in your place." He laughed nervously before taking it off and putting it over the back of the sofa. They had always gone back to his place. "It's nice here, Isla," he said, looking around the walls. "It's very *you*."

"What does that mean?"

"It's creative, homely."

She made the tea and they fell silent for a while, clasping their mugs, until Greg spoke.

"So did you make any headway with your sister?"

She shook her head. "I was over there again. She isn't going to change her mind. I think I underestimated her feelings about it all. I think she has left all of that in the past, back when Réiltín was conceived. I suppose to her it was all done and dusted so when I went and asked her for the embryo she was in total shock."

"Well, maybe she just needs some time to come around to the idea?" Greg asked hopefully.

"You should have seen her reaction. I really don't think she'll ever change her mind."

"You never know – she might in time. Don't give up hope."

"I don't know . . . maybe I should just try to accept it. I did give up any rights I had to the embryo when I donated it so maybe I should have expected this. I just never thought back then that I would be in this position."

"Of course you didn't. Look, why don't you take legal advice? Maybe you have more rights than you think?"

Isla exhaled wearily. "I just couldn't face going down that road. I don't want to get into a battle with my own sister – plus, as I told you, she's a lawyer and I wouldn't stand a chance against her. I just wish she would help me."

"Well, it shouldn't come down to legal rights and contracts and what have you. I know it's not the most conventional of requests but she should want to help you, like you helped her. I'm so sorry, Isla. I feel so bad for you."

"Hey, I'll be fine – you know me." She forced a smile on her face that she didn't feel on the inside.

"I'm so sorry you have to go through this."

They fell quiet for a while until Isla spoke again.

"Greg, I've been doing a lot of thinking lately . . . I was just wondering . . ."

"Oh yeah?"

"I think you're right. I think it's time I started taking control of my life instead of just floating along and seeing where I end up. Maybe if I had done it years ago, I would be a mother by now."

He shrugged his shoulders. "Who knows? Everything always seems a bit easier in hindsight."

She paused for a moment. "I have a big favour to ask you and feel free to say no if you want to –"

"Go on?"

"Well, I was thinking . . . maybe . . . well . . . maybe you could teach me?"

"What? Teach you how to read?"

She nodded. "I mean only if you want to . . ."

"Yeah . . . sure . . . okay, Isla, I think we could do that." His mouth broke into a wide grin.

Chapter 26

Feelings

In the café Isla and Greg had just got over the coffee-to-go rush and the lunchtime sandwich queues, and things were just starting to settle down to the slower afternoon pace that they always welcomed after a hectic morning. They were a person short as Jamie was sick so Michelle couldn't come in to work and Fran was on holidays so he couldn't cover for her. They had worked busily all day without much time to chat.

Suddenly the door swung open, taken by a gust, and Réiltín marched in through it. Her blue hair dye had faded from its earlier electric shade to a softer baby-blue colour. She was wearing her school uniform but her tie was missing. She walked up to the counter where Isla was cleaning the salad trays.

"I want to know what's going on between you and Mum," she demanded of Isla.

"Well, hello to you too!" Isla said.

"I'm serious, Isla. I want to know what's going on!"

"Do you want a hot chocolate? I was just going to make myself one." She turned to Greg. "Can you hold the fort for a few minutes?"

"Work away!"

She took her time making two steaming mugs of cocoa. She was buying herself time to think about the best way to handle the conversation with Réiltín. She made sure to add plenty of mini-marshmallows into Réiltín's mug before sitting down at a table in the corner with her.

"I know there's something going on between you and Mum and you think I don't notice but I do. So are you going to tell me why you've been avoiding us?"

"I'm not avoiding you." Which was technically true.

"I know you're making up excuses not to have to see Mum. You practically used to live in our house and now you hardly come at all."

"I have been over but you were out at the time."

"I want to know what's going on. Stop lying to me, Isla. Please, it's bad enough that Mum and Dad treat me like a child constantly but please don't you do it too. Now tell me what's going on."

"There is nothing going on. Everything is fine – you don't need to worry about anything."

"I know there is something, Isla. You haven't been over to the house in ages and then when you did come you were fighting with Mum. Then Dad and Mum are barely talking even though they pretend to be whenever I'm there –"

"It's nothing. I'll be over again soon, I promise."

"So there is something then. I knew it."

"Look, I'm not fighting with your mum, honestly. I can promise you that. We just have a difference of opinion on something and sometimes things like that happen but it will all blow over soon. You have nothing to worry about."

"But what's it about?"

"I can't tell you that, Réilt, but you just have to trust me, okay?"

"Is Mum being bossy again? Because I know what she's like. She never stops organising people and telling them what they should be doing – ask Dad. But it's just the way she is. She doesn't mean it really. She likes to be in control. Me and Dad have this thing where we just nod to agree with her because it's easier that way and then when she's not there we both laugh about it."

Isla knew exactly what she meant. She had known Jo her whole life so she knew what she was like but she also knew that sometimes Jo could be overprotective with Ryan and Réiltín because she loved them so much. She had been like that with Isla when they were growing up.

"Look, if it makes you feel any better I'll call over at the weekend, okay?"

"Good, because I really miss you." Réiltín leant in and threw her arms around her.

"You know you can call over to see me at any time too, don't you?"

"Yeah, but you're part of our family – it's not the same without you."

Suddenly Isla felt a huge pang of guilt. Réiltín was right. She had to think of her feelings as well.

"Okay, well, I'll call over at the weekend then."

"You promise?"

"I promise."

"I'd better run. I've got piano practice now."

They both stood up and Isla leant in to hug her. She noticed that her hair smelt of cigarette smoke but she didn't say anything.

Chapter 27

Jealousy

The following weekend, before she had even reached the door, Jo could hear the laughter. She stopped to let herself listen to it for a moment, to its carefree and unrestrained notes. She couldn't remember if she had ever laughed like that, really just let herself go without caring what she sounded like or whether she had something stuck in her teeth. Before she even opened it, she knew that the three of them were in there together. She hated to admit it but the three of them seemed to get along better whenever she wasn't around. The old, deep-rooted insecurity was raising its ugly head again. What was Isla even doing here anyway? She hadn't told her that she was calling over. She had a downright cheek to sit in her living room with her family as if nothing had happened after the drama she had caused over the last few weeks.

She steeled herself and pushed open the living-room door.

"What's going on?" She tried to make her tone sound even and calm but she could hear the staccato notes of panic in it. "I didn't know we were expecting you, Isla?"

Silence fell on the room, like they were all in school and had just been caught in the middle of doing something wrong.

Réiltín looked from her mother to Isla and back again.

"Sorry, I only came for a short visit – I promised Réiltín earlier in the week that I'd call in," Isla said quickly.

"I see." Jo took off her coat and folded it over her forearm.

"She doesn't need to tell us when she's calling over, Mum!" Réiltín was angered by her mother's reaction.

"How are you? How was work?" Isla said, standing up and gesturing at Jo to sit down.

In my own house, thought Jo – she is telling me to sit down in my own house.

"Did you get the notes on the Gibson case prepared?" Ryan asked, trying to break the tension.

"It took a while but we should be okay for Monday." Her tone was sharp. "So, what were you all laughing about when I came in? What was so funny?"

"Oh, it was just a joke about a guy on TV," Isla said.

"What was the joke?"

"Well, it probably won't seem funny now," Ryan muttered.

"Well, tell me."

"Oh, it was just a guy on TV was calling himself an athlete and Dad said the closest he would get to being an athlete was using athlete's foot powder," Réiltín said.

Jo knew that she should laugh. Even if she didn't think it was as funny as they all seemed to find it – which she didn't – she still knew that she should give them a laugh so that nobody felt awkward. Be part of the gang. Be in *the clique*. If she laughed it would mean that she was one of them, she would be included in their cosy little gathering, but she just couldn't do it. It was like some stubborn tie had come over her tongue and wouldn't let her do it. They were all looking at her, waiting for her to laugh with them even if it was faked. It was expected of her to laugh but she wouldn't do it.

"So did you eat? We have some takeout leftovers if you'd like some?" Ryan said, changing the subject.

"You had takeaway again tonight? But you had one a few

days ago!" She looked to Réiltín for confirmation but she wouldn't meet her eyes.

"Chill, Jo, it's not like we're eating it every day," Ryan said in that same irksome tone again.

It angered her how he could speak to her like that. Strip her down in front of everyone.

"I'll make myself a sandwich, thanks," Jo said, getting up and closing the door on the three of them.

She went into the kitchen and flicked on the lights. The paper takeaway bags and the empty plastic tubs that the food had arrived in were scattered across the table. She gathered them up and put them into the bin, separating the unsoiled recyclables and putting everything else in the general waste. Dishes and cups lay strewn across the counter. "Would it have been too much extra trouble to put them into the dishwasher underneath?" she asked nobody as she went over to pull out the drawers and load them into it. She noticed crumbs, probably from the morning's toast, were sprinkled along the worktop. She felt her shoulders start to tense as she began to clean up the mess.

Isla had some cheek coming over there after the last time she saw her.

Jo had never told anyone before, because she was too afraid of what they would think of her, but there were times over the last few years when she had almost hated Isla. She had hated her for what she had done for them even though that was completely illogical. Jo knew that she had given them the best gift they could ever have hoped for but she had been so caught up in the excitement of finally being pregnant that it was only after Réiltín was born that the reality of how she was conceived had started to hit her properly.

When Jo had initially got the two pink lines on the pregnancy test she was so elated to finally be at that stage that she didn't care how she had achieved it. She was ecstatic, on a high, and everything was finally good in her world. When

Réiltín was growing inside of her, she was *her* baby. Ryan would ask her how she was doing and she would tell him if she was having an active day or a quiet one. She was the one to tell him when the baby was kicking. Whenever Isla had felt her bump, Jo was able to tell her which way the baby was positioned. Jo could tell her which mound was a head and which was a bum. But when Réiltín was born, she was out there in the world. Suddenly she was everyone else's baby too. Isla or Ryan could just walk in and lift her out of her crib and Jo hated that. She knew it was horrible but there were times where she desperately wished that she could fold Réiltín up neatly and tuck her back inside herself, away from everyone else, where she was hers and hers alone. She would lie in bed at night, wide awake, thinking about it. She felt as though her role was obsolete once Réiltín was born. While she was pregnant, she was doing something – by carrying Réiltín she felt she was contributing to the trio. But she gradually realised that, instead of them being a family on their own, Isla was now intricately involved in their lives forever more whether she liked it or not. She was woven into the fabric of her family – there were four of them in the relationship. While Isla was there, Jo could never forget how they came to have Réiltín. Jo was soon to learn that there were always reminders. Even though they never discussed what they had done all those years ago, something would peep its head up and remind them that they could never forget how Réiltín had come to be.

One time, when Réiltín was about three, Jo and Isla had taken her for a walk along the beach in front of Jo's house. They were walking along the sand, crumbly from the rain the night before. Réiltín was gathering shells and running back to put them into the bucket that they were holding for her. Some were smooth, others were ridged and gritty.

"'Ook I got, Mamma!" Réiltín had said.

They made their way over to her and looked at what she wanted to show them.

"Wow, you got a shell! That's so pretty, sweetheart," Jo said, crouching down to inspect it.

Réiltín threw it into the bucket where it rattled off the other shells she had collected. Just then they saw a woman with a small dog approaching and Réiltín ran across the flattened sand over to it. She bent down and put out a hand to pat the dog. They watched from a distance as it started to snarl at her, its lips rising to show bared teeth. She quickly took her hand away and came running back over towards them, her small face red and streaked with tears. Jo crouched down on the sand and opened her arms wide, ready to take Réiltín into them, but Réiltín's small body collided with Isla's legs and she wrapped her two arms around her knees.

Jo had stood up again, came over to them and said, "I'm here, Little Star, Mummy's right here," but Réiltín still stayed clinging to Isla's legs.

Obviously feeling awkward, Isla had finally managed to prise Réiltín's small arms off her legs and bent down to her level. "Are you okay, Réiltín? Did the bold doggy scare you?"

"Me go home, I-ya. Me no like here," Réiltín had said with her bottom lip quivering.

They did go home. Jo had felt humiliated. She had stormed off down the beach and climbed the steps back up to her house.

Jo felt that if they had used an anonymous donor it would have been much easier to forget and to get on with things but Isla was her sister and she was going to be there every single day for the rest of their lives. Jo could never cut her out even though, if she was really honest, she wished she could at times. She hated herself for feeling like that about her own sister because she loved her so much as well but it was so complex and awful and she felt too ashamed to tell anyone about her thoughts. She was so disgusted with herself for feeling that way. She knew that Ryan would never have understood it if she had told him. From the moment Réiltín had been born, he had placed Isla up on a pedestal of gratitude. Sometimes over the years she'd catch him looking at Isla. She couldn't put into words exactly what it was that she saw but it was a look of admiration, maybe even desire. Ryan had a protectiveness towards Isla that she just couldn't figure out. He seemed to feel it was his duty to mind her. If she needed a lift somewhere, he would be the first one to offer, if her tap sprang a leak he would be straight over there with the toolbox to fix it. Jo couldn't decide if it was a brotherly type of feeling or if it was something else. She didn't like letting her head go there but she couldn't help but wonder if it was because she had given him a child, the much longed-for child that Jo had been unable to give him. She hated seeing the three of them on their own together. She would look at them like a stranger might and let herself imagine that they were a couple and Réiltín was their child. How would their family look to the outside world? Did Réiltín look like them? She didn't want to see it, if she did. She imagined that the three of them had a stronger bond, like a radio fence where you couldn't see it but it was there all right. Sometimes Jo wanted to rip Isla out of their lives like you would tear someone that you didn't like out of a photo and she hated herself for that because she knew that they wouldn't have ever had their baby without her. It was an insane jealousy but she couldn't stop thinking like that. Whenever she watched Ryan and Isla laughing and joking together it made her wonder if anything would ever happen between them. She used to worry that they would have an affair behind her back and run away with Réiltín, leaving her on her own, so she refused to leave the three of them alone together. Then she would feel awful for not trusting them. She knew that she wasn't thinking rationally.

There was one time that Jo would never forget. Réiltín had been three months old. She wasn't long out of hospital at the time and the months of worry were starting to catch up on Jo. The sleepless nights had started and she would fret over every little thing because she was so fragile. She was afraid that she was doing it all wrong. Maybe it was the hormones but she couldn't sleep and would lie there all night long with her stomach churning, worrying about how she was going to cope with tomorrow. Ryan saw the dark shadows on her face, the exhaustion in her body and he said he'd take Réiltín off for a walk and ordered Jo to go back to bed to sleep for a while. She did as she was told without any argument; she was too weary to fight. She climbed back into their bed and slept for hours. When she woke she could tell by the pinky-orange light that was making its way around the curtains that it was nearly dusk outside and that she had spent most of the day asleep. She listened out for sounds in the house but she couldn't hear anything coming up from downstairs. She jumped out of bed, feeling a sensation of wild panic flooding through her. Something was wrong. She could feel it deep inside. She ran down the stairs, taking two steps at a time and ran between the rooms but there was no sign of them in the house. She tried ringing Ryan on his mobile but he didn't answer. *Something has happened, something has happened,* that voice which had been tormenting her since Réiltín was born kept on repeating. *They should be back by now,* it said. She didn't know if it was the hormones or some kind of feral protectiveness of her family but the urgency to find them and find out what had happened was overwhelming.

She threw on her coat over her pyjamas and drove over to Isla's house. She knocked on the door in a panic.

"They're gone," she said. "Something has happened to them!"

"Who is? What are you talking about?"

Jo had looked past Isla and her eyes landed on the pram in the small space behind the door. Réiltín's pram. She felt the blood rush into her ears. Why had he come here? Why was this the place where he had chosen to go? She pushed past Isla and ran up the stairs and straight into the kitchen where Ryan was sitting with Réiltín on his knee, just about to bring a biscuit up to his lips.

"Jo!" he had said, looking startled.

"Don't lie to me!" she said. "I know what's going on here." She looked from Ryan to Isla and back to Ryan again.

"What are you talking about, Jo?" Ryan asked, clearly annoyed. "There's nothing going on. I took the baby for a walk, then went home and saw you were still sleeping – so I said we'd leave you to it, you were obviously exhausted. We went back out again but I needed somewhere to change her and feed her so we called over here. That's it. What has got into you?"

Isla looked bewildered, standing with her mouth open in her kitchen. Well, Jo had thought to herself, I'm certainly not going to let you two play happy families without me. So she walked over and lifted Réiltín, *her* daughter, up out of Ryan's arms. She carried her downstairs where she placed her gently into her pram. She covered her up with blankets to protect her from the elements and then left them to it. She didn't have her car seat so she left her car behind and walked her all the way home in the drizzle in her pyjamas and slippers.

Ryan had driven her car home later and ignored her for the rest of the evening. She was sorry by that stage of course. She'd had time to calm down and even she could see then that her behaviour was irrational. She apologised to him, blaming the tiredness and the hormones and the worry that seemed to creep its way around every thought that she had. He had nodded and taken her in his arms. He whispered into her ear that it was okay. Isla never mentioned it again.

She knew it was an ugly emotion, jealousy, but that was why she could never give Isla that embryo. If she did, she would be strengthening those triangular bonds, which were invisible to her but which she was pretty sure were binding the three of them closer together.

Chapter 28

The Outsider

The bird swooped down on the diagonal. A large gull. He swept down to the green-grey water, picked something up before swooping back upwards again. It was too small for Jo to make out what it was that he had picked up. She noticed that Ryan's car wasn't in the driveway. Surely they should be home by now, she thought. She pressed the button to lock her car and made her way across the gravel to the house.

She opened the door and Oscar rushed out to greet her. She rubbed his silky ears before bending over to pick the post up from the mat. She went into the kitchen and fed Oscar before ringing Ryan's phone to see where he was. There was no answer so she tried ringing Réiltín next but she didn't answer either.

He was meant to be picking her up from piano practice that day. She felt that familiar wave of anxiety winding itself around her, the one that never went too far away. It was always there simmering below the surface. She told herself that she was being ridiculous and began pulling ingredients out of the presses to make dinner. She began slicing a courgette into spiral slices and adding them to the saucepan where they hissed in the olive oil. She added the garlic and waited until it started to dance before lowering the heat. She set the table and then looked at the clock on the wall and wondered where her husband had got to. She dialled his number again but it went straight to voicemail. Anxiety knotted in her chest. She felt her breathing tighten like someone was pushing down on her chest. *What if something had happened to them? What if he had crashed his car?* Then a rational voice chastised her: *Stop being so ridiculous.* She knew that she needed to calm herself down and not to let the old insecurities start causing trouble for them again. She took a deep breath in and let it fill up her lungs. Sometimes she felt as though she was going crazy. She had been doing well for so long and now the thoughts and fears and anxieties were back and they were starting to scare her. Sometimes what worried her even more, though, was that she was turning into her mother.

She set the table and when she was finished she picked her phone off the granite worktop and checked it once again in case he had texted her but she hadn't heard it.

Half an hour later there was still no sign of either of them and the fish was almost cooked. She had tried ringing them both again but there was no reply. Eventually her phone sounded with a text from Ryan: **'Just getting food – see you soon.'**

She felt the anger rise up inside her. They hadn't asked her – she could have joined them on her way home from work, she would have liked that actually, but they never even thought to ask her. To her they had seemed to be as thick as thieves then – they probably didn't want her there, she would cramp their style. She looked at her reflection in the mirror. The lines in her forehead had got deeper, her crow's feet spread out from the corners of her eyes like tentacles. Ryan didn't seem to be ageing as fast as she was. She had to get her colour done now every six weeks or her roots were silver grey. He had only a slight sprinkling of grey. It irked her how time didn't seem to be catching up on him – it wasn't digging its claws into him in the same way that it was doing to her. Réiltín never seemed to give him the disdainful treatment she meted out to her; she seemed to spare him the heavy sigh or the patronising roll of the eyes whereas Jo imagined that there was a reel playing inside her head on a continuous loop, which said 'Here she goes again'. Sometimes she wasn't sure if Réiltín even *liked* her. She longed for the closeness they once had, when she held her hand in hers when she was a little girl and Réiltín would bounce along beside her on the footpath. She had told her friends about it and they all told her not to take it personally – that it was a phase and perfectly normal teenage behaviour. But Jo couldn't help worrying. What if they never regained their closeness? It seemed that Réiltín just tolerated her because she was her mother.

She was feeling the age-old insecurities raise their head again. Was this the normal way for a teenage girl to behave with her mother or, dare she say it, did Réiltín act like this because she wasn't her biological mother? She hated those thoughts but sometimes she just couldn't help herself,

Jo served up the food onto plates and put it on the table to grow cold. She didn't bother eating herself. She was too wound-up to eat. She went into her study and started reading over a report into the economic benefits for establishing wind farms versus the possible negative impact on the landscape. A client had recently asked her for her opinion on whether it would have any legal implications for their future growth strategy. The report was dull and full of technical jargon, which she kept on having to stop and Google. She was beginning to grow frustrated with herself – what was wrong with her? She was used to reading reports like this but she just couldn't get into it today. She seemed to be making such slow progress through it. Her concentration kept dipping and she would find herself staring out at the rain that was running down the windowpanes.

She looked back at the report again and read the same paragraph for the fourth time.

Eventually she heard the door open, after seven. She was fuming. She didn't answer Ryan's cheery "Hiya!".

Then he walked down the hallway and stuck his head around the door of the study. "Hi there."

She didn't bother looking up at him.

"Réiltín wanted to call into Fiona's house for a while to finish off some project they're working on so her mum said she'd drop her home later," he continued.

Jo got up off her chair, stormed past him and went into the kitchen. She pulled open the door of the fridge and started cleaning it out, throwing out the stuff close to going past its use-by date.

"Hey, what's got into you?" Ryan asked from the doorway.

"You could have asked me to join you."

"Oh sorry, I never even thought of it. We were both hungry so we said we'd grab some food. It was no big deal. I meant to say in my text not to bother making us dinner but I forgot!" He gestured to the now cold plates of food that were sitting on the kitchen table.

"Forgot?"

"Sorry."

"Well, you could have asked me to join you, couldn't you?" she said, moving around the room with swift, exaggerated movements.

"Right, sorry, I'll ask next time!" he said huffily. He was tired; he'd had a long day in the office. His branch's loan book was underperforming against the rest in the territory, his personal assistant had fallen over playing tennis and had fractured her wrist and would be out of action for at least two months. She took care of everything – he didn't know how he was going to cope without her.

His response had angered her even more. She wasn't going to let it go – she couldn't help herself.

"I hate that cliquey little relationship that you both have – the whole 'silly mum, let's not ask her' routine is growing tiresome."

"What on earth are you talking about, Jo?"

"I just want to be included, that's all."

"We'll ask you next time then!" Then he walked out of the kitchen and went into the living room, slamming the door shut, and turning on the TV.

Jo put her hands on her shoulders and started massaging her neck. She went back into the study and tried to read the report. She heard Réiltín come home a while later. She waited for her to come into the study but instead she went in to Ryan in the living room and then she heard her footsteps making their way up the stairs. Jo felt her heart sink. She felt as though she was losing Réiltín and she didn't know how to get her back. They were supposed to be a family, yet here they were each of them sealed into their separate quarters. She was sure Réiltín had picked up on the atmosphere between her parents and she felt the guilt start to gnaw away at her.

When she was heading to bed she stopped on the landing outside Réiltín's bedroom. She took a deep breath before knocking softly.

"Yeah?" Réiltín's voice called out.

She pushed open the door and poked her head around the side. "I'm just saying goodnight."

Réiltín was sitting back on her bed with her laptop resting on her knees. "Night." She didn't even look up at her mother.

Jo closed the door behind her and went into her bedroom. She already knew that Ryan wouldn't sleep with her that night; it seemed as though lately he was in the spare room every night. Everything they said or did these days seemed to get on each other's nerves. It would only be something small to set off the gunpowder and then the fighting would start. Sometimes she felt like he was deliberately trying to press her buttons; it seemed as though he was almost enjoying himself when the arguments would start. She was trying her best to shield Réiltín from it but at times her temper was so quick and intense that she couldn't keep a lid on it. And that was always when Ryan, the model of a good parent, would throw down his trump card and say, "You know it's not healthy to fight in front of children". And of course the battle was lost then.

Jo stopped the car at the school the next morning and put on the handbrake. There it was again, that sinking, sickening feeling in the pit of her stomach. She hadn't felt it in years. Why, she wondered, had it decided to return now? Why today?

"Where's your tie, love? I don't want you getting another note home," she said, turning to her daughter.

"It's here," Réiltín said, dragging the crumpled blue tie out of her school bag. "I hate wearing it – it makes me all scratchy and hot."

"Well, you only have to wear it for a few more hours and then it's the weekend. Are you doing after-school study today?"

"Do I have to? It's Friday. I was going to go to Dundrum with some of the girls for food."

"Well, I'd like you to, yes. It's important you get into a routine of studying. You have a big year this year."

Silence.

"So did you finish that Irish essay?" Jo said to change the subject.

"Yes, Mum." Réiltín sighed and rolled her eyes, then she opened the handle of the car door and went to get out. Something urgent called to Jo. Something almost primal. She couldn't explain it but she just felt so unsettled. Her stomach was churning and she didn't know why.

"Réiltín?" Her voice sounded shaky.

"Yes?"

"You do know that I love you, don't you? I love you very much."

She watched her daughter's face as her eyes narrowed in suspicion before she responded with a laugh.

"Of course I do, Mum. I love you too."

"Okay, well, have a good day in school."

She released her handbrake, checked her mirrors and drove on to the offices of Lawson-McBride-Williams Solicitors.

Chapter 29

Discovery

Jo was working in her study on Saturday afternoon. She was bent over her laptop, her keys clacking rapidly as she worked.

"Mum, can I have some money?" Réiltín swung her head around the door.

"How much do you need?"

"Thirty?"

"*Thirty?*"

"Well, we're going to the cinema." She was meeting Fiona.

"Right," Jo sighed. "Bring me in my purse – my bag is in the kitchen."

Réiltín returned after a few seconds and handed her mother the purse. Jo unzipped it and gave her daughter the money.

"We'll have dinner at six so make sure you're home before then."

"Okay, Mum." She leant in and kissed Jo goodbye.

"Have a nice time, see you later."

Jo heard the door slam and then turned back to her laptop and continued typing out the email she was drafting. After a few minutes she felt a presence in the room. She looked up and saw Ryan's broad frame shadowing the door.

"Hi there," she said.

"You're hard at work?"

"I'm just catching up on my emails – what's up?" She took off her reading glasses and rubbed her eyes for what felt like the hundredth time.

"Réiltín's been asking what's going on with yourself and Isla."

"What's she been saying?" She sighed wearily.

"She was asking me in the kitchen earlier. She knows there's something up between you and she wants to know what it is."

"It'll all blow over soon."

"Are you sure about that?" He walked over and sat down on the ottoman in front of her.

"Of course I am! Look, just because I don't want to give Isla that embryo doesn't mean that we have fallen out with each other."

"Does Isla see it like that, I wonder?" There was an unmistakable trace of sarcasm in his voice.

"Why do you always have to take her side, Ryan? I thought you said it was my call?"

"Yeah, but I just don't see your logic. We're never going to use it."

"You know that I have my reasons."

"What? You're worried that Réiltín will find out that she was conceived using Isla's eggs?"

"Well, yes, that's part of it."

"Well, maybe she'd take it better than you give her credit for! She's fourteen years old. I think at this stage she knows who her parents are!"

"Finding out something that big about your origins could really be detrimental to a teenager – it could irreparably damage her trust in us."

"Well, I wanted to tell her all along, I don't agree with her not knowing something so important about herself. It's her whole identity – it's who she is!"

"She does know who she is – she's *our* child, Ryan – yours and mine!"

"You can't just keep ignoring the situation, Jo!"

"What's going on, Mum? Dad? What are you two talking about?"

Jo felt everything stop. The blood rushed into her ears and started to make a ringing sound.

"What are you doing back here, Little Star?" she said, doing her best to keep her voice calm. "Did you forget something?"

"I left my phone in the kitchen," Réiltín said angrily. "Look, I know there's something going on here. I've known for weeks there's something up. You're not talking to Isla, Mum, and now you two keep arguing! So either you're going to tell me what it is or I'm going to go and ask Isla again and this time I'll make her tell me!"

"*Again?* You've been asking Isla?" Jo was horrified. "There's nothing to ask her, Réiltín!"

"Stop lying, Mum – stop lying to me!" said Réiltín in a stony voice. "There has been something going on for weeks now and I want to know what it is."

"There's nothing going on, love – I've already told you that!"

Jo looked desperately at Ryan who remained infuriatingly silent.

"You – Dad – even Isla – you've all been lying to me!" Réiltín was screaming now.

"No one has been lying to you –"

Ryan cut her off. "It's time to tell her, Jo, come on!" He was looking at her angrily. "You can't keep it a secret forever!"

Jo's very worst fears were being realised. She couldn't speak. She couldn't be the one to crush her daughter's world like that. She couldn't do it. She felt as though her whole existence, everything that she had wanted for so long, was falling apart. It was falling down around her in a million dusty fragments and she couldn't do anything to stop it from happening. She could feel the rattle of her heartbeat against her ribcage. Her chest felt tight as though somebody was sitting on her chest. *Breathe in, breathe out*, she told herself, *breathe in, breathe out.*

"Please, Ryan, don't do it, please –" Her voice was trembling.

"Right, well, if your mum won't say it, I will, Réiltín. As you know we tried for a long time to have you. We had a difficult journey where we tried fertility treatment, which didn't work for us, and eventually the doctors told us that we were never going to be able to have a child of our own. Isla did something for us back then that was very generous: she donated her eggs to us so that we could have you. Do you understand what I'm saying, love?"

She was looking at him blankly.

"You were conceived using Isla's egg and my sperm."

They both watched the expressions change on her face as she tried to process what her father had said to her.

Finally it registered.

"So *Isla* – not you," she pointed at Jo, "is my real mother?"

"She is *not* your mother, Réiltín!" Jo started to cry. "I'm your mother and you know that! I'm the one who carried you for nine months and gave birth to you!"

"Oh my God, I can't believe this. Why didn't you tell me?"

"Look, love, I realise that this is an awful shock for you," Jo said, choking back tears, "but, believe me, if you knew everything that we went through to have you, you'd know you were a much-wanted baby. I'd go as far as to say the most wanted baby ever."

"But I'm Isla's child! Dad is my dad but you're not my mum!" Réiltín said with disbelief.

"*Stop saying that!* I am your mother and you finding out that Isla donated her eggs to us won't change anything! She gave them to me as a gift and it allowed me to have you. I wouldn't change a thing though because it made *you*." Jo was sobbing now. "We got you and never have two people wanted a child so badly and been so happy to finally get her."

"But no matter what you say, Isla is my mother!"

"It's not that simple! I carried you, Réiltín, I gave birth to you, I am named on your birth cert – you're my child. No matter what you may think or what you believe, I'm your mother, Réiltín. I carried you in my womb – my blood flowed through you."

"But my whole entire life has been one big lie! You've turned everything that I've ever known upside-down. Do you realise how horrible it is to learn something like this now? Is everything else that you've told me a lie too?"

"Oh, honey, look," Jo said, "when a woman donates an egg she loses all rights to the egg with the act of donation. So once Isla donated those eggs, you became my child. We used your father's sperm and I carried you. Everything else from that point on was our child and not Isla's egg. Without me, Isla's egg would still be Isla's egg, but together with your dad *we* made you. *We* created you. If we didn't do that, you would never have been born. Can't you see that?"

"You keep telling yourself that if that's what makes you feel better – you can twist it around whatever way you want to but at the end of the day it's just like Dad and Isla had a baby together and that baby is me!"

"No, don't say that! It's way more complicated than that – there is so much scientific evidence to suggest that there are many more factors than just the simple egg and sperm. If your dad and Isla had a baby it wouldn't be like *you* because it was my body that determined what way your genes were expressed. Do you see?"

"But why didn't you tell me? Are you ashamed of me? Are

you embarrassed? I can't believe you were all in on this big secret together, you, Dad and Isla. I can't trust any of you . . ." She spun around to face her father then, her green eyes blazing. "Did you ever plan on telling me, Dad? Or were you going to let me live my whole life with this huge secret about who my real parents are? Everyone knew about it except for me – the one person that it affects the most. Why would you keep it a secret from me?" Her anger gave away to tears. "I will never forgive you for this – never!"

"Please, love, I'm sorry we didn't tell you sooner," Ryan said, distraught. "I wanted to, I swear I did, but your mum . . . well . . . she thought it would be better if we didn't."

"I just wanted the best for you, Réiltín – that's all I've ever wanted. I wanted you to have what every other child has – complete security about who your parents are – and I was worried that telling you something like that could sow seeds of doubt in a child's head."

"And what you've done now hasn't done that to me? You think you know your parents, you think your life is a certain way – and then you realise that it's all imagined!"

"I never meant for you to find out –"

"And that's supposed to make me feel better?"

"What I mean is that you are *my* child. You are the same whether or not it was my egg that you were conceived with. What you've found out today doesn't change anything."

"It changes *everything*!"

"If you went to a court tomorrow, they'd tell you the same thing –"

"There you go again! You're not in work now – for once can't you just switch off your lawyer head, Mum?"

"Sorry, I'm just trying to show you what it all means."

"No wonder I always felt closer to Isla. I always wondered why you were so weird about things whenever I was hanging out with her."

"That's not true. I've always encouraged your relationship

with her – she's been a big part of our lives."

"Yeah, but you hate it when me and her do stuff together. I can see it in your eyes. You're jealous whenever we hang out or have a laugh together. I always knew it!"

That stung. It seared deep down inside but Jo knew that Réiltín was hurting. She wanted her to feel her pain too. Réiltín was like a dying wasp, determined to sting before finally giving up the fight. This was all Isla's fault, thought Jo. She cursed her for bringing the whole thing up again. They had been fine until she had started asking for that embryo. They'd had a perfectly normal life until Isla began uprooting things.

Jo could see Réiltín's mind working, trying to take it all in and process all this new information.

"Well, I'm going to live with Isla since she is my mother!"

"She is *not* your mother," Jo said, trying her best to stay calm but she could hear the edge of panic in her voice.

"I'm going upstairs to pack. Excuse me." Réiltín left the room and started climbing up the stairs.

Ryan and Jo went after her.

"You can't go, Réiltín, this is your home," Ryan was pleading. "I know you've had a horrible shock but if you could just stay calm we could sit down and talk about this together –"

"I'm going to live with my *real* mother."

"Please, Réiltín, don't do this," Jo said desperately. "You're angry, I know that, but we're still your parents and you're only fourteen so you cannot leave this house without our permission!"

Réiltín reached her bedroom door and went inside. Jo and Ryan watched from the doorway as she walked over to her wardrobe and pulled her holdall down from the top shelf.

"Oh yeah?" She picked up a pair of boots from the floor and threw them into the bag. "Watch me."

"Réiltín, no – Isla won't take you in if I tell her not to." Jo's voice was a shaky whisper.

"Well, if she won't let me stay with her then I'm on the streets and I don't think my own *mother* would do that to me, do you?"

Ryan ran his hands back through his hair and started pacing around the room before stopping and turning to Réiltín. "Réiltín, this doesn't change anything – you need to know that. You are still our child and we love you very much."

His voice was desperate and Jo hated herself yet again for putting them in that position. All the anger and despair and feelings of failure and insecurity that she'd had years ago about having to use an egg-donor came rushing back up to smother her. She hated herself for not knowing what to say to her teenage daughter to calm her down and tell her how much she loved her. She was paying a very dear price.

Ryan went over to hug Réiltín but she pushed him away.

"Leave me alone, Dad – you were as big a part of this charade as Mum. I'm going to live with Isla."

"Now hang on a minute, love – this is your home," he said, his voice breaking.

"I'm not staying any longer in a house where I don't belong." Réiltín picked up her bag to leave.

"You do belong here. I'm not letting you go," Jo said, standing in front of her, blocking her exit.

"You can't stop me."

"I'm not letting you go, Réiltín. Do you know the pain that we went through to have you? Do you know how small and sick you were when you were born?"

"Yeah, I know, I nearly died twice but you and Dad prayed so hard to keep me here, *blah, blah, blah*!" Réiltín finished the story that Jo was so fond of telling her, the same story that she was so fond of hearing when she was a little girl. She would climb up on Jo's knee, curl her fingers around her hair and ask her to tell her the story of when she was born. Whenever Jo got to the bit about her almost dying, she would hold her breath and Jo would feel her small heart thumping with suspense underneath the palm of her hand.

"Well, that is the exact reason why I'm not letting you go now. No way."

Réiltín went to push past her but Jo grabbed her by the wrist that was holding her bag. She knew her grip was too tight but she needed to hold on to her.

"Let go of me!" Réiltín screamed and jerked her wrist out of Jo's grip. She walked out onto the landing. "It's not your choice, Mum . . ." She paused before delivering her final punch. "Actually, wait a minute . . . shouldn't I be calling you *Jo* now?"

Ryan tried a softer tack. "Please, love – it's not safe where Isla lives and it'll be dark soon –"

"What are you going to do? Lock me up in my room until I'm eighteen?"

"No," Jo said. "We just want you to calm down and when we've all had a chance to think about this rationally, we can talk then –"

"Look, maybe we should just let her go," Ryan said. "She's made her mind up –"

Réiltín hurried down the stairs without a backward glance. They stood paralysed on the landing, watching her go.

"I can't let her go!" Jo's voice was trembling with desperation and despair. "She's my baby, Ryan – she's everything to me. She's my world – this is her home, she belongs here!"

"I know, but can't you see she is going to go whether we like it or not?" Ryan was suddenly yelling. "Short of locking her in her room I don't think we have many options here, do you? This is why I said we should have told her from the start, y'know!"

"She would never have found out if you hadn't taken it upon yourself to tell her!"

"It was time – these things always come out in the end."

His eyes were burning with something that looked close to hatred and Jo wanted to crawl inside herself and hide.

"She's had an awful shock, Jo. She needs some space to get her head around all of this. Her whole world has just been turned upside-down – the person that she thought she was has been wiped out!"

"I'm sorry, Ryan, I'm so sorry," she sobbed. "But she's still our daughter, no matter what she says or thinks. I don't want to lose her."

"And you think I do? Under the circumstances I think all we can do is give her time to calm down and hope that she'll be back home in a few days."

"What if she doesn't come back?"

"I'm not even thinking about that, to be honest, Jo. I'm going to drive after her – hopefully I can pick her up on the street."

"But I don't want her to go," Jo sobbed.

"Well, she's going whether you like it or not. This isn't in your control. Either I drop her over to Isla's flat now and at least we know that she's somewhere safe with someone who cares about her or else we let her roam the streets in that weather where she could meet with every weirdo out there – which would you prefer?"

Jo nodded, resigned to the fact that this was a battle that she wasn't going to win.

Ryan ran down the stairs. At the door he turned to look back at Jo over his shoulder. "Maybe you should give Isla a call and tell her what's happened so she has some time to prepare herself. This has big implications for her too . . ."

Then he hurried outside into the rain after Réiltín.

Chapter 30

Same Hands

Isla turned on the taps until the water thundered into the tub. Her plan for the evening was to take a long soak in the bath and then she was going to veg in front of the TV in her pyjamas. She poured in some sandalwood-scented bubble bath. It was an expensive one that Jo had bought her last Christmas and, while she waited for the bath to fill, she went back out to the hotpress in the kitchen to get a towel. She was just passing through the living room on her way back into the bathroom when she heard her phone ringing. She reached for it on the coffee table and she saw Jo's number come up. Isla knew that she was calling her for a reason. Things had been so strained between the two of them that, save for the day Isla had called over to appease Réiltín, they hadn't been in contact since. She knew that Jo wasn't ringing her for a sisterly chat.

"Isla – it's me, Jo –"

Isla could hear the panic instantly.

"Jo? What's up?"

"Look, Isla – it's Réiltín – she knows."

"What do you mean? Knows what?"

"She knows, Isla, she knows about the donation."

"You mean that she was conceived using my eggs?"

There was silence on the other end of the line.

"How did she find out?" Isla probed and immediately worry spread through her mind when she thought of how she had confided in Vera and Greg.

"We had to tell her – we had no choice. She overheard me and Ryan talking about it."

"Oh my God . . . I'm so sorry, Jo. How is she? How did she take it?"

"Not good – not good at all. She's so angry, understandably, but I don't think she'll ever forgive me, Isla." Her voice broke and she dissolved into tears.

"She'll come round, she's had a shock."

"She's on her way over to your house."

"She's coming over to *me*?"

"Yes – I didn't want her to go but we couldn't stop her." She was sobbing. "You know that this is all your fault, don't you? I warned you that something like this would happen. You had to go and dig up the past. Everything was fine in my life until you started out on your quest to ruin my family."

"Jo, I'm so sorry – I know you're angry but I swear that was never my intention. I'm so sorry. I wasn't trying to upset you. I just wanted to have a baby and that was my only option. I never thought something like this would happen!"

"Well, I hope you realise the damage you've done. You've destroyed my family."

Jo hung up then.

Isla had two minutes to digest what had happened and the implications for her before her buzzer went. She had no idea how Réiltín was going to be feeling about her part in all this. Was she going to be angry with her for donating her eggs to Jo in the first place? Or just mad with her for not telling her? She took a deep breath, went down the stairs and pulled back the door.

"Isla," Réiltín was crying, "can I come in? I've nowhere else to go."

She walked past Isla up the stairs, carrying her hold-all over her shoulder. Isla saw Ryan hesitating on the path outside. She raised her hand in a half-wave. His shoulders were sunken; he looked like a broken man.

He stepped forward.

"Jo called me," Isla said.

"I hope you can take her in?"

"Of course I can, but God I wasn't expecting this . . ."

"She's very upset right now." His voice was choked. "Just look after her for me, Isla, won't you? Just look after her . . ."

Isla knew he was close to tears.

"Of course I will – you know you don't even need to ask me that."

"I know, I'll ring you later on to see how's she doing."

"Try not to worry – it's all going to be okay when she calms down."

"I hope to God you're right, Isla."

Isla closed the door after he had gone and went upstairs to Réiltín, not knowing what kind of conversation would await her.

"Why didn't you tell me, Isla?" Réiltín sobbed as soon as Isla had reached the top of the stairs. "I expect this kind of thing from Mum and Dad but not from you."

"Come here." Isla guided her over to sit down on the sofa where Réiltín fell into her arms. Isla held onto her tightly as she convulsed in tears.

"I'm so confused – I thought Mum was my mum and now it's you . . ."

Isla had had no time to prepare for the onslaught and she wasn't sure how to approach it. She knew the child was devastated but at the same time she knew that it was important to be upfront with her – she didn't want to mislead her.

"I'm not your mother, Réiltín, Jo is. I just gave her some eggs to help her to have a baby which was you but that was

243

as far as my involvement went. After I donated the eggs I was out of the picture and I let your mum and dad at it."

"So you're trying to tell me that Mum isn't my mum, Dad lied to me, you don't want me either . . . does anyone want to think about *me*?" She was growing hysterical.

"Of course we're thinking of you – we all love you but your mum *is* your mum – she gave birth to you – you wouldn't be alive today if it wasn't for your mum!"

"And your eggs!"

"Which part of it is upsetting you more – is it the fact that they never told you or the fact that you were conceived using a donor?"

"I'm so mad that I don't even know the answer to that myself!"

"Come on, Réiltín love, you know you mean the world to your mum and dad. I bet your mum is so upset right now."

"I'm not going back there, Isla – if you make me go back, I'll run away, I swear!"

"No one is going to make you go anywhere, don't worry. You can stay here for as long as you need to get your head around all of this but ultimately you belong with your mum and dad."

"Well, it's too late – she should have told me the truth before instead of letting me find out like this! It's horrible! I feel like I don't belong anywhere."

"You know where you belong,"

"But I'm questioning everything now. Like my hair – we have the same hair colour, Isla – I always thought it was weird having auburn hair when Mum's is black and Dad's is brown. How did I not notice it before?"

"Well, your grandmother, mine and Jo's mum, had this hair too, you know . . ."

"And we have the same hands – look!" She held her hands out and Isla found herself hiding hers under her legs.

"Stop treating me like this, Isla, like you're trying to

distance yourself from me. Why are you on their side? If I don't have you then I have nobody."

"Hey, calm down, it's not like that. There are no sides here, love," Isla said, stroking her hair.

"The whole thing is just . . . crazy! I just want everything to go back to the way it was before I heard them talking." All her bravado evaporated and gave way to tears. She laid her head on Isla's lap and Isla stroked her face and brushed strands of her hair behind her ears until she fell asleep, her chest rising and falling in shallow beats.

Isla rang Jo then and told her that Réiltín was okay but upset and angry. Isla could barely make out what Jo was saying through her tears.

"I can't believe this has happened," she kept repeating.

"Look, tomorrow she'll have calmed down a bit more and she might be willing to talk to you," Isla tried to assure her. "Try and get some sleep tonight, it's all going to be fine. She'll calm down."

"You better be right, Isla."

Chapter 31

A Shooting Star

Isla came in the door and placed her heavy shopping bags down on the worktop. Réiltín was sitting cross-legged on the sofa watching TV.

"Hiya," she said, swinging her head around from the screen.

"So how was your day?"

"Fine." She turned her head back around.

Isla began unpacking the groceries and putting them away. She pulled out loaves of bread, yoghurts, fruit and other things that she wouldn't usually eat but thought that Réiltín might. She had bought so much extra stuff because she wasn't used to shopping for two.

"I bought Coco Pops and Weetabix – I wasn't sure which you'd prefer so I bought both," she said, holding up both boxes. "I also bought smoothies – I thought you might like them for school?"

"Thanks, Isla."

She reached up to put a tin of beans into a press. "Your mum called again today," she said, talking over her shoulder. "They're really worried about you . . ."

"Well, you should tell them to stop wasting their time. I don't want to talk to them ever again."

"Maybe you should just hear them out – it might help?"

"No way – I'm done with them. They said everything the other night – there's nothing more I need to know now."

"C'mon, Réiltín, you're their world, they're devastated! If you heard your poor mum when she called me today – she's so upset!" She opened the fridge and placed a litre of milk on the shelf inside the door.

"Yeah, well, they should have thought about that before they decided to keep the world's biggest secret."

"So how was school?" Isla changed the subject to safer ground.

Réiltín shrugged her shoulders.

"Were you okay today?" Isla tried again.

Réiltín hadn't wanted to go in that morning but Isla had used all of her powers of persuasion to make her go. A teary Jo had dropped her schoolbag and uniform into the café and Isla promised that she would make sure she went in. It had been unnerving to see Jo like that because as long as Isla had known her, she had very rarely cried. She was usually so calm and organised but she had looked frightful standing in front of her in the café. Her skin had looked grey, her eyes were red and puffy. She hadn't bothered with her make-up and her hair wasn't blow-dried like it usually would be.

"When I see the other girls in my class I can't stop thinking that they have no problems," Réiltín said. "Exactly the way that I used to be. I'm so jealous of them. They know who their parents are, they don't have any dark secrets in their past. Their whole lives aren't ruined by what their parents did. They start talking about One Direction and about how hard it will be to get a ticket when they go on sale and I'm thinking is that really the biggest of your worries? Is that *it*? But you know what it is – that is as bad as it gets for them and I can't stand listening to it. They seem so immature to me now when just a few days ago I was just like them. I can't stand listening to it so I get up and walk off. When I did it today I heard Sophie Talbot say real loud so that I'd hear: 'What's her problem?' I know they're talking about me and whispering behind my back but I can't tell them, I can't tell anyone. I'm so embarrassed – oh my God, it's so disgusting to even think about it!" She visibly shuddered on the sofa.

"Hey, you've nothing to be embarrassed about! You should see it as a sign of how much your parents really wanted to have you."

"I just don't know where I belong," she sighed. "And please don't say at home with Mum and Dad."

Isla raised her hands. "I wasn't going to say that. I know this is hard on you but you have three people in your life that love you so much – your mum and dad *and* me. Okay, I get it that this is a big shock but it doesn't change anything in your life. It's not the very worst thing that could happen to you."

"That's easy for you to say, Isla."

"Sorry – I wasn't trying to trivialise it."

"Don't you think it's weird that you're my mum?"

Isla stopped unpacking the bags and looked at her. Because she was so angry with her parents, Réiltín was letting her mind run away with the idea that somehow she had found her real mother. She wanted a connection. Isla could understand that – she had been uprooted and she wanted something to tether herself to. She wanted Isla to be the stand-in but Isla knew that she was treading on dangerous ground and she had to set her straight.

"I've told you over and over again. I'm not your mum – genetically, yes, but that's it – that's as far as it goes, Réilt. Your mother is Jo. She's the one who has been a mum to you. A mother is so much more than just being a biological parent. It's like being adopted – it's the people who loved you and raised you that matter. I can't step in and take credit for everything that Jo has done for you – she has fed you, clothed you, nurtured you, loved you."

"But you would have done all those things too if I was born to you."

"But you weren't born to me, that's what I'm trying to show you – she has been your mother from day one. If she didn't use my eggs then you wouldn't be here today so if you think about it, she *did* create you. Réiltín, you know that I love you more than anything but I've always only been an aunt to you. I could never let you take that away from your parents."

"So you don't want me either, is that what you're saying? Because, if I'm putting you out, I can go and pack my bags and I won't inconvenience you any longer!" She got up off the sofa.

"Sit down, you know that's not what I'm saying," Isla sighed. "Why don't I make us a hot chocolate before I start on dinner, huh?"

Jo turned and looked out the floor-to-ceiling glazing at the view down over the wide swell of the Liffey. People hurried along to their lives on the streets below. She missed that. She missed hurrying home from work to see Réiltín and Ryan. She missed knowing there were people who loved her, waiting for her to come in the door. She was in a hurry nowhere any more.

She had tried ringing Réiltín, texting her. She had written her a letter explaining everything and how much they both loved her and telling her that, no matter what, she was still their daughter, their very much wanted daughter. She had turned up on Isla's doorstep but Réiltín had refused to see her. She had emailed her, she had even set up a Facebook account so she could send her messages that way but they all went unanswered. She had begged Isla to try and get her to talk to her but Réiltín was adamant that she didn't want to see her.

She left the office after four. She knew that people were

looking at her as she put on her coat and wrapped her scarf around her neck. She could feel their eyes following her movements. They were not used to seeing her head home at that time, save for when Réiltín had a match on or something which she had told them about. She couldn't remember leaving that early before without a reason but the truth was that she didn't want to be there.

Jo's work life was a disaster. She couldn't concentrate in meetings – she kept checking her phone to see if it was Isla calling with an update or even better still a call from Réiltín saying she was finally able to talk to her. The other partners would come to her with decisions that needed to be made about the firm, things that needed to be signed off but she just didn't seem to be able to do the simple things any more. It was like everything in her life was futile now. Nothing mattered any more. It was like the colour had been sucked out of her world and everything existed in shades of grey, if her daughter wasn't in her life. She was tired. She was exhausted actually. She hadn't slept since the day Réiltín had left. She went to her doctor for some sleeping tablets but they didn't work.

Isla had assured her that she was feeding Réiltín well and making sure that she went to school every day and did her homework in the evenings. Jo had had to give in and bring over some more of her clothes and other things like her iPad even though it killed her to facilitate her staying with Isla for a day longer than was necessary. Isla had said that she would come round when her anger faded but she had been saying that since the whole thing happened and Réiltín still hadn't softened. Jo didn't know what to do any more. The life that she knew and loved was slipping away from her and she didn't know whether to fight back with all of her strength and risk damaging her relationship with Réiltín forever or to give her the space that she wanted and hope that Isla and Ryan were right and that she would make the choice herself to come home.

Earlier that day she had called into Réiltín's school to speak with her year head. Without going into all the details, she told her confidentially that they were having some family problems. Jo could see that the rotund woman who sat across the desk from her, nosiness propelling her forward, was almost salivating to hear more. She wanted to know what goriness could be going on beneath the surface of their outwardly perfect family but Jo didn't say any more. Jo asked her if she could keep an extra close eye on Réiltín in case it was affecting her schoolwork and the year head had promised her with a scowl, which Jo had taken as disappointment, that she would. Jo had stayed in her car afterwards and waited for the home bell to ring. She finally saw Réiltín coming in the distance and savoured watching her from afar. Her tie was loosened in a way that usually made Jo want to tell her to tighten it up but it didn't matter now. Her reddish, wispy curls hung loosely around her face as usual. Jo smiled. As she got nearer to her she had seen Jo watching her and had looked back at her with burning hatred in her eyes and gone in the other direction. Her own daughter.

Jo arrived home and switched on the lights. The house was chilly, having been empty for most of the day. She saw a note on the worktop from Aurelia asking her to buy bleach and bags for the vacuum cleaner. Damn it, she thought, that was the second time that Aurelia had asked her to buy them. She never usually forgot things like that. She put a reminder into her phone so that she wouldn't forget again.

She looked around the kitchen and saw that Ryan still wasn't home. He had been doing that a lot in the days after Réiltín had left – it was like he couldn't stand to be in the silence of their house. It felt eerily quiet and empty without Réiltín's music resonating off the walls or the sound of her moving about upstairs. Time seemed endless in their house with her gone. Ryan and Jo were barely on speaking terms. They couldn't meet each other's eye; it was like they were afraid of what they would see reflected there. He had barely said two words to her since the night that he'd driven Réiltín over to Isla's place. With Réiltín gone, she had become painfully aware of the fact that she had been their sole topic of conversation for a long time and without her they were just two people sharing a house. Réiltín had gone and she had taken the heart from their home. She knew Ryan was heartbroken but her heart was hurting too much from Réiltín's absence to have room to let his pain come in as well. The soul of their lives had been stripped out of it. As their marriage went, she knew that they were not in a good place. Like all couples they'd had their ups and downs through the years. There were times when they were getting along brilliantly and other times where they got on each other's nerves, but this was the very worst. Since Isla had started the whole drama about the embryo, things had been very strained between them and now, with Réiltín gone, he wouldn't even look at her. When she tried to talk to him, just general chitchat about their day, his eyes wouldn't meet hers. Jo would tell him that she had made shepherd's pie if he wanted some but he wouldn't even turn around and answer her. Then later she would listen as he moved around the kitchen fixing himself a sandwich.

Jo knew that he blamed her. Of course he did – she blamed herself too. She knew that he would never admit it but she was sure that he was thinking that if it weren't for her faulty eggs, then they would never have needed to use a donor and wouldn't be in the awful situation they now found themselves in. It was her infertility that had brought them down that road initially and while he had been unsure about using a donor, Jo had pulled him along with her and convinced him to come down the path of using Isla's eggs. Then it was her unwillingness to be upfront with Réiltín from the start about her conception that had became a moot point between them over the years so she knew that Ryan believed that the situation that they were in was all down to her.

She looked around the room with its dark wood furnishings. It all looked like someone else's life. It seemed foreign to her. The wallpaper that she'd had made in a replica of the period that would have originally been hung on the wall, the furniture she had bought at auction. She traced her fingers over the jacquard fabric of the bolster cushion. To think she had spent hours of time choosing between fabrics and colour schemes. Had she really dithered so much over patterns and textures and period detailing, like any of it was of any consequence? It seemed unbelievable that they were the things that had once mattered to her.

The last of the evening light had faded purple pink and, as she walked over to the French doors to draw the curtains, she caught sight of a blazing trail of yellow light tracking across the sky. It was so bright that she assumed it was a firework and waited for its customary explosion into millions of smaller lights. But then it was gone again just as fast. A shooting star. She made a wish for her own star to come home.

Jo moved away from the window and looked around the cool sitting room which just four weeks ago was echoing with noise and laughter and happiness. It seemed so long ago now. It was like a movie playing in her head that she had watched years ago. It seemed so distant to her now. The people seemed so different to her, like they were all actors. She didn't know them any more. How had this happened? How had they ended up here?

She felt an overwhelming sense of tiredness. She felt so worn out by it all. She was sick of fighting battles that she wasn't winning. She poured herself a glass of wine and sat down into the wingback armchair. She let the wine warm her and soon felt herself slip away into a distant fuzziness where she was in a subdued world just beyond the pain that simmered at the surface.

As the wine soothed, she had hazy thoughts about all of them. Her eyes felt heavy and she let them fall closed. She saw Isla laughing – she was in Mr Taylor's house, she was calling to her but she wouldn't come out to her. But when she looked again it wasn't Isla but Réiltín. She was calling her: *Mamma, Mamma, help me, Mamma, help!* She ran towards her, her heart thumping. She was almost in touching distance of her when Isla came in through the back door behind them and threw her arms around Réiltín, pulling her in close against her chest. They were both smiling at her serenely like the statue of the blue-cloaked Virgin Mary holding Baby Jesus in her arms outside the principal's office in their secondary school. Then the two of them started to laugh at her.

Chapter 32

Stubborn

The day went past in a blur of buttered bread and steaming mugs of tea as Greg, Fran and Isla worked in the café. Isla barely had time to think, for which she was grateful. She was wiping down a table later that afternoon when the café door opened and Jo strode in through it. She could tell instantly by her brusque manner that she was going to go off on one.

"I want to see her, Isla," she almost hissed at her across the tables. "Come on, it's going on too long now!"

Heads swung around to watch the scene. From the corner of her eye Isla could see Fran nudging Greg behind the counter and she knew that Greg was wondering whether or not he should intervene.

"Not here, Jo. Come out the back with me."

Jo followed Isla through the kitchen, passing the stainless-steel ovens and the open shelves stacked with crockery. Isla opened the latch on the fire-exit door and stepped out onto the back lane.

"What more do you want me to do, Jo?" Isla said. "I didn't tell her to come stay at my place. I'm not stopping her from leaving."

"You have to do more to get her to come home. Can't you talk some sense into her?"

"Look, I know you're frustrated but I'm doing all that I can. What do you want me to do? Do you want me to throw her out on the street and hope she goes home to you, Jo?"

"Of course not," she mumbled.

"Look, you need to give her time. I'm doing all that I can, believe me."

"I know," Jo sighed. "I know." She ran her hands down over her face before softening her tone. "I'm sorry – I shouldn't be going off at you. I'm at my wits' end, Isla – I can't sleep, I can't eat – I don't know what to do." She found herself in the position of being angry beyond reason with her sister for making this whole business raise its head again but also needing her, as she was the only link to her daughter at that moment.

"I know, I know . . ." Isla came closer and put her arms around her.

"You said she'd be home by now!"

"And I thought she would be but your daughter is stubborn."

"How much longer is this going to go on? If she would only just talk to me at least . . . it's killing me, Isla! I miss her so much . . ." Her voice broke off into tears. "She's my daughter, no matter what she thinks!"

"I know," Isla soothed.

"Her school play is on in a couple of weeks – did she mention anything about it to you?"

"Well . . . she's been doing rehearsals most days after school."

"No, I mean about Ryan and me going to it?"

"Oh, well, I don't know . . ."

"Are you going, Isla?"

"Well . . . I said I would," Isla admitted hesitantly.

"Ryan and I should be there too, you know."

"Of course you should. Why don't I sound it out with her tonight?"

Jo nodded.

"Here, come on back inside for a cup of tea."

Jo shook her head. "I need to go. I'm supposed to be having a meeting with the other partners but God knows I'm going to be so ineffective. I haven't prepared a thing for it. If it were anything else, I'd just cancel it. I can't concentrate on anything – I can't sleep at night, then I'm wrecked all day long."

"Look, I'll talk to her again tonight. I'll tell her how upset you are – maybe that'll make her come round."

She nodded. "Please, Isla, I need her back at home. I can't bear it any longer."

"I'll do my best."

"Is she eating okay? Taking her inhalers? Doing her homework at night?"

"She's doing fine." Isla didn't tell Jo that her behaviour was nearly too normal. That the whole debacle didn't seem to be disturbing her nearly as much as it was her parents. In fact, if Isla was honest, Réiltín actually seemed quite happy with how it had all worked out. Isla knew that in Réiltín's head she almost saw them as flatmates. Réiltín knew that Isla wasn't going to assert the same authority and protective parenting style of Jo and she was enjoying the freedom. Not that Isla was letting her do anything that Jo wouldn't but Isla believed that it was a temporary arrangement so she wasn't taking on the full responsibility that a mother would, like keeping an eye on her grades in school.

"Watch her maths – make sure she's not falling behind on it. She has to work hard at that."

"I'm the last person you want helping her with her maths homework."

The corners of Jo's mouth turned up in a smile at that.

"How's Ryan?"

"He's barely speaking to me. It's horrible. The atmosphere in the house is so tense. I just think if she comes home we'll be able to sort it all out but the longer she's away the more things are getting worse between the two of us."

After she had gone Isla felt terrible. She knew that Réiltín wasn't going to back down and now Jo had gone home with a small chink of hope that maybe Isla would be able to convince Réiltín to talk to her. She felt totally caught in the middle and she didn't know how to get out of it.

It was only when they had closed the door behind the last of the customers and she was sweeping the floor that she had time to think. She knew that she and Jo were on dangerous ground. It saddened her that Jo was the only family that she had left in the whole world and yet there was a massive gulf between them. Réiltín was adamant that she wasn't going home and Jo blamed her for bringing the whole thing up. She was also trying to accept the fact that she was never going to have a child of her own. It was all getting too much for her. She felt the weight of tears building behind her eyes, threatening to push forward and spill down her face.

"I printed off a few more sheets for you – we can do them afterwards if you'd like?" Greg said after they had said goodbye to Michelle.

"I can't tonight, Greg, sorry."

After she had asked him for help, Greg had gone home and looked up the topic of adult literacy on the Internet. He had found a website for a support group and learnt all that he could about how to be a tutor. He had printed off worksheets and taught her how to sound the words and blend them together and every day, after they closed the café for the day, they sat down and worked on them for an hour. It was a buzz when the words began to come to her. She realised that she was starting to read and she wanted to do more. So Greg found more challenging books and sheets and they started working on them. Time flew past in his company – one hour would roll into two and two to three and then they both would be hungry so he'd cook them something to eat. She liked it when they sat close together, poring over the pages he had printed out for her. It never seemed like work – they had too much fun for it to feel like that. They would stay late into the evening and then he would walk her home afterwards.

She had also started to wear her glasses again, now that she no longer needed the excuse of not being able to see. Isla found herself looking up at a street signs and sounding out the place name or in the supermarket she would try to read the signs that hung above the aisles like *'Pasta'*. Words she had spent so much time running away from, now she would try and give them a go. She might not always get them right but sometimes she would.

She thought about how good it had felt waking up beside him the previous weekend. The closeness, the knowledge that there was someone there for you at the end of the day, waiting to take you into their arms. She thought about how he smiled with his eyes and how he always sang along with the wrong words to the songs on the radio that played in the café. She thought about the lesson they had done the last day and how, as she sat there moving her finger along underneath the words, she had found herself reaching out with her other hand and taking his. He had looked up at her and she had looked into his eyes, and she knew that something had changed between them.

"Is everything okay, Isla?" Greg asked now.

"No, Greg, no, it's not." Suddenly her voice broke and the tears came streaming down her face.

"Hey, what's happened?" he said, leaving down his brush and rushing over to her.

He put his arms around her. It was the first time that they had ever done anything like that in work and it felt daring, dangerous even, but she liked the security of his arms around her. She wished she could stay there forever.

"Families, who'd have them, eh?" Isla said, biting down on her lip with a sad smile.

"Does this have something to do with your sister coming in earlier?"

Isla nodded. "Sorry about that, Greg."

"Don't be – you wouldn't be normal if you didn't have a few whacky relys. I could tell you a few stories about some of mine! Do you want to talk about it?"

"It's all just such a mess. I wish I never asked her for the embryo." Isla sighed heavily. "And she definitely won't give it to me now. Réiltín found out that Jo used my eggs to conceive her."

"Oh, Isla, I'm sorry. How did that happen?"

"She overheard them arguing about it and she demanded to know what was going on so Ryan told her."

"Oh God! How's she taking it?"

"Not good, not good at all. She's so angry that she's moved in with me. Jo is devastated and I'm stuck in the middle between the two of them. It's all such a mess!" Her voice broke into tears.

"Why don't I walk you home? I can mop the floor when I get in tomorrow morning."

"You don't have to."

"I know I don't but I'd like to."

They went outside and he locked the door. It was a warm evening and the streets were full of al fresco diners and people crowding merrily into beer-gardens.

They walked until they reached the door to Isla's flat.

"Do you want to come up for tea?"

"What about Réiltín?"

"She's at rehearsals for her play so she won't be home for a while yet."

She put the key in the lock and he followed her up the stairs. She flicked on the lights and he sat down on the settee. She went into the kitchenette and made two mugs of tea and then sank down beside him.

"So how long more do you think she's going to stay?"

"I've no idea," Isla sighed. "I actually like having her here, she's no trouble at all, but for Jo's sake I wish she'd go home. Jo blames me. She's so mad with me – she thinks it's all my fault because I brought up the subject of the embryo again after all these years. God, it's such a mess . . ." She rubbed her hands down over her face.

"Well, maybe she should have just given it to you in the first place without any drama and then perhaps Réiltín would never have found out in the way that she did."

Isla shrugged her shoulders. "Well, it's too late now. I feel so awful about it all. I wish I had never asked her for it."

"Everything happens for a reason, Isla – maybe it's a good thing that Réiltín found out now instead of down the line."

"Maybe, but Jo doesn't see it like that. I'm worried that I've just lost the only family I have." Her voice trembled.

"She'll calm down. I know she's angry right now but these things take time. You're sisters – you'll work it out, I'm sure of it."

"I hope so, Greg, I really do."

They heard footsteps making their way up the stairs, then the door opened and Réiltín came in.

"Hiya, Réilt," Isla said, blushing a little. "You know Greg, don't you?"

"Hi, Greg," she said with a smile on her face.

"Hi, Réiltín." He stood up off the sofa and drank the end of his tea. "I'd better head on."

"Don't go just yet," Isla said.

"Well, I need to grab a few bits in the shop before it closes."

"Alright, I'll walk you down so."

She followed him down the stairs and he stepped outside onto the footpath. She longed to invite him to stay, she longed to lie in his arms and to feel his skin against hers and to wake up to his smile in the morning with the birds chattering outside her window – but she couldn't with Réiltín staying there.

"Will you be okay?" he asked.

"Of course I will."

"Maybe we could go for a bite to eat at the weekend?" he asked hopefully.

"Yeah, you know what, that sounds good. Réiltín mentioned something about going to the movies with her friends – a six o'clock showing – so maybe we could get an early bird? I don't want to leave her on her own at night-time – I know Jo wouldn't be happy and besides she's a bit vulnerable at the moment. How about that new tapas place on George's Street?"

"I've been dying to try it – good choice."

"Greg?"

"Yes?"

"Thank you for everything. You've been a rock for me over the last while, you know, with the reading and everything . . ." She still felt embarrassed about it. "I don't know how I'd cope without you."

"Don't mention it," he said, his cheeks reddening. He leaned in and kissed her on the lips and then he walked on down the street. She stood in the doorway for a moment, watching him as he walked away. She climbed the stairs with a smile on her face.

"What's got into you?" Réiltín asked, looking up from her iPad as soon as Isla came back into the living room.

"Oh, nothing – can't a person smile without having a reason?" Isla flopped down onto the sofa beside her.

"You're so strange sometimes," Réiltín said with a grin.

"Eh, watch it, lady," Isla said, laughing with her.

Réiltín turned back to the music video on her iPad.

"Your mum called into the café earlier," Isla continued.

"Again? You should consider taking out a barring order."

She didn't lift her eyes from the screen.

"Now, now, Réiltín, you should see how upset she is – how upset they both are. Why won't you just hear them out at least? If you don't like what they say then you can still stay here with me but at least give them a chance to explain."

"No way, Isla – there is nothing they can say to me that will change anything. They have kept this huge secret from me my whole life and I will never forgive them for that."

"They want to come to your play next week."

"Well, I don't want them there."

"Réiltín, come on," Isla pleaded.

"Well, I don't."

"You're very stubborn."

She shrugged her shoulders. "I guess I get that from you."

Chapter 33

What If?

It had become their routine that Isla would wake Réiltín for school in the morning, they'd both grab some toast, then Isla would walk to work in the café and Réiltín would walk in the opposite direction to school. Isla had got a key cut for her so, if she was home before her, she could let herself in. Réiltín would make a start on her homework and then when Isla came home in the evenings she would perch herself on the end of the counter and chat to her about her day while Isla chopped vegetables for dinner. After dinner they would do the dishes together – Réiltín would wash and Isla would dry. Then they'd watch some TV. Sometimes, as they sat together on the sofa, Isla would catch Réiltín staring at her hands. She would be moving hers alongside Isla's and Isla knew that she was trying to size them up. Isla would then move hers away and distract her by stroking her hair. Then they would go to bed around eleven and then the next day would start all over again. Of course she would never dare to say it to Jo but the longer Réiltín was staying with her, the more Isla was amazed and partly frightened by how easily they had both seemed to settle into normalcy.

She knew that Jo was still distraught and Ryan too. He had called into the coffee shop one day and begged Isla to let him come over that evening to see Réiltín. Instead of his usual well-kept appearance, Isla noticed that he looked scraggly. He had let his facial hair grow and she observed that he had started to grey more. Previously he had only had a few grey hairs peppered through his black hair but now they were clustering at the temples. But it went beyond his appearance: his eyes looked listless, the sparkle was gone.

"I have to see her, Isla – it's too awful – I miss her desperately –"

She could see tears in his eyes. "Hey, I'm not stopping anyone from seeing her but she warned me that if I bring you or Jo over, she's going to walk out of my place and God knows where she'll end up then."

"Please, Isla, this is killing me."

"Look, Ryan, I'll try and talk to her again to see if she'll see you but don't get your hopes up. She's still very angry."

He nodded. "Thanks, Isla – I'd really appreciate that."

But Réiltín had stubbornly refused to see him so instead he made a habit of calling into the coffee shop to see Isla just for an update on how Réiltín was doing. He would give Isla money to buy stuff. She would tell him it was fine, that she had it covered, but he would insist that she take it. Isla knew that he felt it was the only way he could help out in the situation. She felt sorry for him. She felt sorry for all of them. The guilt for her role in all of it was getting worse for every day that Réiltín was away from home.

Isla didn't see much of Jo. Jo couldn't call over to the flat and Isla didn't want to leave Réiltín on her own by calling over there. And anyway she wasn't even sure what she could possibly say to Jo. Whenever Jo saw her, she wanted reassurance that Réiltín was calming down. She wanted to hear that she would be home soon. Isla could hear the eager bating of breath for good news whenever she was at the other end of the phone. She wanted Isla to say that Réiltín was missing her and that she felt that she would be ready to see her soon. Jo wanted hope but Isla couldn't give her that.

It was only now that the consequences of what they had done all those years ago were starting to hit her. Although she'd had counselling when she donated her eggs to Jo, at the time she had never given it a second thought. It hadn't really given her cause for consideration over the years. At the time, she hadn't looked upon her eggs as being anything special. She'd had no emotional attachment to them. To her it was like when you donated blood to the blood bank – yes, it was yours originally but you forgot about it soon afterwards and you didn't obsess about it all the time, wondering about the person who got your blood and how they're doing and what your blood was doing now inside them. Isla had donated her eggs and had pretty much forgotten about them afterwards. Yes, there had been a certain part of her that was curious when Réiltín was born to see if she had inherited any of her features but it was in the same way that you would look at any niece to see if they had inherited characteristics from your side of the family, like your mum's nose or an aunt's high cheekbones. Jo had needed eggs and Isla offered them like she would have if she had needed a kidney but it was only now that she was beginning to realise that it wasn't like donating a kidney, that there was so much more to it than that. Isla now found herself wondering what it would have been like if Réiltín had been born to her. If *she* had carried her, nourished her and given birth to her. If she had been the one to bathe her for the first time and buy her tiny clothes. If she had dithered over choosing which school she should attend or put a plaster on a grazed knee. Isla started to imagine that scenario. She would indulge herself in the quieter moments in the café and let it all play out in her head. Instead of just being aunt and niece, if Réiltín were *her* daughter what would it be like? She wasn't sure if it was because she was already longing for a child that this was now impinging on how she was feeling or if she would have felt like that anyway? Was she secretly enjoying all of it? Then she would feel nauseatingly guilty afterwards like she had done something horribly wrong and she would try to bring it up with Réiltín again that she should really think about meeting up with her mother for a talk. Was she doing enough to talk Réiltín around into going home to her parents? She needed to remember that she was her aunt at the end of the day. What would happen when it was time for Réiltín to go home? Isla knew that realistically there would probably come a point when that would happen. She couldn't stay with her forever but Isla had grown to like having her there. She enjoyed her company and she knew that Réiltín liked hers too. And she had to wonder if their bond was closer than it would be to that of a 'normal' niece. Because they shared fifty per cent of their genes, did it link them not just biologically but also deeper than that? Nevis had told her once that some people believed that we were attracted to people with the same blood types as our own and Isla couldn't help thinking of that now. She wondered if it extended to genes? Her head was spinning in confusion and part disgust at her own feelings. She felt she was doing something awful to Jo by even letting the thoughts grow wild and untamed in her head.

Then she would think about the embryo, the baby that could be just like Réiltín. The embryo that could be *her* child, if Jo would only sign the consent forms. Would having her own baby banish those thoughts? She had certainly never meant for the whole drama to happen but she never could have imagined that her feelings would have been so complicated either. Isla knew that Réiltín wasn't her child, deep down she knew that. She belonged to Jo and Ryan but a dark place deep within Isla kept whispering *what if*?

Chapter 34

Spite

It was the evening of Réiltín's school play. They were performing a modern adaptation of *Romeo and Juliet*. Jo had phoned Isla in the café at lunchtime to ask her whether she had made any progress with Réiltín and Isla had to relay it back to Jo that she was still insisting that she didn't want to see them. Jo had said defiantly that she was going anyway and what kind of mother would she look like if she weren't there in the audience to support her daughter? It was clear that she had already made up her mind about it so Isla decided not to say anything to Réiltín and see how it went that night.

Isla arrived at the school that evening and followed the signs to the hall. She had to search the rows of seating in the room for Jo and Ryan and when she saw them she made her way over and slotted in beside them.

"Hi, Isla," Ryan said.

Jo's greeting was a curter "Hi".

Ryan handed Isla his programme to look at. Jo shot him a look. They sat in awkward silence and Isla was glad when the lighting dimmed, the curtain parted and the play commenced with Sampson and Gregory strolling through the aged streets of Verona.

While Jo watched Réiltín deliver her lines as she played the part of Juliet's mother, Lady Capulet, she felt the most acute longing to be with her. She felt a force pulling her off her seat to go and reach out to her. She wanted to climb onto that stage and wrap her daughter inside her arms but instead she stayed sitting on that hard plastic seat. She couldn't help thinking back to the time in her own school hall when she had been on the stage. She could still recall the musty smell of the red-velvet curtains. It was her first memory of excruciating embarrassment. She could still remember that knot of anxiety and the fear that she was going to be in trouble. She looked over at Isla's face, which was fixed on the stage. She wondered if Isla ever thought about it since? If she even remembered it now?

Jo had been six years old and her class had been practising the Christmas nativity over and over. She was overjoyed to be given a part as one of the angels. Even though everyone wanted to be Mary, she didn't because she knew that the angels got to wear the prettiest costumes. She had seen the two dresses hanging in the cupboard at the back of the classroom since they had gone into it on the first day of September. She had loved those costumes from the moment she set eyes on them. They were beautifully made from gossamer silk and were stitched with a shimmering silver thread. There was a halo made from tinsel to wear around the head. She had been singing all the songs at home for weeks, practising them over and over again, determined to get them right. Isla had known all the words just from listening to her singing and would copy her. On the day of the play, Jo had been so excited. They had peeked out from behind the stage curtain and watched as the hall filled up with their parents. Then it was time to take their positions like they had rehearsed many times and the curtains parted. The class had the parents captivated with the nativity scene and had just started to point up to the Star of Bethlehem hanging from the ceiling before breaking into *Twinkle Twinkle Little Star* exactly as they had practised many times before. Suddenly a ripple of laughter broke out in the audience, distracting the children who looked around and saw a determined-looking Isla climbing the steps to the left of the stage. Jo could still remember her expression: her face was scrunched up and she was earnestly biting down on her tongue. She still made the same face even now when she was concentrating hard on something. Jo had watched in horror, waiting for someone to stop her before she reached them but she came running over to her, her two feet echoing noisily off the wooden floor of the stage as she ran across it in her thick-soled winter boots. Jo still remembered the sickening panic, the sinking feeling in her stomach. Before she knew it, Isla had reached out to hold her hand and was singing *"De-Da, De-Da, ickle daaaaar!"* at the top of her voice with the rest of the class who were now starting to laugh and giggle. Jo desperately tried to find their mother's face in the audience but the lights had bleached everyone's faces. All she could see was a sea of people staring up, pointing and laughing at them, and it was all because of Isla. She couldn't understand why her mother wasn't coming up to take her down. Then eventually her eyes landed on her mother's face and she was smiling, which seemed outrageous to her. She was dreading the song ending because she was worried that she was going to be in trouble from her teacher Mrs Franklin but when they got off the stage she wasn't cross at all. Instead she lifted Isla up in her arms, rubbed her silky auburn curls and said "I think we have a true star in the making". She hadn't even looked at Jo.

Jo switched her mind back to the play in front of her. They watched as Romeo drank the potion and died and then as Juliet, roused from sleep, tried to kiss Romeo in vain and so used his dagger to take her own life too. Jo felt tears spring into the corners of her eyes but she quickly wiped them away.

Then they all stood up to clap as the cast took a bow and the curtains drew closed.

"That was great," Isla said afterwards. She could see Jo and Ryan were beaming with pride.

"I think I'm going to go backstage and see if I can see her," Jo said.

"Are you sure that's a good idea, Jo?" Ryan said.

"I just want to tell her how proud I am of her."

"Well, it might not be the best time," Isla said.

"Are you trying to stop me from seeing her?"

"Of course not, Jo, but I just don't know if she's ready to see you."

"What's that supposed to mean?" Jo asked through gritted teeth.

"Okay, you know her better than me."

"I think I'll wait here," Ryan said.

Jo pushed past Isla and walked down the corridor between notice boards, glass cabinets displaying sporting trophies and project displays.

Ryan and Isla were left alone together.

"I don't think it's a good idea that she's going back there," Ryan said nervously. "God only knows how Réiltín will react when she sees her!"

"I don't think we could have stopped her."

"So how's Réiltín been?" he asked.

"She's okay – she's still quite angry though."

He nodded. "Of course she is. I mean this whole thing – it's a nightmare. It all seems so surreal to be honest."

Isla could hear the wobble in his voice. She reached out and placed her hand on his arm. "Look, Ryan, she'll calm down. She's had a big shock. She's at a vulnerable age anyway where any little thing will cause a huge emotional reaction but just give her time."

"You see, I can do that but Jo . . . this is killing her."

Less than two minutes later they saw Jo coming back down

271

the hall towards them. Her steps were brisk and purposeful. Her face was flushed and her eyes red.

"What happened?" Ryan said as she got close to them.

"What do you think? She told me to go away – she told her own mother to go away – in front of everyone! All the other parents were looking at me –" Her voice choked. "Come on, Ryan, let's go. There's no point in us hanging around here." She turned to Isla then, "I presume you'll wait here until she's ready to go home?"

She nodded. "Yes, of course I will. Look, Jo, I'm sorry, I really am . . ."

"It's too late for sorry now, Isla." Jo turned on her heel and walked away.

After Jo was gone Isla was left standing in the chilly reception area on her own. She felt awful. In a way Jo was right – this was all her fault. If she hadn't asked for that embryo then the topic of Réiltín's conception would never have come up again and she would never have overheard her parents arguing about it. She felt wretched and wished she could turn back the clock. No one had won. Jo wasn't going to give her the embryo and now her world had fallen apart, which had never been her intention. She was starting to think that maybe her mother had been right all those years ago. Maybe she did bring trouble, maybe being born in that heat wave meant she was destined to hurt people her whole life.

When Jo got up the next morning her head was fuzzy with tiredness. As she lay back against the pillows, she felt like Goldilocks waking up in Baby Bear's bed, her own life seemed so alien to her now. She had lain awake all night long thinking it through. She had two columns in her mind – the reasons *For* were on the left and the reasons *Against* on the right. She had spent all night putting arguments into each column. Sometimes she would take them out again but then she'd mull it over some more and she'd put them back in again. The end result always came out the same and her mind was made up for her.

As soon as the clock read nine, she lifted her phone off her bedside table and dialled the number to the clinic. It rang for a long time before Dr Collins' secretary answered, out of breath. Jo imagined her running to get to her desk to answer it.

"Hello, the Dublin Reproductive Centre, how may I help you?"

"This is Jo Kingston. I have a storage licence which is due to be renewed in the coming weeks." Jo held the letter in front of her that had arrived in the post earlier in the week and quoted the reference off it.

"Just give me a moment while I pull up your file. Would you mind if I popped you on hold for a moment?"

"Not at all." Jo was instantly rewarded with an ear-splittingly, squeaky version of 'Für Elise'.

"Yes, I have your file here on the screen." The woman was back on the line.

"I was just ringing to say that my husband and I have given it a lot of thought and we have decided that we won't be renewing the storage contract but we would like to donate our embryo to medical research."

"Well, that is very generous of you. I'll have Dr Collins call you back as soon as he is available and he will talk you through the necessary steps and of course the dreaded paperwork that needs to be filled out." She gave a little laugh.

"Ah yes," Jo groaned playfully. "I knew we wouldn't escape without some paperwork."

"I always joke that if I want to use the bathroom here I nearly need to sign a consent form. Okay, well, thanks for that, Mrs Kingston, and Dr Collins will be in touch shortly."

"Thank you for your help."

After she had hung up the phone Jo stayed lying where she was. She couldn't get out of bed. She couldn't face the world.

Chapter 35

Calamari

Isla stood back from the mirror and looked at her appearance. It was Saturday afternoon and she was meeting Greg for an early bird. She had thrown on jeans and a sweater initially but then had second thoughts and pulled the sweater off over her head and instead put on a silk blouse that she thought looked a little more sophisticated. She tied up her hair into a ponytail and put on her eyeliner as usual. She was just about to switch off the light when she remembered the bracelet that Greg had given her for her birthday. She opened the box and carefully lifted the bracelet out and placed it around her wrist. She fastened the clasp and held her arm out to admire it. She didn't usually wear jewellery but he had chosen well. Then she put on her parka and set off to the restaurant where they had arranged to meet.

She came upon the building with its bay window lit by the yellow glow of candles inside. She pushed back the door and scanned the dark interior. A young guy was standing at the back of the room, playing the Spanish guitar. His fingers plucked and teased out a lively song. She followed the waiter down to the table. Greg hadn't yet arrived.

While she waited, she looked up at the blackboard with the daily specials written in chalk. She let her eyes run along the words as she tried to sound them out inside her head. *Ca-la-mar-i*. She was amazed by how far she had come – just a few weeks ago she would have avoided looking at that blackboard because the inner shame of not being able to understand it was too much.

She knew that she was growing ever closer to Greg; she was falling in love with him. It scared her if she was honest. She felt vulnerable opening herself up to him like this – she had nothing left any more – she had exposed her very biggest fears to him – but then she would look into his clear blue eyes and know that he wasn't going to hurt her. She liked being around him and, whenever anyone else was there, she couldn't wait for them to be gone so that they could be alone again. He had seen the one thing that she had been so fearful of. She had laid herself bare; he had seen the real her and he hadn't run away screaming. In fact it was the opposite – he wanted to help her. Isla had never imagined in a million years being able to open up to anyone the way she had with Greg and it felt amazing. It was liberating not to be carrying around secrets any more. Not even Nevis had known that she couldn't read. He had never noticed.

Greg appeared a few minutes later, dressed in jeans and an open blue checked shirt, showing a T-shirt underneath.

"Sorry, I'm late, Isla – the bus took forever!"

"No worries at all. I'm only just here myself."

The waitress came and handed them menus. Greg chose a steak with chips on the side. Isla, with a thumping heart, decided to be brave and to order the calamari. She hoped that she had read it correctly – her big fear was that the waitress would tell her there was no mention of it on the menu and that she would look stupid. But then she remembered what Greg had said about believing in herself and pushing herself outside her comfort zone. She was elated when the waitress wrote it down without hesitation. It was a simple thing but Isla felt the door to a whole new world was slowly opening up to her.

"Well done, I'm proud of you," Greg whispered as soon as the waitress had left them alone.

She smiled across the table at him.

They chit-chatted some more until their food was served.

"So how's Réiltín doing?" he asked after a while.

"She's doing alright. I really thought she'd have gone home by now but she's not calming down." Isla picked up her fork and speared a piece of rocket from her side-salad.

He leant in across the table conspiratorially to her. "So I presume you haven't raised the topic of the embryo with Jo again then?"

"Are you mad?" Isla put down her cutlery and leaned back in her chair. "No, not after everything that has happened. I can say goodbye to that idea." She sighed. "It was a crazy idea anyway."

"Well, at least you tried. Wouldn't it be worse if you had never plucked up the courage to ask Jo for the embryo and then you looked back on all of this some day and wondered what might have been?"

"Maybe, but at least then my niece wouldn't be living with me and my sister would still be talking to me."

"Réiltín will come round – she just needs time."

"But what if she doesn't? The longer it goes on, the more comfortable she seems to be with the situation. I'm stuck in the middle."

Greg reached across the table and placed his hand over hers.

"It'll all work out, Isla – these things always do."

He walked her home and they kissed goodbye outside.

"I wish you could stay," she sighed.

"Me too," he said, leaning in and kissing her on the

forehead. "But there'll be lots of time for that. Goodnight, Isla."

"Goodnight."

She put her key in the lock and climbed the stairs. When she came into the living room she saw that Réiltín wasn't home yet. She flicked on the TV and watched a bit of the News but when she looked at the clock on the wall again she saw it was nine thirty and there was still no sign of Réiltín. She decided to ring her to see where she was. She dialled her number but it went straight to voicemail. *Hi, this is Réiltín, leave a message!* the phone sang back to her. Every time she checked the clock, the big hand seemed to be moving ever slower. When she still hadn't appeared by ten she tried her number again and again until she began to lose count of the number of times that she had heard the same message. It wasn't like Réiltín not to call. Something told Isla this wasn't right. She made up her mind that if she didn't appear in the next half an hour, she was going to ring Jo. She knew that Réiltín wouldn't be pleased but she felt like she didn't have any choice. Ryan and Jo needed to know something like this.

The longer the minutes ticked on, the more the worry wrapped itself around her. Her mind was imagining all kinds of awful scenarios and she had to push the thoughts out of her head. She still didn't ring Jo, she didn't want to upset her when Réiltín would probably walk in the door any minute.

She turned to the clock again and watched the big hand inch forward until it reached the top, sitting bang in the centre between the '1' and the '2'. She was wavering on a knife-edge of anger and worry.

She picked up her phone and dialled Jo's number. Her mouth felt dry as she waited for her sister to answer.

"Isla – is everything okay?" Jo asked quickly.

Isla could already hear the panic in her tone even though she hadn't even said anything yet.

"Réiltín hasn't come home – she was going to the movies.

The film started at six and she was meant to be home by nine but that was two hours ago and there's still no sign of her. Her phone is switched off too."

"Well, who was she meeting?"

"She just said she was going with some of her friends."

"Well, who were they?" Jo demanded in a heightened tone.

"I'm not sure," Isla said in a small voice.

"You mean to tell me that you let her off somewhere without even asking who she was meeting? Jesus Christ, Isla!"

"I'm sorry, Jo, I didn't think –"

"I knew something like this would happen, I just knew it! I'll call some of their parents and see if they know where she is. Ring me straight away if she shows up the meantime."

"Of course."

Jo hung up and immediately dialled Réiltín's friend Fiona's mother's number. The other woman answered her phone sleepily and told Jo that her daughter was tucked up in bed and hadn't been out that evening. Jo felt a sinking feeling deep within. When she had seen Isla's number calling her, she just knew in her bones that something had happened. Call it instinct or whatever but she had always known that something like that was bound to happen with Isla in charge. She went into the kitchen and over to the fridge where she had a list of phone numbers belonging to the mothers on the parents' association. She ran her finger down through the names until she found the number for Charlotte's mother Sarah. She dialled her number with trembling fingers.

"Sarah, hi, it's Jo – Réiltín's mother. I'm sorry for calling you so late but Réiltín hasn't come home. I believe she was going to the cinema with some friends and I just wanted to check with you whether Charlotte was with her?"

"Hi, Jo – yes, Charlotte was at the cinema earlier and she said that Réiltín was going too but, I'm sorry, I picked Charlotte up from the bus-stop just after nine."

Jo felt her heart plummet like someone had just poured it full of lead.

"Hang on a minute until I go and check with her to see if she knows where Réiltín might be. I'll just be a sec."

"Thanks, Sarah." Jo could hear a tremor in her own voice.

After a few minutes Jo could hear the sound of footsteps getting closer to the phone. She could hear a mumbled conversation taking place in the background but she couldn't make out what they were saying. Finally Sarah picked the handset up again. "I'm so sorry, Jo, Charlotte said that Réiltín was at the cinema with them but she left and went home early."

"Oh, God." Jo felt her palm grow sweaty around the handset.

"I'm sorry, Jo, I wish I could help you, I can imagine how worried you are right now."

"Thanks, Sarah, I'd better go."

"Well, if there's anything I can do, let me know."

Jo hung up the phone then and climbed the stairs to the spare room where Ryan had already gone to bed. She knocked gently on the door before entering. He was sitting up in bed reading a Harlan Coben novel under the lamplight. He put down the book and looked at her.

"It's Réiltín, she's gone missing. Isla rang me to say she was due home at nine o'clock but she never arrived. She went to the cinema with some friends earlier on but I spoke to Charlotte who was with them and she said that Réiltín had left the cinema early and gone home."

"Oh, shit." He jumped up and reached for the jeans that he had been wearing earlier. He thrust his legs into them and pulled a sweater down over his head. "Her friends must know something – they must know where she is. C'mon."

"Where are we going to go?"

"We'll drive over to Charlotte's house and talk to her."

"But she said that Réiltín left early and went home!"

"And you believe her? She's a teenager. I bet she knows more than she's telling us."

Jo nodded silently and followed him down the stairs and into the car.

She rang Isla to update her on the way.

"Any sign of her?" Jo asked.

"No," Isla said, feeling useless.

"Well, we're calling to one of her friends now to see if she knows anything."

"I'm so sorry, Jo – I really am."

At least she has the good grace to sound upset, thought Jo. "Just stay where you are in case she comes back."

"Of course – if I hear anything, I'll let you know straight away."

"I'd better go – we're here now."

Jo hung up just as Ryan was pulling up outside Charlotte's house.

He hopped out and ran up to the front door with Jo running behind him.

Sarah answered immediately to Ryan's knock.

"Sarah, sorry for calling so late," Ryan said, "but I was wondering if we could talk to Charlotte for a few minutes to see if we can find out where Réiltín is?"

"We're very worried," Jo added and immediately felt stupid. It was after eleven o'clock at night and they were knocking on this woman's door – it was obvious that they were worried.

"Sure, of course. Come in and sit down while I go and wake her."

They followed her into the small living room and sat down on a well-worn sofa, which was moulded into the shape of the people who sat on it. The TV was showing some US cop drama. The wall above the fireplace was crowded with mismatched frames of family portraits. There were children on their first day of school, Communions, Confirmations, family weddings and graduations. She knew that Charlotte was one of five children and Jo couldn't help but reflect on how different this room was compared to her own orderly living room with its symmetrical frames and complementary artwork. There was something soothing about the room. It was warm and relaxed and she could imagine them all seated around watching *The X Factor* together or something. Jo never watched *The X Factor*; she couldn't stand those types of shows. Réiltín loved it of course. She suddenly felt the most acute wave of sadness in her heart as she realised that she never watched TV with Réiltín. She should have watched it with her. Even if she didn't like the same shows, she should have just watched them for her sake. An involuntary choking sound escaped her mouth and tears made their way down her face.

Ryan stood up when Sarah came back down the stairs with a sleepy-looking Charlotte following behind her.

"I'm sorry for disturbing you, Charlotte," Ryan said, "but Réiltín never came home this evening and apparently you were with her at the movies earlier?"

Charlotte nodded vigorously. "I was, but she left the cinema early," she said quietly.

"But why would she do that?" Jo asked.

Charlotte shrugged her shoulders. "I don't know – she's been acting weird lately anyway so we just thought that she wanted to go home early or something."

"Well, do you know where she went?" Ryan demanded.

"I thought she was going home but she obviously didn't."

"Is there anywhere else you think she might have gone?"

"I don't know." She looked panicked and her eyes darted towards her mother.

"Charlotte, you need to tell Jo and Ryan everything," her mother said sternly. "They need to know what happened for Réiltín's sake."

"Look, we're so worried about her, Charlotte. Please, do

281

you know where she is?" Ryan pleaded.

"Please, Charlotte, think for a minute," said Jo. "Is there anywhere at all she might have gone?"

Charlotte was silent for a minute, then she said, "Well . . . maybe you should try the beach . . ."

"Why on earth would she go there at this hour of the night?" Sarah asked, shocked.

"Rick and some of his friends usually hang out on Seals' Rock. Sometimes we head down there too," Charlotte answered sheepishly.

"Who's Rick?" Jo asked once again, feeling that she barely seemed to know her own daughter any more.

"A guy Réiltín is into – they've been together a few times – it's on-off all the time."

"Okay, thanks, Charlotte," Ryan said. He turned to Jo. "C'mon, we'd better go and see if we can find her."

Chapter 36

Alone

Réiltín knew that she was drunk. Her head was starting to spin. She eventually spotted Rick and his mates at the rocks. She kept walking and climbed up onto one of the rocks near where they were sitting. She purposely didn't go right up beside them but close enough so that they saw her there. She wobbled a bit before catching her balance again. Nobody said hi to her as she sat down on the slanting face of a large stone and hugged her knees against her chest. She couldn't figure Rick out at all – one minute he was all over her and then the next day he blew cold again. It was all Doireann Walsh's fault. He had been really keen until she came on the scene. She watched from outside the group as Rick and his friends wittered on about some YouTube video with a dog. A dog who could sing apparently and they thought it was the funniest thing they had ever seen. They were taking turns passing the phone around to watch it. She lifted the Coca-Cola bottle to her mouth and took another gulp of the Coke and vodka she had mixed together. The wind blew the wispy strands of her hair into her face and she tucked them back behind her ears. She drank some more but he still didn't come over to her. Eventually she decided to get up and go over to talk to him. She wanted to have it out with him but she slipped and lost her footing again as she crossed over the treacherous rocks. Her leg scraped against its jagged sharpness and when she looked down she saw that an angry red gash had appeared along her shinbone. It was stinging like mad. She sat back down again and tried to clean it up with a tissue from her bag. She looked around but nobody seemed to have noticed. They were all too busy crowding around the phone. Everyone was getting excited about that silly dog video and here she was with the biggest secret and nobody knew about it. No one knew she was staying with Isla; she had managed to keep it hidden from them all. She didn't want anyone to know what was going on. She would be mortified if anyone ever found out.

After a while she saw a group walking up the beach towards them. She couldn't make them out in the darkness but as they drew closer she saw that it was Doireann and some of her friends from the year above. Réiltín's heart sank as Rick climbed down from the rocks and made his way across the sand to them. She watched him walk with his jeans low-slung and his hoody pulled up over his head. She looked on as he put his arm around Doireann's shoulders. Then they both climbed back up onto the rocks and sat down beside each other. He leant in and whispered something to Doireann. They both turned to look over at Réiltín and then they started to laugh. She felt the hurt grow inside her. Someone passed the phone to Doireann and she threw her head back and laughed at the dog video.

She knew she should just go home. She knew that Isla would probably be wondering where she was but she didn't care. She didn't care about anything any more. She stood up again and climbed down from the rocks. She slipped at the bottom and righted herself before sitting back down to steady her head.

After a while she saw Doireann's blurry shape stand up and heard her announce that she had to go home before her parents came looking for her. Réiltín watched as Rick jumped up and offered to walk her home. His friends soon got up and trailed after them, leaving Réiltín on her own. No one had even said goodbye to her, not one person. Certainly not Rick and Doireann. Soon they were all out of sight.

She dragged herself up again and walked past the steps. She knew that she was stumbling and falling over but she didn't care. She didn't care about anything any more. She kept on going along the sand until she was standing below her house on Sandymount Heights. The light in the living room was still on. She stood on the strand under the moonlight and stared up at the house. She watched as a shadow moved behind the curtain. She wished things could go back to the way they were before. She longed to breeze in through the door and say 'Hi, Dad, how was your day' or 'Hi, Mum, what's for dinner?'. She even missed Oscar's wet nose nudging her for a rub behind the ears. She longed for the carefree existence that she had before, when she knew who her parents were. Where she could watch that dog video and laugh at it like everyone else. Everything had fallen apart on the day she learnt about how they had made her. This beach had been her playground as a child, fishing for periwinkles, poking crabs with sticks, chasing off gutsy seagulls, throwing sticks for Oscar, clambering over the slippery rocks with her mum calling to her from the sand to be careful. It was all a fabrication – her whole life to this point was a lie. She walked down towards the water, which was gently lapping the shoreline. She took off her shoes and felt her weight sink down into the squidgy sand. The water was cold as it hit her ankles. She stayed standing there. She turned behind her to look up at the house. The light was still on. She started to cry. Tears came streaming down her face and she couldn't stop them. She wanted to be a little girl again; she wanted her mum to hug her close. She

285

wanted all this to stop, for someone to take the pain and the lies away. She wanted things to go back to the way they were before, when her parents were her parents. She didn't ask for this, she just wanted to be safe in that house and know that she was wanted. Suddenly she felt an awful sensation. Her chest felt tight like she had been winded. She felt her chest grow even tighter, like her ribs had locked into position and wouldn't move, like there were one hundred men sitting on her chest. She reached into her pocket for her inhaler and realised that she had forgotten to bring it out with her. Her breathing turned into a wheeze and she felt the familiar closing of her airway. She began to panic as she tried to fight it but she knew that that was the worst thing she could do. *Tight, tight, tighter.* She fell down onto the hard sand and the water rushed in around her.

Chapter 37

Searching

Isla sat on the sofa and fumbled with the phone in her hands. Her trembling fingers had to make several attempts to dial his number.

"Isla?" a sleepy voice answered.

"I'm sorry for calling so late, Greg, but Réiltín has gone missing."

"What happened?"

"Well, she didn't come home this evening when she was supposed to. I'm so worried about her, Greg." Her voice choked with tears.

"Oh no, Isla – I'll be straight over."

Fifteen minutes later, the doorbell went. She went downstairs and let him in. He climbed the stairs after her and when they reached the top he took her in his arms.

"So tell me what's happened."

"I don't know. She was meant to be home by nine but when she didn't come home by eleven I was starting to worry. I rang Jo and they're trying to find her now. I have to wait here in case she comes back to my place. Apparently she was with her friends at the cinema but she left the cinema early withou* them and no one has seen her since."

"Sit down there and I'll make a cup of tea for us, yeah?"

She sat down on the sofa and he placed a throw around her shoulders before going over to fill the kettle.

"I'm sorry for calling you like this, Greg, and dragging you out at this hour but thanks for coming. I couldn't bear to be on my own."

"She probably just lost track of time or went to a party somewhere – you know what teenagers are like," he said as he flicked the switch on the kettle.

"I hope so, Greg, I really do. It's all my fault – I should have kept a closer eye on her."

He made the tea and sat down beside her. She looked up at the clock on the wall and saw it was almost midnight. The longer it went on the worse the sense of dread that grew inside her. All kinds of thoughts were jumping into her head and she couldn't stand it.

"Anything could be happening to her, Greg. What if she's met some creep – oh God, it doesn't even bear thinking about. I will never forgive myself if anything happens to her, Greg!" She turned and sobbed into his shoulder.

"Don't think about any of that stuff now. It's pointless and isn't going to help anyone. She's probably fast asleep in a friend's house somewhere, I'm telling you." He placed his hand over hers.

"I'm so glad that you're here – I don't think I could cope without you."

"Hey, I'm glad to be here with you." He leant in, put his arm around her shoulders and kissed her hair gently and it was then that she finally realised that this was where she felt safe. Why had she stopped herself from feeling this for so long? Here in his arms was where she belonged.

Ryan and Jo were hurrying along the beach, stepping over seaweed and driftwood, calling Réiltín's name as they went.

Jo had rung as many of Réiltín's friends as she could on the short journey to the beach but nobody seemed to know where she was. As they hurried up the beach Ryan swept the torch in an arc from right to left and back again. There was no moon in the sky and the sound of the gentle waves lapping the shore seemed sharper, more intense now compared to during the daytime.

"*Réiltín? Can you hear us, Réiltín?*" Ryan shouted.

But the only response was the *whisssssssssh* of the waves as they gently broke on the shoreline.

Finally they reached the sleek black crop of stones known as Seals' Rock but it was deserted. Ryan clambered over the rocks, shining the torch across their backs. They glistened black, sleek and treacherous in the torchlight. A crumbling cliff face hugged the rocks from behind.

"Where do we go now?" Jo was forlorn.

"Come on, we'll check down the other end of the beach – if we don't find her there, then we'll have to go to the Gardaí."

"Oh God," Jo cried, placing her palms over her face.

Ryan put his arm around her shoulders and gave her a squeeze. "Come on, we need to hurry."

They turned and made their way back along the beach, tracing the path they had just come. They went past the steps and kept going until they were in front of the street where their house was. Ryan stopped and shone the torch again in a three-hundred-and-sixty-degree circle.

"What's that?" he said as he spotted a dark lump lying at the water's edge.

He ran towards it, Jo following behind.

Then they saw her illuminated by the torchlight, lying on the sand, in a shallow bath of seawater.

When the reached her they saw that her lips were purple, her usually porcelain skin blue.

"*Réiltín? Réiltín?*" Ryan roared. "Oh God, no!" She was

unresponsive and when he placed his palm on her chest her ribcage was only barely moving. "I think she's had an asthma attack!"

He fished his phone out of his pocket and with trembling hands dialled the number for the emergency services.

"Oh, Réiltín, love," Jo cried, tears streaming down her face. She hugged her daughter's head close to her chest. Her skin was cold to the touch. "I can't lose you. You're strong, Little Star, you're a fighter," she whispered in her daughter's ear.

Eventually the glare of the blue flashing lights broke the darkness up on the road overhead. Ryan ran up the beach to meet the crew and brief them on Réiltín's medical history.

As the paramedics set to work, Ryan and Jo stood back helplessly and watched. They hooked Réiltín up to an oxygen mask before carefully lifting her onto a stretcher. They followed behind numbly as the crew carried her across the sand and up the stone steps leading back up to the road.

"We can only allow one in the back with her so which one of you wants to go?"

"I will," Jo said quickly, looking at Ryan with begging eyes.

"Sure," he said. "I'll follow in the car."

"Okay, let's go," said the paramedic.

A shaking Jo got into the back of the ambulance and held onto her daughter's icy hand.

As they sped through the city she caught glimpses of familiar buildings through the orange tint of the ambulance windows. Eventually she saw that they had reached the hospital. As soon as they stopped, the back doors flew open and Réiltín's stretcher was wheeled out by the paramedics and into the hospital where she was greeted by a team of doctors who rushed off with her, leaving Jo and Ryan to cling to each other in the foyer.

They found a row of hard plastic chairs and sat down. As

they sat there under the bright hospital lights the waiting seemed interminable. The whole thing felt surreal. Jo felt as though she was an actor in someone else's life. In just a few short weeks her whole world had been turned upside down and was barely recognisable to her any more. The hardness of the chair underneath was the only reminder that this was all real life and not some awful nightmare.

At some point Jo remembered to phone Isla and let her know that they had found her.

Eventually, after what seemed like hours later, a doctor came to talk to them.

"You're Réiltín's parents?"

They nodded, unable to articulate a response.

"Well, the good news is that she's stable now. You found her just in time. Her blood-oxygen saturation levels were very low – dangerously low. If you had been any later getting to her, it might have been a very different outcome."

Jo buckled into Ryan's arms. "Oh my God," she sobbed into his shoulder.

"Has she been taking her medication like she's supposed to?"

Jo dissolved into tears. "I – I – I don't know."

"Look, her body is responding well now and she's going to be okay but asthma is a very serious condition. Most of the time it can be kept under control when a patient takes their medication correctly but you cannot take any chances. Children by their very nature cannot be relied upon to remember their medication – that's your job as a parent. Your daughter had a lucky escape tonight. The next time she might not be so lucky."

Jo nodded, unable to speak with distress.

They followed the doctor inside to the room where Réiltín was lying on a bed, hooked up to monitors. She was sleeping peacefully. Jo noticed a small patch of drool on the fabric of her pillow. She sat down and stroked her hair, which looked wilder than ever. She was relieved that her skin felt warmer to the touch now. Ryan took a seat on the other side of the bed.

"It's okay, Little Star, it's all going to be okay," Jo whispered in her ear.

After a while they heard someone come into the room and when they turned they saw Isla waiting hesitantly against the doorframe.

"Sorry, I can come back later if you want?" she said.

Jo noticed that Isla's face was pale and her green eyes were large with worry. She got up off the chair, walked over to her sister and threw her arms around her. They stood there clinging desperately to each other under the bright hospital lights.

"I'm sorry!" Isla started to cry.

Jo shook her head. "No, I'm sorry. I shouldn't have snapped at you like that – it wasn't your fault."

"I'm just glad she's okay," Isla said.

"We got such a scare – if anything were to happen to her –" Jo's voice broke as the night's events hit her in a fresh wave again.

"She's safe now, that's the main thing," Isla said.

"Come in and sit down," Jo said.

Ryan stood up and gestured for Isla to sit on his chair. She walked over and sat down at Réiltín's bedside.

Eventually Réiltín started to stir. Her eyes flickered open before closing down again. "Mum!"

"How are you feeling, Little Star?" Jo whispered.

"Tired."

"Well, it's going to take a while for you to build your strength up again, so for now you need to rest," Ryan said gently.

"I'm sorry – I'm so sorry for not bringing my inhaler with me."

"Ssssh, love," Jo said, raising a finger to Réiltín's lips. "It doesn't matter. None of that matters now. We're just so glad that you're okay." She lowered her face down to her daughter's, letting their foreheads touch. "You don't know how much I have missed you." Her voice broke into sobs.

"You gave us such a fright!" Isla whispered to her niece.

"I'm okay, Isla – I'm so sorry for making you worry."

"Hey, don't fret about it."

Réiltín's lids grew heavy again and she drifted back off to sleep.

Ryan squeezed Jo's hand across the bed. "Thank God, thank God – she's going to be okay."

Chapter 38

Back Home

The doctors discharged Réiltín the following morning and Jo was relieved when she said she wanted to go home to their house. The journey home from the hospital reminded Jo of the day they had brought her home from the special care unit when she was an infant. She felt the same emotional seesaw of excitement and worry for her child. Réiltín let her father lift her into her childhood bed like she was a baby once again while Jo tucked her up and stayed with her, stroking her hair until she fell soundly asleep.

Jo could hardly dare to believe that Réiltín was home. The events of the night before were exhausting but then she could feel waves of ecstasy and relief flood through her as well. The last few weeks had been wretched but now as she watched her daughter sleeping her heart soared. She didn't care about what Réiltín was doing that night or the fact that she had been staying with Isla. All that mattered right at that minute was that she was asleep in the bed where she belonged. Jo bent down to kiss her on the forehead before creeping out of the room and pulling the door closed softly behind her.

"How is she?" Ryan asked when she came back down to

the kitchen.

She couldn't help but notice the dark shadows under his eyes, the grey in his hair. The last few weeks had taken their toll on him too.

"Exhausted. She was asleep within minutes. The doctor said it would take her a few days to regain her strength."

He nodded. "I've just made some coffee."

She sat down at the table and noticed that the mugs Ryan had used weren't from a matching set. She always used matching ones . . . but then she stopped her train of thought and remembered that after everything that they had been through over the last few weeks, the matching mugs were the least of her problems. Her daughter was home.

"It's such a relief to have her back home again." He paused for a moment. "Look, there has been something that I've wanted to say to you for a while. I'm sorry if you felt that I was taking Isla's side in this whole thing. I never meant to make you feel like that and you didn't deserve it. Yes, I am very grateful to her for all that she has done for us but I'm also so grateful to you – you're the one who carried Réiltín and gave birth to her and you're an amazing mother. You're the woman that I love, Jo."

Jo felt the pressure of tears building in her eyes. She took a deep breath before speaking. "I've always found it difficult, you see. You and Réiltín and then Isla too . . . well, sometimes I imagine that all of you have a stronger bond because you're both biologically related to Réiltín, whereas, well, me . . . I'm not . . ."

"Jo, you know that's not how it is. You even saw it there last night when she was in hospital – *you* were the person that she wanted by her bedside. You're her mother and no one else could ever take your place with her."

The tears started to roll down her cheeks and Ryan reached forward and brushed them away with his fingers.

"You know, I think maybe I underestimated what we did all those years ago," Jo whispered.

"How do you mean?"

"Well, I thought that accepting that I had to use Isla's egg was going to be the hard part but it was only after she was born that I realised my worries were only beginning. I thought that once I had a baby I would be fine about the whole thing – I mean, I'd had the counselling and everything – but I still carried a lot of anger and resentment and the more Réiltín grew, the more fearful I became of losing her. Does that make sense? I'm so sorry, Ryan. I know being married to me hasn't always been easy. And you were right about telling Réiltín . . . we should have told her the truth from the start. I never thought I would say these words but I'm glad she knows now. This whole drama has given me perspective. Réiltín wouldn't be Réiltín, she wouldn't be the beautiful girl she is today, our beautiful daughter, without Isla's involvement – so even if I had been able to have a biological child of my own, it still wouldn't have been Réiltín. This was the path we were meant to take – it's just taken me a long time to recognise that."

That evening Isla called over to see them.

"I just said I'd stop by to see how you're all doing?"

"We're doing okay," Jo said. "Réiltín has been asleep for most of the day."

Isla placed Réiltín's hold-all down on the floor at her feet. "I . . . eh . . . thought she might be looking for this – it's her iPad and stuff."

"Thanks, Isla," Jo said, taking the bag. "I'll take it up to her room."

After Jo went upstairs, Ryan cleared his throat. "Isla, I have something that I want to say to you. I know Jo might not appreciate me saying this but, well, I just want to say thank you, Isla. Thank you for everything that you have done for us over the last few weeks. They certainly haven't been easy but, although she wasn't here, at least we knew she was in the next best place and that was with you."

Isla felt the heat work its way up her cheeks.

"I don't want to experience that ever again," Ryan continued with a shudder. "But all that matters now is that she's okay – and she's back home."

"Don't mention it," Isla said. "I'm just glad that she's back where she belongs."

But her words didn't match the hollow feeling deep within her. She knew that she should be thrilled for Jo and Ryan and she was, but she also felt . . . well . . . she wasn't sure how she felt exactly but it was something close to sadness. Her heart felt heavy whenever she thought about it. She knew that this was the house where Réiltín belonged, deep down she knew that, but it didn't mean that she wasn't going to miss her a hell of a lot.

A few days later Jo opened up her wardrobe and lifted down the memory box that she had been keeping for Réiltín since the day she was born. She delicately removed the lid and saw her hospital bracelet and the pink certificate that had hung at the end of her crib giving her parents' names, her time and date of birth and her weight. It also contained the first blanket she had wrapped her in on the day that they were taking her home from hospital. If she brought it up to her nose she could still get that newborn smell of baby mixed with a faint trace of antiseptic.

She lifted the box gently and walked down the landing to Réiltín's bedroom. She knocked softly and let herself in. Réiltín was lying in bed, reading something on her iPad.

"I was going through some stuff and I thought you might like to see your memory box again." Jo put the box down on the bed. "Here, look at this . . ." She handed her the tiny hospital bracelet with her name on it.

"I can't believe how small my wrists were," Réiltín said, slipping the bracelet around her index finger.

"Yes, you really were our miracle baby," Jo said. "I never

imagined I could be so lucky in life as to have you. We love you very, very much – you do know that, don't you?"

"I know, Mum. I know I was horrible to you over the last few weeks but I was so angry I just needed some space to get my head around it all, you know?"

"I understand, love, I understand it was a huge shock for you and I'm sorry – I'm sorry you had to find out that way. I'm sorry we didn't tell you from the start – it's a big regret. I think in hindsight your dad was right – it would have been better."

"Look, it's all been a bit weird, I'm not going to lie to you – in fact, the whole thing is a bit fucked-up."

"Hey, watch your language!"

"Sorry, Mum," she said contritely. "But even you have to admit that it's all a bit crazy. *EastEnders* will be asking us for script ideas next!"

Jo laughed. "At this stage, darling, I think we're more Jeremy Kyle than *EastEnders*!"

"Mum?"

"Yes?"

"I know you had to use Isla's eggs because your own weren't working properly but I'm glad you did it – I'm glad I was born to you." She threw her arms around her and squeezed her tight.

Jo felt the pressure of tears filling behind her eyes. "I'm so glad you were born to me too. I never thought I'd say this but in a way I'm glad your dad and I had to go through all that we did because all of that heartache led us to you. We were meant to have you, Little Star."

Chapter 39

Sisters

Isla had just settled down on the sofa with the remote control when the buzzer went. She groaned and pulled herself back off the sofa to answer it.

"It's only me – can I come up for a minute?" Jo's voice said.

Isla went down the stairs to open up the door.

"How are you?" Jo asked, bouncing up the stairs.

"I'm good," Isla said. She couldn't help but notice how much better Jo looked. She had looked exhausted over the last few days, but she definitely was a different woman today.

"Do you want a coffee?" Isla asked.

"Yeah, go on," she said.

Isla made a plunger of coffee and set two mugs down on the coffee table.

"How's Réiltín?"

"She's great – she's getting stronger by the day and the doctor said she could go back to school next week." She paused for a moment. "We also had our first session with the family counsellor."

"So how did it go?"

"Well, Réiltín hadn't wanted to go at first but, as soon a⁵

299

she started to open up, she found that talking through her problems helped her to process them."

"That's good. I'm glad everything is getting back to normal."

"Me too! We're taking things slowly but we're getting there. Things are also a lot better between Ryan and me. We've talked over stuff going back years – now it feels like the whole slate has been wiped clean. We're getting a fresh start and we're all the better for it. And you'll never guess what I did today?" There was an excited glint in her eye.

"What?"

"I booked a trip to South America for the three of us this summer for a month."

"South America, Jo? Are you sure?"

When Isla heard people talking about their travels to South America, they usually recounted tales of people having sex beside them in hostel dormitory bunks or eleven-hour bus journeys with chickens in the aisles. Or sleeping on a beach under the stars and waking up to find your passport and money stolen. It didn't sound like the kind of thing Jo would be into.

"I know it's a bit mad but I'm excited. Now we won't exactly be backpacking but, still, it's going to be an adventure! It'll do me good to step out of my comfort zone for a while – in fact, I think it will do us all good as a family."

"Wow, Jo, that's great. What made you decide to do it?"

"Well, the last few weeks have opened my eyes up to lots of things. I just felt I needed a break away from the relentless client demands and I wanted for us to do something fun as a family." She felt the need to relinquish control, to see where life took her and this trip was to signify all of that.

"You never do things by halves, that's for sure."

"Look, Isla, the real reason that I'm here is that I want to talk to you about something."

"Oh yeah?"

"Everything that has gone on between us over the last few weeks, well, it was dreadful . . . They were the worst few weeks of my life and I wouldn't wish it on anyone but it taught me that all that matters in my life is my family – everything else is just secondary. It makes me wonder what I've been fighting for, for all these months."

"What do you mean?"

"Well, the embryo in storage – it kind of all seems futile now. It makes me wonder why I was so against you having it in the first place. Everything that has happened has taught me a valuable lesson. I've been doing a lot of thinking and the reason I was so against you using the embryo was because I was jealous of you, if I'm being completely honest. There was a part of me that felt I always did things properly and you never did. I did well in school, I went to university, I got a first class honour in my degree, I got married, and then I had a baby. I did everything the right way around whereas I always felt that you had never planned or set your life in motion. You just seemed to fall into things and I hate admitting this because it makes me sound like a selfish cow but I didn't want things to fall into place for you. I felt you didn't deserve it. I didn't want you to have a child of your own so easily after the struggles that I had experienced to have Réiltín. Deep down I was resentful of you potentially being able to have a genetic child of your own. I was jealous of you in so many ways."

"You were jealous of me?" Isla asked in disbelief.

"I think I've always been jealous of you, Isla. I am jealous of how you can just be yourself, your freedom, the way you don't seem to get caught up in the day-to-day pressures of life, the way you don't seem to give a toss what anyone thinks of you. I know I blamed you for me having to be the responsible older sister growing up but the truth was I am too afraid. I've always been too afraid to move out of my comfort zone, which is why I always played the good girl. It was the safe option."

"I never knew that – you always seemed so confident, so content with the structure in your life."

Jo shrugged her shoulders. "I don't think I knew any other way. I feel like I've been trying to please people my whole life. I've been on a career trajectory since I was five years old. The teachers in school always pushed me on – don't get me wrong, I'm glad they did, but I never really stopped to think if being a solicitor was what I really wanted. I think it was just expected of me because I had enough points." She averted her eyes to the floor. "I was also jealous of you and Ryan."

"But why would you be jealous of us?"

"I was afraid, you see, I've always been afraid of . . . of . . . you and Ryan . . . and Réiltín."

"What?"

"I know it sounds mad but the people I love most in this world are the people who scare me the most as well."

"How could we scare you?"

"I was so afraid you were going to get together, the three of you as a family, and leave me without my baby – the thing I loved the most."

"Jesus, Jo, are you for real? You thought me and Ryan would . . . eh . . . y'know?"

"It's crazy, isn't it?"

"I would never do something like that! I would never betray my own sister. Hell, he's not even my type!"

"I know you wouldn't. It was all me and my head running away with itself. I was so insecure, you see. I hated the fact that we had to rely on you to conceive our baby. It took me a long time to accept it."

"I thought I did the right thing –"

"You did! Sorry, that came out all wrong – what I mean is that it was all me – I wasn't well in the head. I was so jealous and angry and I think it only really hit me after Réiltín was born – the extent of what we had done. I thought the hardest part was behind us but, for me, it was only then I started to realise that it was only just beginning. I couldn't switch off from her origins – it became even more real once she was born. I used to obsess over her. I would spend hours just staring at her or poring over photographs I had taken wondering if I could look at her and say she had my eyes or lips or chin. Do you remember the day Ryan brought her over to your house in the buggy so I could get some rest?"

"Uh-huh. You came in and started shouting stuff at him and at me. I didn't know what was going on to be honest. I thought it was some fight you were having."

"Well, that was part of it – the madness. I couldn't think straight. I was so paranoid, so insecure. It was horrible. I always felt I hadn't really given Ryan what he should have had. I never felt good enough. That I hadn't proved my worth as a woman. Oh I know it sounds ridiculous and irrational but that was how I felt. So I would cause huge jealous arguments and accuse him of all kinds of things. There was one time when it was the office Christmas party and they were all staying in the hotel overnight like they do every year but there was one year, I think Réiltín must have only been about two, and I couldn't get the paranoia out of my head. I kept imagining all sorts – that he was having sex with his PA or then it would be one of the branch managers. I had no reason to suspect anything but my mind was running away with itself. So I bundled Réiltín into the car at one in the morning and we drove to the hotel. When I got there he was there with a few of his colleagues in the bar. He was stunned to see me and then I realised I was in my pyjamas. In the end I pretended Réiltín had been sick and I was worried about her but he knew. We ended up in marriage counselling for a long time afterwards."

"I never knew you found it so difficult – I'm sorry."

"It wasn't your fault, Isla – it was all me."

"Look, it's in the past now, Jo. Don't worry. I don't hold it against you."

303

"You were always so forgiving, so loving." Jo turned and looked at Isla. "I never said this to you before but, you know what, you'd be a brilliant mum."

"Do you really think I would?" Isla smiled a sad smile.

"You have a lot to give – love, patience, kindness. Look, Isla, the reason I came here was that I need to tell you something . . ."

"Go on –"

"This isn't an easy thing for me to tell you but I need to say it – I rang the clinic last week to tell them that we wouldn't be renewing the storage contract any more. I told them that we wanted to donate the embryo to medical research, so perhaps they could find new ways to help couples who struggle to conceive like Ryan and I did."

"I see." Isla looked down at the floor. That was it, she thought. Whatever small glimmer of hope she had retained deep inside her was gone now. She would never get to experience what Jo had with Réiltín. She felt the pressure of tears filling her eyes.

"But after I had hung up," Jo went on, "I knew I had done the wrong thing. I was doing it out of spite and even I knew that I wasn't in the right frame of mind to do something like that. I'm sorry, Isla. What I came here to say to you and I know I'm going about this in a very long-winded way but what I wanted to say is that I have a beautiful daughter thanks to you and I can't deny you the chance to experience what I have with her. I'm sorry I was so selfish. I was looking at it all wrong before now. It's not about the egg and the sperm or cells or DNA – it's quite simple really – it's all about love. So it's yours if you want it."

"What is?"

"The baby – the embryo. I didn't sign the paperwork yet so it's still there. I never should have tried to stop you from having it. It's more yours than mine, but I was afraid, Isla, can you see that? I was so afraid that it would make a unit out of you, Ryan and Réiltín once and for all and I would be pushed aside. I know that sounds stupid now. I was trying to cling to Réiltín, I was trying to prove that *I* was her mother. That's why I didn't want her to know the truth, I was always so worried that she would leave me, just like she did, but now that she's home I can honestly say that it was one of the best things to ever happen to us. I am her mother, she loves me as her mother and I learnt that by letting her go she figured that out for herself. It's made us much stronger. I love you, Isla, and I love being your sister."

"I love you too, Jo," Isla said, throwing her arms around her older sister and burying her head in her hair.

"I'm sorry I'm such an awful sister," Jo went on. "I'm embarrassed admitting it and I hate myself for it. I hate the way I can be so manipulative. Sometimes I feel like such a bad person, when you have so much goodness in you. Sometimes I think you and I are like oil on water. It's like I got all the dark scum at the top and you got everything good that is hiding underneath. But now I've nothing to fight for any more and, besides, I'm too tired. The baby is yours if you want it. You have our full consent. I will need to check with the clinic though about how we proceed from here."

Isla felt stunned. She had wanted this so much but now that Jo was giving her what she wanted, she didn't feel ecstatic – instead she just felt hollow, almost deflated.

"I'm sorry, Jo," she said slowly, pulling back from Jo's arms, "but I can't take it now – not after everything that has happened – it's not right."

"Oh for heaven's sake, Isla! It's taken me a long time to work up to this decision and then you go and change your mind!"

"It wouldn't be right, Jo. I mean your family was almost broken up and I can't help but feel that I caused it all . . ."

"Look, if you don't take it I'm going to donate it to research so, please, I'd rather it was you." She reached out for her younger sister's hand.

"Are you completely sure about this, Jo? Maybe you should take some time to think it through properly – I mean you've had a stressful few weeks . . ."

"I am sure. Absolutely sure."

"Okay then," Isla said with tears glistening in the corners of her eyes. "Thank you, Jo, thank you so much." She threw her arms around her sister and the two of them started to laugh.

As Jo drove home to Sandymount Heights, she let herself cry. Just the once, just for everything that had been lost. Her hopes and dreams, the ones that she'd had as a teenager. The longing for a loving mother, the longing for a brood of children of her own. But then she thought of all that she did have. She had a great husband and a daughter who filled her with more love and pride than she had ever dared to dream of. And although they'd had a difficult relationship at times, she loved her sister dearly. Isla was her very best friend and her very worst one too. She was the person who annoyed her most on this earth but they shared the strongest love as well. Isla had pushed her to the point of fury more times than anyone else in this life but she knew that that's what sisters were like: magnets. You couldn't explain the charge pulling you together, yet at times you wished you could repel each other as far away as possible. But Jo knew that that was why sisters were so special: because a bond like that could never be explained. There were no words to describe it. Isla knew her better than anyone else she would ever meet. She was there for everything that had happened in their shared childhood. Isla saw the side of her that her friends didn't. The side of her that she wouldn't dare to show her friends. Isla knew better than anybody the things that motivated her, made her cry or what happened at her sixth birthday party. It was a volatile love, the one between them, and there were times when it had left her feeling smothered but, without it, she would be unable to breathe. Jo knew that a sister was a little bit of childhood that could never be lost – sisters were the threads that tie us together through the generations. She knew that some people go through life without experiencing any of that and she knew that she was blessed.

Chapter 40

New Beginnings

Isla walks around the corner and feels the full force of the wind against her face, blowing back her hair. It fills her ears and is strangely calming. It's a day full of power and energy: a nice day for the start of a new life, she thinks. She stops to cross the road. She looks up at the street name and now she doesn't turn her eyes away – she lets them follow the letters across as she tries to sound out the word in the way that Greg has taught her.

She is elated. It is the morning after her conversation with Jo and she is walking to work in the café.

After Jo had gone home the night before, it had taken Isla a while to figure out exactly what the feeling was but then she realised that the feeling she was experiencing was happiness. She knows that that is what it is because it bubbles up inside her and she can almost feel it frothing over and spilling out of her. She can't remember ever feeling anything as pure, as joyous. She has a smile plastered on her face as she walks down the street and she knows that she must look crazy but she doesn't care. A secret part of her was worried that when Jo said that she could have the embryo that the ugly self-

308

destructive part of herself, the part of her that never wanted her to be happy or to have something good in her life, would try to sabotage her efforts. She was worried that she would change her mind, that the fear would get the better of her. But it hasn't happened and instead she is left feeling joyous because she might finally get to have a child of her own. There is so much running around inside her head.

She has made up her mind to go into the café and tell Greg how she is feeling. She is going to tell him everything – how she loves being around him, how she loves him. It has taken her so long to be able to let down her walls and let him in. Maybe she and Jo were more alike than she thought – she has been too afraid to step out of her comfort zone for so long but she's ready to let go of the fear now. She is going to tell him about Jo's change of mind and how she hopes that he will join her on the journey. She wants to do it with him. It has taken her a while to realise it but she knows that they will be great together. It has all fallen into place at last. It feels like this is the moment that she has been journeying to for her whole life. For the first time in her life she isn't going to run away from it or be scared off by the commitment that she is entering into. Something good is going to happen.

* * * **THE END** * * *

Note on Donor-assisted Reproduction

The Children and Family Relationships Act 2015 changed family law in Ireland to extend parental rights and responsibilities to non-traditional families. It also addresses, for the first time, donor-assisted reproduction and provides for a National Donor-Conceived Person Register, whereas previously couples could elect to use an anonymous donor. The Department of Justice has delayed enacting this section of the Act until 2016 to allow a transition period for people currently undergoing anonymous donor-assisted reproduction, after which point people using a donor to conceive a child will have to ensure that the donor is named and traceable on the register.